# BLACK BOTTOM EXODUS

# BLACK BOTTOM EXODUS

## JOURNEYS OF SALVATION

---

*A GREAT MIGRATION TALE*

## Kirk P. Mullen

ISBN-13: 9780997185904
ISBN-10: 0997185902

*Author's Note*

**Black Bottom Exodus** is a work of fiction. In this novel, fictitious characters interact with persons who actually lived in places which may or may not have existed. Although the novel is laid out in a chronological manner, the verifiable events may have or may not have taken place on those specified days.

The inspiration for this Great Migration tale came from two sources, first, the opera *Porgy and Bess* by DuBose Heyward and George and Ira Gershwin and second, the journalistic masterpiece, *The Warmth of Other Suns* by Isabel Wilkerson.

If after reading this story, you find that you are thinking positively about it, then please mention it to a friend. The book may be ordered from Create Space. The URL is as follows:

https://www.createspace.com/5844896

Thank you for choosing to read **Black Bottom Exodus.**

## Dedication

*This novel is dedicated to Alain Locke, Langston Hughes, Richard Bruce Nugent, Countee Cullen, Wallace Thurman, Aaron Douglas, Zora Neale Hurston, Walter White, Arna Bontemps, Harold Jackman, Carl Van Vechten, W. E. B. DuBois, A'Lelia Walker, Anne Spencer, Dorothy West, Alice Dunbar Nelson, James Weldon Johnson, Claude McKay, Jean Toomer, and Arturo Schomburg. Although they did not live to see the Harlem Renaissance, this novel is also dedicated to Booker T. Washington, Madam C. J. Walker, and Paul Laurence Dunbar. Further, this novel is dedicated to the millions of African-Americans who lived in and died in the Jim Crow South, those who were lynched during the Jim Crow era, and those who fled to the North and the West during the Jim Crow era. This novel is also dedicated to those Caucasians who played major and minor roles in moving racial relations in the United States in a more equitable and inclusive direction. Naming just a few of them: Viola Liuzzo, Sarah and Angelina Grimke, Felix Adler, Abel Meeropol, Andrew Goodman, Michael Schwerner, and Julius Rosenwald. This novel is also dedicated to those men and women who are working to end religious bigotry and who understand that there are sacred paths as well as secular paths which lead to salvation. Lastly, this novel is dedicated to all the lesbian, gay, bisexual, transgender, and straight individuals worldwide, working on issues of gender and sexual orientation equality.*

## Thank You

I want to acknowledge the encouragement of two individuals with regard to the writing of this novel. Ms. Rosemary Klein, a poetry editor, a creative writing teacher, and my friend, heard my thoughts for this story and encouraged me to develop the story. I was also encouraged in this first attempt at writing a novel by Mr. James Foster, a playwright, actor, director, producer, and my longtime friend. The manuscript for this novel was made a little nicer due to the technical support of Dr. Duane Thomas. Thanks, Doc. This novel was also read by Ms. Linda Joy Burke, a published poet, educator, performance artist, and friend. Thanks for your feedback, Linda Joy. This novel was also read by Dr. Argentine Craig, an Organizational Psychologist and my friend. Thanks for your feedback, Argentine. I want to thank my brother, Michael Mullen, a semi-retired businessman, for his very keen proof-reading skills and manuscript comments. Thanks, Mike. I also want to thank my cousin, Mr. Edward Rogers, a retired librarian for his technical support and advice. Thanks, Eddie. Also, I have to thank my good friend, Bob Jacobson, a semi-retired social worker for donating his proofreading skills towards the development of this book. Thanks, Bob. My friend, Mr. Gordon Stills, a retired school principal, offered quite insightful comments concerning my novel. Thank you, Gordon. I must also thank my friend Avalon Thompson, a florist and the owner of Enchanted Petals in Baltimore,

Md. She made the palm frond cross which appears on this book's cover. Thank you, Avalon. Lastly, I want to thank my friends and fellow bibliophiles, Mr. Leslie H. Saunders, Jr. for his technical support and manuscript comments and Mr. Roland Handy for his proofreading skills and manuscript comments.

# TABLE OF CONTENTS

Johnson Genealogy · · · · · · · · · · · · · · · · ·xiii

Chapter 1   In The Beginning  · · · · · · · · · · · · · · · · · 1
Chapter 2   Yea, Though I Walk Through
            The Valley Of The Shadow Of Death  · · · · 11
Chapter 3   Your Secret's Safe With Me · · · · · · · · · · · 19
Chapter 4   An Avoidance Of Negative Publicity · · · · · 24
Chapter 5   Your Balm In Gilead· · · · · · · · · · · · · · · · 26
Chapter 6   Wild Life Dreams· · · · · · · · · · · · · · · · · · 29
Chapter 7   Woven Profits· · · · · · · · · · · · · · · · · · · · 33
Chapter 8   Shadows  · · · · · · · · · · · · · · · · · · · · · · · 37
Chapter 9   The Angel of Shadows · · · · · · · · · · · · · · 41
Chapter 10  The Transition Of Angels · · · · · · · · · · · · 45
Chapter 11  Getting To Know You · · · · · · · · · · · · · · · 59
Chapter 12  He'd Never Had It So Good · · · · · · · · · · 114
Chapter 13  The End Of The Woodland Feast · · · · · · 126
Chapter 14  A Royal Mess · · · · · · · · · · · · · · · · · · · 132
Chapter 15  Nominal Consequences · · · · · · · · · · · · · 146
Chapter 16  Moving On  · · · · · · · · · · · · · · · · · · · · · 188
Chapter 17  The Nurturing Womb Of Education · · · · 203

Chapter 18   The Lone Ranger · · · · · · · · · · · · · · · · · 219

Chapter 19   Shady Lady · · · · · · · · · · · · · · · · · · · · · 226

Chapter 20   From Deanwood To Downtown
And Back · · · · · · · · · · · · · · · · · · · · · · 234

Chapter 21   Funerals Are For The Living · · · · · · · · · 239

# Johnson Genealogy

**Chinualumogu Ogidi**
b. 1793 - d. 1860, captured in 1803 and taken to Charleston, S. C.
Name changed to Jeremiah at the Trevor Johnson rice plantation.
**Jeremiah - Matilda**
(The parents of 5 boys and 3 girls. One son was named Jubal).

↓

**Jubal Johnson - Nellie (nee Lawson)**
b. 1825 - d. 1884, a musician and a carpenter who preferred to stay in the islands after Emancipation.
(7 children were born, 4 girls and 3 boys. One son was named Seth).

↓

**Seth Johnson - Albertina (nee Grayson)**
b. 1850 - d. 1925, stayed in the South Carolina barrier islands as an adult.

(6 children were born, 3 boys and 3 girls. One boy was named Hiram Johnson).

↓

**Hiram Johnson - Loretta Mae (nee Marshall)**
b. 1885 - d. 1930, lived on Black Bottom Island.
(One child born, a son, named Rocky Johnson).

↓

**Rocky Johnson**
b. 1910 - Rocky was born and raised on Black Bottom Island.
He was named after the fish his parents loved.

# CHAPTER 1

# IN THE BEGINNING

*Thursday, September 14, 1933*

TENSION GRIPPED HATTIE'S FACE AS she peeped through the shutters. Scanning the neighborhood revealed that the raped harlot and her lover were the only living entities near the well. The lover, Hattie's friend, needed help. She had to do something.

The storm was over and the air was cooler; the sun would soon set. Rocky looked as though Death would soon be flaying him. There was nothing that he could do to halt his demise; he had to stand up to Big Jim. His protest, his fighting for Vanda Mae, would be symbolic. All of Black Bottom would know of his courage . . . or maybe, his foolishness. They would see it from their windows. He couldn't expect any help. He knew it would be a lost cause, but his love for Vanda Mae had to be made known to her. She had to understand how deeply he cared for her. Even though he would lose the fight with Big Jim, he would always be in her heart.

Big Jim wouldn't be able to take that. Rocky looked up and saw that Bobby was walking towards him. He had kind of a stiff legged walk that was barely noticeable, but with Rocky's preparation for Death, the slightest of variations in the way things usually went was being noticed.

Bobby spoke first. "Hi, Rocky. I need to talk with you inside your home and we need to do it right now."

"O.K., Bobby. Let's go."

Rocky really liked Bobby. Bobby treated him with respect. Bobby had built a cart for him so that he could more easily get around Black Bottom. Bobby built that cart when they were eight years old, fifteen years ago. It was his gift to Rocky. It had been built from discarded materials. All of Black Bottom knew that Bobby was real good with his hands and that he could build and did build all sorts of things. Rocky and Bobby were friends before the cart, but the cart made their bond stronger.

The two friends entered the home. Rocky's home consisted of one big circular room which had a fire pit in the center, the purpose of which was the provision of light and heat. Bobby had built the house for Rocky, with the permission of his father and Rocky's father. When Bobby had spare time, he would transplant bamboo from the grove at the edge of Black Bottom to the present site of the home. The bamboo was trained to take the shape of a dome. Bobby found a discarded shutter and made that the home's one window. Then he, his father, Rocky's father, Rocky, and anyone else who wanted to lend a hand, coated the structure with tar and placed clay, twigs, and dried vines along the seams of the bamboo. They started at the top of the structure, filling in the spaces around the chimney which

Bobby had created and over the weeks, worked their way down the frame to where it went into the ground. Closer to the ground, Rocky helped the men and Bobby. Inside the home, pegs protruded through the wall at an upward pointing angle so that various things such as mirrors, pots and pans, and clothing could be hung. Bobby built a scale model of the home when he was twelve and convinced his father and Mr. Johnson (Rocky's father), that a larger version could be built. When they said that the house would wash away with the first rain storm, he countered that hills with grass don't wash away. He stated that he would transplant dirt and grass and that it was worth a try. The parents eventually dropped their opposition to this diversion from fishing and gave their permission for these twelve year olds to build their playhouse. That was eleven years ago. Seven years ago, when Rocky was sixteen, he permanently moved from his father's home into his own home. When he made baskets, he would hang them on the extra pegs which Bobby had placed through the wall. Now Bobby wanted to talk to him in private. He thought that this might be a goodbye talk. If they shared some dried fish and lemonade, it would be a Last Supper talk. Rocky had two chairs, a card table, a few milk crates, and an icebox inside his home. They both sat in the chairs at the table. Rocky spoke first.

"Would you like a cup of water Bobby? I ain't got nothin prepared to offer you."

"This ain't no social call, Rocky. Your ass is about to be slaughtered. Do you really think that fighting for her to stay here with you is worth your life?"

"Bobby, the Vanda Mae of today ain't like the Vanda Mae of a few months ago. She takes care of me. She's tender with me. Vanda Mae helps me with the baskets. Vanda Mae likes to give me a bath and I like to give her one. I ain't never had a woman before, Bobby. Bobby, you're good lookin and you're smart. You got Melissa. Would you fight for Melissa? I ain't gonna get another woman, not anytime soon, anyways. Vanda Mae don't want to go with Big Jim. Someone's gotta stand up to him. Bobby, I gotta be a man."

"Does being a man mean that you have to die or worse, becoming more crippled than you already are?"

"Suppose it was Melissa who was raped? Vanda Mae ain't even in her right head. She just sit there staring off at the sea or at the hills, like she's shell shock."

"O.K., Rocky," Bobby said as he was standing up. He undid the button at the top of his pants and took out a two foot long piece of bamboo.

Rocky saw it and stated, "I thought you was walking funny. Is that supposed to be a weapon?"

"This is my prayer for you. I hope that it protects your life. I made it after Big Jim killed Byrd. My mind was wandering and I came up with this little piece of protection. Bamboo is light weight, but real strong. You got fat bamboo and you got skinny bamboo. This prayer combines the two. The fat bamboo was hollowed out. The skinny bamboo moves inside the fat bamboo. This first handle here, moves the skinny bamboo forward. When you move the handle to the end of the slot and lock it in place, the razor blades and the fish hooks are exposed and at the very tip, there is a four edged arrow head. You have to lock the skinny bamboo in place to keep the spear from moving backwards."

Rocky looked on in amazement. "I ain't never seen 4 edges on a arrow head."

"I made it from one small discarded window pane," replied Bobby. Then he added, "This back handle here goes in your armpit. That way, you will have more control over this prayer."

"Rocky," Bobby continued, "Big Jim is huge. It will be as though you're fighting a full grown bear. You gotta out think him. He can't see the spear coming. If he is charging you or if he is falling toward you, then, move the handle on the prayer. When he sees the blades, arrow head and hooks, it'll be too late. If you use the prayer too soon, he'll take it from you and you will die a very painful death.

"Bobby, let's pray at the altar."

"Rocky, you got those African masks by the cross."

"We an African people, Bobby. I got African angels, Bobby. You said I'm going to be fighting a bear, well my angels need to change me from a chipmunk with a bad foot into a porcupine with a bad attitude. All I got Bobby is your prayer and my prayer."

Bobby placed the prayer in Rocky's cart and then took a chair over to the altar. Rocky sat in it. Bobby kneeled beside Rocky. Rocky picked up one of the masks and held it to his chest. He asked Bobby to pick up the other mask, but Bobby refused, saying that this prayer was too close to calling on Satan.

"Bobby, I'm not calling on Satan. I'm calling on our African angels. The ones that kept us alive as we crossed the ocean; the ones that gave us hope during slavery; the ones that take our souls to heaven when we're swinging from trees. I'll hold the other mask if you pass it to me." Bobby passed the mask and he noticed that his fingers did not tingle. Rocky held both masks in his left hand and took hold of Bobby's left hand with his right. Rocky asked Bobby to ring the altar bell three times and this he did.

Rocky began the prayer:

*I am asking the angels which have helped us so far to help us again. We understand that you are there, in spirit to help us here, in the flesh. Please take this prayer for safety and for thanks, to Jesus, His Father, God, and to the Holy Ghost. I normally come to you alone in prayer, but today, I bring a friend. I am thanking my friend for his prayer for me and I hope and pray that you can bless and protect him. He has been so kind to me over the years. Ghost, I know that you know this, but I am asking you to continue blessing this man and also his wife, Melissa. Help me please, Ghost to be a victorious David over a brutish, uncivilized, murderous Goliath. Please help Vanda Mae to put the brute's rape of her, behind her. Ghost, Vanda Mae is broken. Please help her to move forward and to become a better person and a whole person. Please let her get her mind back and please bring her heart back to mine."*

*"The Lord is my Shepherd, I shall not want."*

They both recited the 23rd Psalm.

*"He maketh me to lie down in green pastures. He leadeth me beside the still waters. He restoreth my soul. He leadeth me in the paths of righteousness for his name's sake. Yea, though I walk through the valley of the shadow of death, I will fear no evil, for thou art with me. Thy rod and thy staff they comfort me. Thou preparest a table before me in the presence of mine enemies. Thou anointest my head with oil; my cup runneth over. Surely goodness and mercy shall follow me all the days of my life and I will dwell in the house of the LORD forever. Amen. Ache'."*

"Rocky, what's that Ache' stuff?"

It's an African way of saying Amen.

"O.K. One more thing Rocky, I didn't answer your question. I would fight Big Jim if I had to, but I would prefer to kill him from a distance; a safe distance.

Bobby left Rocky's home as Hattie was coming to his door.

"Rocky, can I come in?"

"Sure, Hattie. Can I offer you a cup of water? I haven't prepared anything to eat."

"No thank you, Rocky. I came because I wanted you to have this knife. If you fight Big Jim, he can't think that you have a weapon. He might not see the knife if it's in your shoe or in your belt. You might be able to surprise him. Maybe, stab him in the back of his neck."

"Thank you, Hattie. Is Vanda Mae still near the well?"

"Yeah, Rocky."

"Well, that's where I'm headed."

Rocky tucked the knife into his belt and pulled his shirt over it. He limped over to his cart and then rolled out of his home with Hattie following. He knew that a wanted criminal like Big Jim would show up when it was dark and so he waited for him at the well. As soon as he told Vanda Mae to go back to the house, they heard a voice say, "Nah, Vanda Mae, stay right there."

"She ain't goin wit you, Big Jim. Be a man and face the facts, she don't like you. You need to get on out of here while you can, before the law comes rolling through here."

Vanda Mae started screaming, but Big Jim didn't care. He came out of the shadows and walked towards her. He grabbed her and started pulling her into the shadows. He punched her in the face and then she was quiet; it was then that Big Jim started lifting her. Rocky pushed his cart towards Big Jim and hit the back of his knee, as hard as he could, with the bamboo prayer. Jim lost his balance, dropped Vanda Mae, and then turned around only to get jabbed in the stomach by the bamboo prayer. The pain of the jab was immediately intensified when Rocky pushed the inner bamboo spear into Jim's stomach and locked it in place. Jim fell forward onto Rocky and grabbed his neck. He would not die alone. They would both die. He would strangle Rocky. His hands were on Rocky's neck and then his hands were limp. He didn't understand why they weren't working. Before he lost consciousness, he realized that Rocky had stabbed him in the back of his neck. The cripple had won.

Big Jim died on top of Rocky. The cripple had to wiggle as best he could to get from under the giant. Rocky's clothes were now covered with the giant's blood. Rocky knew that he couldn't tell the police anything regarding this night. He knew he would be charged with the murder of Big Jim and that Bobby and Hattie would be charged as accomplices. He was so anxious. What to do first? He told himself to calm down. He thought that he had to get rid of his clothes, he had to get rid of the weapons, and he had to get rid of the body. Which one to do first? He knew that Black Bottom eyes were on him. He was being watched from the other side of several windows. He pushed his cart over to Cecelia Byrd's home and asked for help in moving the body. He had just killed the man who had murdered her husband; of course she would help. Cecelia said "No," but she did give a pair of pants and shirt. Rocky thanked her and asked if she could put the clothes in a bag so that blood wouldn't get on them. She complied and closed the door in his face.

Bobby had come from his home to help Rocky. Standing over the dead giant he said, "Rocky you gotta get rid of those clothes. Take them off right now, but first push your cart under the water pump. I'll clean it up.

Bobby cleaned the cart while Rocky awkwardly disrobed, washed his hands and face and then put on the clothes which Cecelia had given to him.

Bobby was concerned that they would not be able to place enough rocks in the pockets and in the shirt of Big Jim to keep the body from eventually rising to the surface of the ocean and floating back to shore. He thought that Big Jim should be left in place.

Rocky thought that Jim should be tied to the pier, below the low tide point; in that way, the crabs could eat him. Bobby pointed out that, that was difficult for two people and that Rocky didn't swim.

Rocky's bloody clothes were filled with rocks, after which, the bamboo prayer was pulled out of Big Jim's body. The rock filled shirt and pants were tied around the prayer and they and the knife were thrown in the ocean. Everything immediately sank to the ocean floor.

Vanda Mae had awakened and started walking around looking at the corpse. She said to the two of them, "We gotta get out of here."

"Bobby," Rocky said, "I think it's a mistake to leave this body here."

Vanda Mae implored, "Bobby, Rocky, we got to get out of here. . . You know what, y'all can talk this over; I'm going back to the house." Vanda Mae was out of sight within seconds.

"Where do you want to put the body, Rocky? If we move the body behind someone's house, that person will turn us in to the police. If we move the body on your cart, the blood will be on it and on you, and on me. Let's let the body stay here, by the water pump."

They didn't have anymore time to discuss the body because they saw headlights turn onto their street. If the car came most of the way down the street, the driver would see them and the corpse. Both guys immediately ran and rolled for the shadows. They both knew that no one who lived in Black Bottom owned a car.

"See ya Rocky."

"See ya Bobby."

They split for the shadows and their respective homes.

# YEA, THOUGH I WALK THROUGH THE VALLEY OF THE SHADOW OF DEATH

---

### *Friday, September 15, 1933*

IT WAS 8:45 A.M. THE Medical Examiner was driving the morgue's van because his assistant hadn't shown up to work. The assistant didn't have a phone line in his rooming house and even if he had, it wouldn't have mattered because the storm had downed many phone lines. So, the Medical Examiner would be working by himself today. He'd get any bodies which the undertaker didn't take. The unclaimed bodies, the unwanted bodies, the bodies which carried the taint of legally questionable deaths, were his domain; the domain of Josiah Jefferson Jones. He used to be called Triple J when he was young, but when he got in high school, he renamed himself T. J. He thought that it was a cool, regular guy type of nickname. He had been T. J. ever since.

As he drove the van down Black Bottom's unpaved road, he saw O'Brien's and Brown's police car. As he got closer, he could see that a body was lying on the ground not too far away from the pump. He realized instantly that Coloreds weren't walking around or standing around trying to get a good look at the corpse. They knew something. Yep, this was foul play.

Ofc. Brown spoke first. "Hey, T. J. How ya doin? Did the storm mess up your home?"

T. J. thought that he could smell alcohol on Brown's breath but said nothing of it. "I'm O.K. and the house is O.K. Who's dead?"

Brown continued, "We got Big Jim here. Remember, he's the one who killed Byrd."

"So he got what he deserved, I guess, with no known suspects. We're closing one case and what are we doing with the other?" asked T. J.

"We're solving this murder" said O'Brien. "I need more money and I might get a raise if I solve this murder. I already got a suspect."

T. J. wanted to know who the suspect was and was told, Cecelia Byrd. "You honestly think that a woman killed this big ass man?"

O'Brien replied, "I think she knows who killed her husband's killer."

Brown asked, "Doc, what do you think was used to make such a large raggedy hole in Big Jim?"

"I don't know. The raggedy part is what baffles me." Turning to O'Brien, T. J. said, "Did you inspect the area for a weapon?"

"No, I didn't. The weapon is probably in the ocean by now. I'm focusing on Cecelia Byrd." With that said, O'Brien started off in the direction of Cecelia Byrd's home; Brown was following after him; and T. J. started strapping Big Jim onto the gurney. Big Jim's next stop would be the morgue.

As Brown and O'Brien were nearing the home of Cecelia, she stepped outside and closed the door behind her. She would protect her children by keeping the police away from them.

"Hi, Cecelia" said O'Brien, "I sure wish you had some hot chocolate for me this morning. Some hot chocolate would really get me going this morning. It would put a smile on my face and some pep in my step. You got any hot chocolate for me this morning, Cecelia?"

Cecelia stood in her doorway and said nothing.

"Cecelia, did you hear me talking to you? You got any hot chocolate for me?"

"I heard you Mr. O'Brien, but I ain't got no hot chocolate for you."

"Well, maybe you will later on, after you have had time to think things over."

"I gotta go to work, Mr. O'Brien."

"It's Officer O'Brien. That's how you speak to a policeman. Say, Officer O'Brien."

Cecelia complied, "Officer O'Brien."

"Your mouth is very pretty when you say the word, Officer. Say it again."

Cecelia waited a few seconds and then said, "Officer."

"That's real nice, Cecelia. Since you won't give me any hot chocolate this morning, I'll have to settle for the beauty of your mouth forming the "O" in 'Officer.' "

O'Brien continued, "But, this ain't no social call Cecelia. I'm here on official police business. I want you to confess to the killing of Big Jim. You killed Big Jim, didn't you?"

"Mr. O'Brien,"

"Officer," he reminded her.

"I put the children to bed right after the storm was over and I went to bed also. When I got up this morning, I saw the body near the water pump. I don't know nothin else about the death of Big Jim."

Brown asked, "You got a shotgun, Cecelia? How'd you put such a large hole in Big Jim?"

"I ain't put no hole in Big Jim. I ain't do nothin to Big Jim. I don't know how Big Jim died. I was in the house with my babies and my mama."

"You know, Cecelia, someone put a big old hole in Big Jim. Think about that, Cecelia. A big old hole in Big Jim." With that said, O'Brien took Brown's nightstick and rubbed it up and down the middle of Cecelia's bosom. Cecelia remained quiet. She was determined not to show fear. She had on her husband's blue jeans and work shirt and she was ready to shuck oysters, not be O'Brien's whore. O'Brien took the nightstick and lowered it to the crotch of Cecelia's pants. "Does this jog your memory, Cecelia? Who killed Big Jim, Cecelia?" The baton was tapping on her crotch now.

"I don't know Mr...., Officer O'Brien. I don't know who killed Big Jim. I went to sleep early last night. I gotta get to work. I got a job at the cannery once my husband was buried."

O'Brien and Brown let her walk away. O'Brien smiled as he viewed her from behind. He said to Brown, "Her husband is dead and she needs someone to take care of her when she is hot and bothered. I think that I should be that guy. Of course, I'll give her a few dollars to help take care of those children. It'll be a mutually beneficial relationship. Yeah Brown, I could develop a taste for some hot chocolate." Then he yelled down the street, "Cecelia, when I write my report, I'm going to name you as a suspect, cause you got a reason to kill Big Jim." Cecelia kept walking and never turned around.

Brown said to his partner, "Well, that was a nice little interview."

"Yes, it was. I feel better already; a little more refreshed; a little more relaxed."

"Yeah," replied Brown. "You got a smile on your face. Who you gonna fuck with next?"

O'Brien was lightly chuckling at his partner's comments. "Well, now who can I make squeal like a little pig?"

"What about Gopher?" Gopher was Brown's private name for Rocky because his house was made of dirt and twigs.

"Yeah, O.K., let's go get Gopher."

O'Brien and Brown weren't as cordial with Rocky as they were with Cecelia.

The Officers drove their car up to Rocky's home, blew the horn, got out of the car, and started to knock on the door as Rocky was opening it.

O'Brien looked down at Rocky sitting in his cart and gruffly said, "Rocky, Big Jim is dead. Who killed him?"

"I don't know Ofc. O'Brien. I've been in my home. Ever since the storm let up, we been right here. I don't know who killed him, Ofc. O'Brien." Rocky knew that they did not believe him.

"I say that we take him to the station and maybe on the ride there, he'll remember who killed Big Jim." Brown spoke like he was ready to do damage to Rocky.

"No. Please don't" cried Vanda Mae. "He don't know nothin about the death of Big Jim. He was here with me."

"Come on out here Vanda Mae," said O'Brien.

When she was standing at the front door, Brown exclaimed, "Damn, Vanda Mae, what happened to your face?" He then looked at Rocky and said, "You been whippin her ass, Rocky? You been battering Vanda Mae? You know that's against the law!"

"O. K., enough talking," said O'Brien. "Let's go to the station." Both officers grabbed Rocky by the arms, lifted him up, and while placing him in the car, slammed his head against the roof of the car.

Rev. Belton had just left City Hall and was walking by the police station when Brown and O'Brien drove up and stopped. He watched them get out of the car, open the back door, and grab Rocky under his arms and drag him up the steps. As they were dragging him, he shouted, "Reverend, I don't know nothin' about the death of Big Jim. Pray for me." The Reverend knew of Big Jim and knew that he was a killer who was wanted by the police. If someone killed Big Jim, why were they making such a big deal out of it? Surely, they didn't think that a crippled basket weaver such as Rocky, a man who needed a crutch and a leg brace to walk, could be the killer. He knew that he had to consult the Bishop about what he witnessed today.

Rocky was sat up in a chair in the station and immediately backhanded by O'Brien. Blood started to trickle from his lip. "O.K., Rocky, now that I got your attention, I want to know who killed Big Jim?" O'Brien waited a few seconds for an answer and when it didn't come, backhanded Rocky again, but this time, Rocky fell out of the chair. He started shouting, "I don't know who killed Big Jim."

O'Brien ordered Brown to sit in the chair and grab Rocky's hands. He then told him to place his feet on Rocky's shoulders and pull.

"No. . . no" whimpered Rocky. "I don't know OWWWWWW!!!!" His scream could be heard at the front desk. O'Brien was standing on his clubfoot. Rocky's brace was protecting the foot until the baton slammed into its sole. Rocky wished for the Lord to take his life at that point. The pain was so intense. Death would have been a blessing.

"Hold him tightly, Brown, while I take this brace off of him." Rocky heard these words, but there was nothing which he could do except wait for the next torture. "Rocky, I want you to tell me the truth, who killed Big Jim?" He looked at Brown and said "While he's thinking over his answer, you want a Lucky Strike?"

"Nah, Pete." Peter was O'Brien's first name. "You know I like Camels."

O'Brien lit the cigarette and took a puff. He pulled another chair near Rocky and sat facing the cripple. The chair was placed between Rocky's knees. O'Brien sat in the chair and placed his right foot on Rocky's crotch. He pushed the foot into the crotch hard and then let up a little and said, "You know Rocky, it wouldn't take much to make you into a flat chested girl."

Rocky's thoughts were on Vanda Mae. All of the pain he was enduring was because he loved her so deeply. He would die knowing that she knew that he loved her. Rocky was having an out of body experience. He knew that his good leg had been picked up and was resting on the thigh of O'Brien. He knew that the shoe and sock were being removed from his right foot. When the cigarette started burning his foot, he knew that he was screaming, but his cries seemed muffled to him. O'Brien kept the burning going and Rocky could smell his flesh being cooked. Even though he was physically struggling, Rocky had mentally detached himself. There was nothing that he could do. He didn't know how much time had elapsed. It eventually occurred to him that he was being dragged from the room and placed on the floor of a cell. His brace, his shoe, and his sock were thrown in after him. As he was falling asleep, he knew that his foot was a bloody mess and that getting up on the cot was going to be a problem for him. He resolved that when he had the energy, he would try to get on the cot. He would just have to rest on the floor of his cell and he did; he did with a slight smile on his face, because the police still didn't suspect that he was the killer of Big Jim. He hadn't given them anyone's name and he hadn't implicated Bobby or Hattie.

# CHAPTER 3

# YOUR SECRET'S SAFE WITH ME

———◆———

*Friday, September 15 & Saturday, September 16, 1933*

REVEREND BELTON SAT DOWN IN his office at the church and called his Bishop in Atlanta. Hopefully, he could help. Bishop Lowry picked up his phone and listened to Reverend Belton describe Rocky, Big Jim, and the reputations of the policemen, O'Brien and Brown. The Bishop thanked the Reverend for the news and told him to pray for Rocky's soul. He told the Reverend that he would see what could be done for Mr. Johnson.

Bishop Lowry looked at his watch and hoped that his friend was in his office. He called the operator and stated that he wanted to make a long distance call and he would speak with anyone at Hamilton 5-5137 in New York City. He waited for the connection.

"NAACP," a female voice answered.

"Hello, this is Bishop Lowry in Atlanta. I'm a friend of Walter White. This is an emergency; I need to speak with him right away. Is he in the office?"

"He's in a meeting Bishop. I'll have him call you."

"No. He would want you to pull him out of the meeting. Let him know that this is a matter of life and death. Tell him imminent life and death. Please tell him that now. I'll wait on this line until he picks it up."

After about two minutes, the Bishop heard, "Richard, what's going on down there in Atlanta?"

"Walt, the problem isn't in Atlanta, it's in Charleston. This morning, the police snatched a crippled beggar off of the streets of Charleston because they think that he knows something about the murder of a 6 foot 7 inch, 312 pound stevedore who was a known murderer and who was wanted by the police. Big Jim was the stevedore's name. Mr. Johnson may not see tomorrow if he spends the night in that jail."

Walter White wrote down the entire story and then repeated it back to the bishop. He wanted to gather as many details as possible regarding this incarceration. "Richard, you pray for him. I'll see what can be done on this end."

"Walter, we have to talk under better circumstances."

"Yes, Richard, we do."

Walter White was a courageous and crafty man. He was Colored on the inside and the color of fresh cream on the outside. His hair was straight and his eyes were blue. He frequently went down south and infiltrated Klan meetings and would give warnings to targeted Coloreds. Having as light a complexion as he had and dealing with as many light skinned Coloreds as he had over the decades, afforded him the ability to easily distinguish Quadroons, Octoroons, and Mustefinos. For security reasons, his picture had never been taken for publication. When the young reporter from the New York Times wanted to interview him regarding lynchings in the South, he'd agreed as long as there were no pictures taken. The young reporter, P. D. Deveraux, was speechless when he saw Walter. Their eyes scanned each other, for a second longer than usual thought White, before shaking hands. This short silence wasn't the usual silence which Walter encountered from white reporters who were surprised to see what appeared to them to be a white man in charge of the NAACP. Walter would quickly explain to these reporters that Colored folks come in all colors and that he was a Colored man. Those reporters quickly adjusted and moved on with the interview. This reporter was different.

"Hello, Mr. Deveraux. Can I offer you a cup of coffee or tea?"

"No thank you, Mr. White."

Walter noted that this kid seemed nervous. How else to explain his pronunciation of 'White' with almost two syllables?

'Where are you from, Mr. Deveraux?"

P. D. was nervous. Tell the truth and face whatever consequences which might unfold or tell a lie and be safe, at least momentarily. He tried to avoid everything about his past; but he knew that to be taken seriously as a journalist, openness and honesty had to become second nature for him. He also knew that if he revealed too much about himself, everything for which he was working, would most likely fall down around him. P. D. was a cub reporter with the Times and he had been on the payroll for only two months. He needed this job. It was his sole source of income and he had no one on whom he could rely. No friends, nor family, were close by. He would walk a tightrope and not reveal too much of himself. "I'm from New Orleans. How about you

Mr. White, where are you from?" He wanted to switch the subject away from himself as quickly as possible.

Walter told him Atlanta and then quickly asked, "Are you related to Josephine and Dominick Deveraux, the school teachers?"

P. D. gasped and then bit his lip. His eyes began to water. He had done so much to hide his past, to get this job. He had gotten a real nice room in Brooklyn, which now might be in jeopardy. He wiped away the tear as it started to roll down his cheek. "They're my grandparents," he said. "My middle name is Dominick. I'm Pierre Dominick Deveraux."

Walter calmly told him, "Your secret's safe with me. Now let's get on with this interview so that you can file your story and continue to earn a paycheck. I hope that you will use what God gave you to help the downtrodden."

"I will Mr. White."

"When we're together, meaning face-to-face and alone, you can call me Walter."

"Thank you. When we're together, and the same, you can call me Pierre."

That meeting was two years ago. Walter had kept Pierre's secret and Pierre was slowly advancing at the New York Times. Walter dialed the number for the Times and asked for Mr. P. D. Deveraux.

"Mr. Deveraux, this is Mr. White from the NAACP. I wanted to let you know of a Colored cripple who was snatched off the streets of Charleston, South Carolina this morning."

Walter elaborated from his notes on Rocky, Big Jim, and the police. Pierre stated that he knew that he could get the story in tomorrow's paper; he just wasn't sure on which page it would run. "I'll do the best I can," he told Walter.

Pierre immediately called the Capitol building in Washington, D. C. and asked for the offices of Senators Smith and then Byrnes. He also called the Governor of South Carolina, Ibra Charles Blackwood. He planned to query the three of them regarding the picking up of crippled beggars off of the streets of Charleston and throwing them in jail without charging them. Was this what the tourists coming down from New York City could expect? Should they get off the cruise ship or stay on it once they docked in Charleston? Pierre figured he'd speak to the politicians' aides and not the politicians and this was fine with him. He knew the word would get back to the politicians. All he really wanted was the names of the aides so that they could be placed in his news article. He told the aides that it had already been verified that the Charleston police had picked up a crippled beggar and thrown him in jail. What was yet to be verified was whether the beggar was also blind! He told them that the paper would run another article once they verified that the beggar was blind.

As luck would have it, he got a few lines of his story on page one of Saturday's paper, right beside a much larger article on lynching. The rest of his story appeared in the back of the "A" section, right beside a cruise ship advertisement. The article appeared in the September 16th edition of the Times.

# CHAPTER 4

# AN AVOIDANCE OF NEGATIVE PUBLICITY

<hr>

### Saturday, September 16, 1933

CAPTAIN RODHAM ENTERED THE REAR of the police station and heard the screams coming from Rocky's cell. He looked through the bars at Ofc. Brown sitting on the cot with his feet on Rocky's shoulders. He was pulling Rocky's arms back towards himself. Rocky was lying on the floor screaming and Ofc. O'Brien was sitting in a chair, the leg of which extended over Rocky's good right ankle. This prevented movement of this leg. O'Brien had his left shoe firmly planted on Rocky's crotch. Rocky's left pant leg was ripped open along the seam. Rodham could smell Rocky's flesh burning. He noticed that O'Brien was no longer focusing on the sole of Rocky's good foot. No, now the cigarette burns were going up Rocky's left calf and would soon be outside the braced area, onto his thigh. Rocky's bad ankle rested on O'Brien's shoulder and O'Brien was saying that he was going to play Rocky like a bass fiddle. He would make him sing. Rodham thought that this was the right time to intervene.

"Good morning, gentlemen."

"Morning, Captain," the officers said.

"Is everything O.K., Captain? You're usually at work 5 - 10 minutes before your shift starts; but, you're more than a half hour late today."

"Yeah, I had to stop at the Mayor's home this morning. The Mayor got a call last night from the Governor. What do you think they were talking about?"

The officers looked at each other and shook their heads.

"They were talking about how much money tourism brings into Charleston. They were also talking about a blind crippled beggar who had been snatched off the streets and not charged. A blind crippled beggar who was right here in our jail."

"Rocky ain't blind. Right Rocky?" laughed Brown. "But we can make him blind!"

"Brown, what you can do is let go of his arms. O'Brien, stop playing him like a bass fiddle. I want both of you to come out of this cell. I don't want you to go back into it until Monday and at that point, you're going to take him home. You got it?"

"Yes, Sir," they said in unison.

"Rocky," said Rodham, "did you kill Big Jim?"

"No."

"Do you know who killed Big Jim?"

"No."

"Gentlemen," looking to the officers, "this case is closed because I don't care who killed Big Jim. One of these days, I'm going to run for mayor, and I don't need any negative publicity associated with me. What you do out in the woods with darkies is your business. What you do in the police station is mine. I don't want to have to explain a thing. Is that clear?"

"Yes, Sir," again, in unison.

# CHAPTER 5

## YOUR BALM IN GILEAD

———◆———

### Monday, September 18, 1933

ROCKY HADN'T BEEN ABLE TO stand since he'd been back-handed by O'Brien. His feet hurt too much to try and stand on them. Getting up on the cot in his cell was a problem which couldn't be surmounted. Dragging himself to the toilet was possible, but actually getting up on it was more difficult than trying to get onto his cot. He decided that he could unbutton his pants, push down his underwear, and relieve himself while lying on his side. Thankfully, the urine ran away from him. He existed this way for three nights and most of the last day. He had no food and he had no water. On the fourth day, near the end of O'Brien's and Brown's shift, they picked him up and placed him in their police car and took him back to Black Bottom where they left him, his shoes, his socks, and his brace near the pump and not at his home.

The root man saw the dumping of Rocky and went to his home to retrieve the cart. He and others helped Rocky into the cart and then pushed him home. Upon entering, his first words were, "Where's Vanda Mae?"

No one answered Rocky. He kept asking and all they did was lift him off of the cart and onto his bed. Bobby arrived at the door as all but the root man were leaving. The root man said, "She left yesterday." Bobby said, "No one thought that you would be back here. Everyone thought that you were going to confess to killing Big Jim and that you would be kept in jail for trial."

"She left with Smooth," said the root man. "He came into your home and started giving her dust. After that, it was easy for her to let you go."

"I save her from Big Jim and she abandons me. I kill her rapist and she don't hang around to see what happens to me. I take her in when she was homeless and she don't keep my home ready for my return. I feels like my stomach has been ripped out of me. I feels like I just discovered that my balls been removed in my sleep. I conquered Goliath, but I ain't got Goliath balls; I ain't got David balls. What I got is nothing. I ain't no man. I ain't even no foolish man. I'm just a fool."

Bobby, hearing this last statement spoke up. "Rocky, you're not a fool. You tricked Big Jim. You outsmarted him. You went to Hell when you went to that police station. You came back, beat up, but you'll heal. The police still don't know that you killed Big Jim. You outsmarted the police, Rocky. Rocky, you gotta stop calling yourself a fool. You're a man, Rocky and you got all of your man parts. You got your brains and you got your balls."

"Rocky," said Olatunji, the root man, "...you can't walk for a few days. You goin' to need someone to help you on and off the pot; you goin' to need someone to prepare meals for you, if the women folk don't bring you food; and you goin' to need someone to take care of those wounds. You need to let someone take care of you. You're the warrior who protected our community. You need to let us be your Balm in Gilead. We appreciate everything you done for us Rocky."

Tunji stayed with Rocky and took care of his wounds for the next three days and then visited him every day for the next five days. He brought him sweetgrass so that he could get back to making baskets for sale. Rocky accepted Tunji's kindness and the kindness of his neighbors. Everyday someone brought enough food for both of the men. Rocky began to feel better about himself and his outlook changed with regard to Vanda Mae. He felt as though Smooth recognized that Vanda Mae wasn't in her right mind and that he took advantage of her. He felt that Vanda Mae had been tricked into following Smooth and that the dust kept her from dealing with the problems she had. He convinced himself that Vanda Mae was essentially kidnapped from Black Bottom and now what was he going to do about it?

# CHAPTER 6

# WILD LIFE DREAMS

———•———

*Monday, September 18 – Saturday, September 23, 1933*

BABIES DON'T CARE HOW THEY look: They just cry. They don't wipe away their tears, they're not ashamed of how they look. They're upset and crying is their expression of that feeling. This is how it was with Rocky. Each night, he went to sleep with tears in his eyes. Memories of the good times which he shared with Vanda Mae were routed by visions of her giving her body to Smooth and selling her body to other men. He dreamt of her as Smooth's slave and dust as the manacle of control. Every night he had visions of his woman lying nude on a bed while a hard erect Smooth straddled her chest and shot dust up her nose. This pollination was followed by an endless number of drones diving into her love triangle and then suddenly, flying out, and copious amounts of honey streaming from the dark patch. The nightly dream ended with a bear lumbering up to an undulating Vanda Mae and licking honey from the triangular patch.

Rocky awoke in a pool of sweat, with his eyes burning, and his heart racing. He didn't think that he was losing his mind, but this nightly dream was a bad sign. He knew he needed help. He felt that he had to talk to Tunji and Bobby. They wouldn't make fun of his dream and when he got both of them to his home; he told them what he saw every night when he slept.

Bobby's reply was that, time would heal his wounded heart; just like it did with his feet and legs. Tunji, a man old enough to be Rocky's father and a man who was the spiritual teacher of Rocky said that time does heal, but so does correctly applied action. "If Vanda Mae is a captive slave, then the manacle must be broken. It will be Vanda Mae's decision then as to whether she wants Smooth or you and you must accept that the decision could come down against you. If she chooses Smooth, you would have to walk away knowing that you'd done everything in your power to have her in your life."

"Ya sayin' I gotta do somethin' to get Vanda Mae off of dust, right?" said Rocky.

"Rocky, Vanda Mae didn't have a good mind when Smooth gave her dust. She had gaps in her brain. Those gaps were filled with dust and dust is like a spider's web, it reaches out and gets into other parts of the brain. Vanda Mae won't think about you until she has been off of dust for at least a few months. She won't really care about Smooth either; as long as he is supplying her with dust. Rocky, she won't care about all of the other men going up inside her as long as she can get dusted. Dust is the key, Rocky. Ya gotta get her off of dust." Tunji, looking back and forth between Bobby and Rocky, continued speaking. "Getting her off of dust ain't goin' to be easy when right now it seems as though she don't want to come off of dust. So, about all that you can do is pray on it. Pray that she gets off of dust and then decides to come back to Black Bottom, in a few years, for a short visit."

"Tunji, Bobby, I want her off of dust and I want her in her right mind, but I also want to be in her heart, cause she's in mine."

Bobby interrupted, "Rocky, Tunji is talking sense right now: real good common sense. Vanda Mae ain't goin' to be givin' her heart to you, if you ain't around. Even if she comes off of dust, you ain't gonna be around. And prayer is good, Rocky, cause it gonna help heal your heart, but prayer ain't gonna bring a healed Vanda Mae back to Black Bottom. Rocky, it would be like you praying that the sun turns blue tomorrow. It ain't gonna happen. You can ask all your African angels to intercede, still the sun ain't gonna be blue tomorrow and Vanda Mae ain't comin' back to Black Bottom."

"Rocky," said Tunji, ". . . you know my son is up in New York City. You know he works for the railroads and I see him regularly for short periods of time when the train stops in Charleston. Rocky, if my son were assigned to a different route, I wouldn't see him at all. My son tells me all of the time, once Coloreds go north, they come south for funerals and those funerals are for close relatives and then they go right back to the North."

"Rocky," said Bobby, ". . . heal your heart with some prayer and some basket weaving because it is over between you and Vanda Mae.

"You know, I hear both of you and you make sense," said Rocky. "Thank you for coming to talk with me, you have helped me to get things straight in my mind. I gotta get Vanda Mae off of dust before she can give me her heart;

that is if she's gonna do that. Uhm-huh, so I'm gonna go to New York City."

Bobby asked immediately, "How you gonna do that, Rocky?"

The reply was, "I don't know."

CHAPTER 7

# WOVEN PROFITS

---

### Sunday, September 24, 1933

IT WAS GETTING CLOSE TO supper time yesterday, when
Bobby and Tunji were trying to change Rocky's mind. Just
because he had killed Big Jim didn't mean that he could
take on the Klan and the Klan was everywhere, waiting for
an innocent Colored man to step out of his place. The Klan
always wanted to teach a Colored guy a lesson. Bobby joked
that the adults wouldn't be bothered with Rocky. He said
that they would let their twelve year old sons string him up.
It would be a training exercise for them; an initiation into
the Klan. The adults would watch them and take over just
in case he somehow got the better of the 12 year olds.

Well, that was last night and before the moon had come
up, Bobby had told Melissa and Melissa had told Hattie and
Hattie told every adult she came in contact with, living on
Black Bottom Island.

Rocky was more hopeful regarding his prospects for traveling to New York City than the others were. He had decided
to go to the city by boat but didn't tell anyone that because

he didn't want anyone to know that he had saved a significant amount of money. Basket weaving had paid off for him and he didn't want to be robbed. He let everyone think that he would panhandle his way north.

Inside his home, with no one there, he absorbed the quiet. He looked at the altar he had created; a cross in the center with two small African masks on either side of it and candles on the outer sides of the masks. There was a small branch with leaves sitting in a glass of water and these were beside an empty bowl. His altar also had a bell which he picked up. He rubbed the bell on his chest, on his forehead, on his face, ears, and neck. He rubbed the bell on his thighs, on his crotch, and then on both arms. He finished by rubbing the bell between his hands and then placing the bell on his lips. He kissed the bell three times and then set it on the altar. He was settling into himself, readying himself for prayer.

Looking at the masks reminded him of his grandfather, Seth Johnson, a man who died in 1925 at the age of 75. He was a man who told Rocky that he had memories of his grandfather who had been born in Africa. Seth Johnson conveyed memories of working in the rice fields of South Carolina. Granddad had told Rocky to always be cautious around white folks and to trust them only while they were in sight. His grandfather told him to learn as much as he could and to always be thinking how a situation could be made better for himself. Granddad also taught him to pray every day and to hold his African ancestors in esteem. Granddad and dad smiled when Rocky demonstrated that he could name his ancestors back to the African.

Rocky picked up the bell and flicked it three times and waited. He repeated this two more times. His prayer began:

*Please, Jesus, enter my body. Please, Mary, enter my body. Please, Eshu, enter my body and place me in the presence of Obatala. Place me in the presence of God. Place me in the presence of Orunmila. Place me in the presence of the Holy Ghost. Let their love surround me and take over my body. Let their love wrap around me like a blanket around a baby. Let their love heal the wounds on my body and in my heart. Eshu, I am asking that you put me in the presence of my African angels, my parents, my grandparents, my great grandparents, my great great grandparents. Please put me in the presence of all those men and women who fought for freedom. Please put me in the presence of Denmark Vesey. Please let me be guided by righteousness and humility.*

*Obatala, Orunmila, Ghost, I am asking for your guid-ance and for your protection. Lemanja, I am asking for your guidance and for your protection. You know that I am considering something that is extremely dangerous. You know that traveling by land and by water opens me up to all sorts of perils. Please help me to be strong and to make the best decisions for my situations. I put my faith in you. I put my trust in you. Ache'.*

Rocky took the branch from the glass and poured the water into the bowl. He dipped the leaves of the branch into the water and then shook drops onto the altar. He dipped the leaves again and then flung water around his home. Lastly, he dipped the leaves into the bowl and shook water onto himself. He rested with the branch in his lap.

Later in the night, when everyone had gone to sleep, he dug underneath his altar and removed a bag of money. No one knew of this hiding place, not even Vanda Mae. Basket weaving had been profitable and he had saved his money. When Vanda Mae had been with him, he kept the cash in his pockets and rarely transferred anything beneath his altar. Now, as he was about to embark on his journey, he needed all of it.

Rocky slept with the money beside him. He dreamed of his grandfather. He saw his grandfather on his death bed. He saw the root man, Olatunji, and he remembered their praying over him. The ritual involved the gentle sprinkling of warm herb infused water over granddad's body. They made him comfortable and they prayed. They rang the bell and they prayed. They continued praying and ringing the bell and sprinkling water after they knew that he had died. Rocky saw himself sitting beside his grandfather waiting for the undertaker to take him away. He saw his grandfather being lowered into a grave at the potter's field.

## CHAPTER 8

# SHADOWS

———◆———

*Monday, September 25, 1933*

IN THE MORNING, ROCKY STARTED packing his altar into an old suitcase which had to be held together by rope. He put his clothes into a different suitcase which was held together by a belt. He used an old shirt to wrap around his money bag and then tied the sleeves around his waist. Ladies from the community started bringing him shoeboxes full of fried chicken. They were wishing him well on his journey and suggested that he travel by night and hide out during the day.

Hattie brought a shoebox of fried chicken to Rocky and told him that the trip was too dangerous to make. She told him that it would be impossible for him to panhandle his way to New York City. Rocky acknowledged the dangers of going to New York City by goat cart and told her that God was on his side. He said that he killed Big Jim, a man that was as wide as a door and as tall as a door. He said that he survived being tortured by the police. He told Hattie that a lot of bad things could happen to him, but he was just as likely to die from pneumonia or rabies before he got to New York.

"That ain't a good thought, Rocky. In fact, going to New York by goat cart makes about as much sense as if you put that cart in the water and paddled up north."

"You know Hattie, I never thought of that. It would be a way of avoiding all the race hating white folks though. Right?"

"Rocky, you got scrambled eggs for brains. I'm going to continue praying for you." With that said, Hattie walked out the door.

At dusk, Rocky pulled his goat cart into his home and piled the suitcases and the baskets on it. There was barely enough room for him to kneel on the cart.

That night, he left Black Bottom. It was dark and he was afraid. He questioned if the goat could pull him all of the way to Charleston. The road was relatively flat, but still it was a goat and not a mule. He thought of Vanda Mae as he traveled down the road. All he could see was his woman lying underneath Smooth. His woman snorting dust and doing things to Smooth that she used to do to him. As the goat pulled him into the night, he continued to see Smooth as a dominant man; Smooth as a free man with money. Smooth went up and down the East Coast when he chose and how he chose. He was the trickster in the stories which his grandfather told him. He lived for pleasure and he exuded charm. He could get a woman and he could keep a woman. Rocky imagined Smooth bone hard and naked, taking Vanda Mae in all sorts of positions which he could never achieve. Through tears, Rocky saw a naked Smooth standing on the bed; the bed on which Rocky and Vanda Mae made love.

Smooth was more than naked and erect, he was wearing an African mask. At his knees was Vanda Mae, also naked and wearing an African mask and servicing him.

Rocky told himself that if he continued with this thinking, he would go crazy. He told himself that he was as much of a man as Smooth and although he had a problem getting around, he had done things that Smooth hadn't. It had taken him time, but he had honestly saved up a significant amount of money; he had endured torture; and Smooth had done neither. He had killed Big Jim and Smooth hadn't. Rocky replaced his mind's images of Smooth with images of himself taking down Big Jim with his prayer. He was David conquering Goliath. He was the porcupine with the bad attitude that no animal wanted to mess with.

These images helped Rocky, but he thought that he would still stop the cart and rest and eat some of the fried chicken. He wasn't hungry, but he wanted to put his mind on other things. He'd eat and feed his goat corn meal and after resting a spell, he'd get back on the road.

Rocky loved the fried chicken which had been prepared for him. The ladies of Black Bottom thought that they would most likely not see him again; certainly not as a living, breathing, talking human. If they saw him again, he'd be a charred corpse. Yes, it was better for him to focus on his demise, than on Vanda Mae and Smooth.

As he was sitting on the side of the road eating out of the shoe box, he thought that he saw something. Movement in the shadows, he told himself, was nothing to be scared of. Rocky knew that all sorts of animals could be out there and that probably, the smell of the chicken was drawing an animal. It was probably a fox, a solitary creature which wouldn't bother him. This time though, the movement seemed closer. Rocky told himself it was his imagination. Nothing was out there. He was startled though when the goat started bleating. Then he started thinking that maybe it was the Klan sneaking up on him, getting ready to string him up. He clearly saw a shadow move this time. His mind was racing. The movement didn't make sense though, if it were being generated by a human. Then the shadow was beside him and even though it was dark, he knew that this apparition, this phantom, actually had substance. Rocky could feel the warm breath of a big and powerful dog. The dog was quietly watching Rocky. Rocky could see that the dog had the outlines of an American Bull Dog, the breed which was used to catch his runaway brethren. The goat's bleats were nonstop at this point, but the dog had not attacked. It was still watching Rocky and it occurred to him that maybe the dog was not going to attack. Maybe the dog wanted something to eat. Rocky pulled chicken off of the bone and stretched out his arm to the canine and the animal ate. More chicken was pulled off the bone and handed to the dog and it was quickly devoured. Again and again and again he fed the dog. He patted the dog. He sang to the dog. He named the dog, Bell. He pushed the empty shoe box toward Bell and she licked its insides. Rocky sat with his back to the cart and started singing a hymn and Bell stretched out beside him and placed her head in his lap. He stroked her head and was happy that the movement in the shadows had been friendly. He couldn't sleep soundly, though. Sleep came and went. He was uncomfortable, but he was content with how the day had ended.

# THE ANGEL OF SHADOWS

*Tuesday Morning, September 26, 1933*

LYING DOWN ON THE GROUND did not suit Rocky's mind or body, that was why he leaned against the cart the entire night; sleeping on his left shoulder, then on the right, then with both shoulder blades against the side of the cart. Bell had no problem with the ground. She was on it with her head in Rocky's lap. She was quite content, though her right ear was twitching. Rocky lifted her head up and gently tried to maneuver himself from under it. The dog yawned, stretched, and watched Rocky struggle to get up. Once he had achieved a comfortable standing position (with the aid of his crutch) the morning urge to void came upon him. Stepping away from the cart, he looked to his left and saw nothing down the road and then to his right and saw nothing down the road except last night's shoebox and trees. He undid his fly, leaned forward a little, and relaxed. That was when the rabbit appeared. He and Bell saw it at the same time. Bell chased the rabbit through the bushes, through the weeds, and off into the woods. Rocky watched as his night time companion ran further and further away. He knew that he would have to be moving on soon. He hobbled over to the shoe box, picked it up, and then placed it before the goat. He got some water from his cart, drank some, and then poured some into the box for the goat. He'd wait a few minutes for the goat to finish drinking, before leaving the dog.

Off in the distance, he could see a car driving up the road. Rocky thought, that it was day light and he shouldn't have any trouble. He'd tell the truth; he was on his way to the dock to sell his baskets. That was the story he would give to any white or Colored person who inquired of him. There was no need to mention his intention to leave the state by an ocean going vessel.

The car drew closer and Rocky could make out that it was a police car and that the driver was O'Brien. Rocky hoped that the car would not come to a stop, but it did. O'Brien stepped from the car, walked up to Rocky, punched him in the stomach, and then punched him in the jaw. When Rocky hit the ground, O'Brien took the crutch and started beating him with it.

"Who killed Big Jim, Rocky? Ain't no point in keeping it a secret. It's just me and you, so you might as well talk."

"I don't know who killed Big Jim. I swear I don't know."

"Yeah, Rocky. You don't know but, maybe a little birdie will tell you. Let's see, where can we find a little birdie? I know Rocky, we can find a birdie in a tree." He took Rocky's crutch with him to his patrol car, dropped it beside the car, and opened the trunk. O'Brien removed the rope and walked back to Rocky. He stood on Rocky's good foot and tied the rope around Rocky's braced foot. He then proceeded to drag Rocky down the knoll into the woods.

Rocky was trying to hold onto bushes and weeds but nothing could prevent O'Brien from finding a tree with a low enough and strong enough branch. O'Brien threw the rope over a branch and started hoisting Rocky. Rocky was screaming. "I don't know who killed Big Jim." The pain was excruciating. O'Brien pushed the hanging man away with his foot and when he swung back, he pushed him harder. Rocky thought to protect his face because he knew that a kick would greet him on his swing back. Rocky found himself screaming again as his body was suddenly hoisted. The scream stopped when his body slammed into the trunk of the tree and he fell to the ground. He heard O'Brien screaming but he couldn't see what was happening. He heard muffled sounds and then he heard a snap and a fall.

Rocky was still looking up into the trees when he realized that he was no longer being tormented by O'Brien. When he rolled over onto his stomach, he saw that Bell was underneath O'Brien and clutching him by the back of the neck. She was trying to shimmy out from under him and when she had, she grabbed the cop's adam's apple and ripped it out. If the snapping of O'Brien's neck hadn't killed him, then this final assault would.

Rocky was resting by the tree catching his breath when he realized that O'Brien's car was on the road and that he was sitting on the ground near O'Brien's lifeless body. Rocky started crawling up the knoll, back to the road. When he got near the road, he realized that he was still pulling O'Brien's rope. He had to roll onto his side, untie the rope, and then resume crawling to the car. Looking both ways, he crawled to his crutch and struggled to stand. He closed the trunk and then got into the car and noticed that the keys were not in the ignition. He did not want to go back to the body to retrieve the keys, but he knew that it had to be done if he were to hide the car in the woods.

Bell had been following him all through his crawling, standing, and hobbling. When he got back to the corpse, Bell squatted on O'Brien's face and urinated.

"Yeah, Bell. You got the right idea." Rocky then unzipped his fly and rained on O'Brien's face. It wasn't enough revenge, but it would have to suffice.

"You're wasting time on revenge," he told himself. "Get the keys and get out of here."

Hobbling back to the police car, Rocky threw his crutch over to the passenger's side and jumped into the front seat. He then drove the car deep into the woods. Outside of the car, he grabbed soil from the ground and smeared it on the door handle and steering wheel and any other part of the car that he thought that his hands may have touched. He then used his crutch to hobble back to his goat cart and get another box of chicken. Quickly heading back to the police car, he rolled down the driver's side window, threw the chicken into the car, went through his soil smearing routine again and then hobbled back to his cart. He and Bell were now on their way toward the dock. He hoped that he had covered his bases and that nothing would be traced back to him. All of this time, his heart and mind were racing. He thought that his story should be simple; he hadn't seen O'Brien. That was his story for Colored people; that was his story for white people; and that was his story for cops. That would be the story that he'd stick to. Bell followed beside him.

CHAPTER 10

# THE TRANSITION OF ANGELS

———•———

## Tuesday, September 26, 1933

ROCKY PULLED UP ONTO THE dock and made himself comfortable. He set his baskets out and he placed Bell behind himself. He sat on his two suitcases and yelled out, "Beautiful baskets for sale. Beautiful island sweet grass baskets for sale. Give them as gifts or use them in your home or use them at picnics. Baskets for sale."

Rocky saw a well dressed Colored man coming down the dock. When the man was closer, Rocky said, "Hi, Mister. Why don't you buy a basket for the Mrs.?"

"I don't have a Mrs."

"You could buy one for your girlfriend."

"Sir, I don't have a girlfriend either."

"Well a prosperous looking man like you, why don't you part with a dollar or two so that I can earn enough money to get to New York City?"

"Are you going to take a boat to New York City or are you going to take that goat cart to New York City?"

"I wanna take a boat to New York. I figure that it'd be easier on my body. I got this bad leg you see."

"Well that's the boat up there. That's the SS Caribbean Yankee and it's leaving for N.Y. in 90 minutes. I don't know if the Captain would allow you to bring your pets, but if he did you'd probably have to pay for them to go in the hold of the boat and you'd probably have to have them in cages and since it doesn't look like you got any cages for your critters, you'd have to rent their cages. All of that would add to the price of your ticket."

"How much would it cost me to go to New York City?"

"Probably about $30.00. Maybe $50.00 if you got your own room."

"I ain't never bought a ticket before in my life. Would you help me? I don't want to appear foolish."

"Sure that's not a problem, but do you have enough money for a ticket?"

"I got enough for a ticket. Say, what's your name?"

"Langston's my name. Langston Hughes."

"Rocky's my name. Rocky Johnson. Oh, shit. See this cop coming up the dock? He's going to begin hassling me."

Ofc. Brown approached Rocky.

"Hi, Rocky."

"Hi, Ofc. Brown."

"You seen Ofc. O'Brien?"

"No, Sir."

"Rocky, it ain't like him not to come to work."

"I ain't seen him."

"Rocky, how come you selling your baskets here and how come you're so dirty?"

"I can get better prices from the tourists here on this dock and I had to sleep outside last night."

"Rocky, you always got answers. You're a smart man Rocky. You'd be something more than a basket weaver if you'd gone to school. That's why we put laws in place to keep smart darkies like you from competing with good white folks like me."

Ofc. Brown casually took out his gun and aimed it Rocky. "Rocky, who killed Big Jim?" Langston's mouth opened in amazement.

"Oh my God. Don't shoot me. Please don't shoot me. I done told you, I don't know who killed Big Jim. I don't know nothin about Big Jim's death."

"You're lying Rocky. I know you're lying. I might have to run you in for vagrancy. The judge won't like sentencing a cripple to the chain gang, but you can spend another night in jail, right? It would be better than sleeping outside again, right?"

Brown looked around himself and saw that a crowd of Coloreds and whites had gathered. Everyone was watching Rocky beg for his life. Brown remembered that he was supposed to be looking for Ofc. O'Brien. "You know Rocky, I want you gone from this dock by sundown or I'm going to arrest you for vagrancy. Rocky, while you're selling those baskets, I want you to think about going back to jail and also think about who killed Big Jim. OK?"

Rocky was speechless. He just looked at Brown.

"Rocky, I'm talking to you. Do you hear me talking to you, Rocky?"

All Rocky could do was nod his head.

Brown was speaking in such a mellow tone that Bell didn't get upset. Brown wasn't swinging at Rocky and Rocky wasn't screaming. Bell had no reason to protect him.

"Think about this also, Rocky," and the bullet exploded into Bell's head. The crowd gasped and mumbled. How could a cop kill a crippled man's dog? Brown heard them talking as he walked away.

When Brown was out of sight, Rocky started crying. Langston stooped down and hugged him.

"A Colored man's life ain't worth nothin' down here. Ain't worth nothin. I gotta get out of here. Can you help me, Mr. Hughes?"

"It's Langston and yeah, I'll help you. Let's put this stuff in the cart and go on up to the boat."

While loading the cart, they both realized that the crowd had gotten quiet again and then they realized that Brown had not gone that far.

Brown came out of the crowd and said to Rocky, "I'm a real bastard for shooting your dog, Rocky. Only someone who has ice water and booze running through his veins could do something so cold and so heartless. But shit, if I wasn't on duty, I'd have a beer right now, to keep my alcohol level up. But I am on duty right now Rocky and I gotta find O'Brien."

Brown was quick on the draw. When the bullet entered the goat's skull, blood, bones and brains flew onto Rocky and Langston.

"Remember Rocky, I want you off this dock by sundown."

Langston tried pushing a seated Rocky and his suitcases the 75 feet toward the Caribbean Yankee but Rocky was horrible in keeping the cart going in a straight line. Langston figured that Rocky's nerves had gotten the better of him. Although he didn't want to assume a beast of burden position, Langston decided that he could more efficiently pull the cart the remaining distance, than continuously push, stop, change direction, and then start again.

At the boat, Langston talked with the captain and asked for help in getting a potential passenger on board. Captain Edwards sent two of the Colored attendants down to the pier to help Rocky get up the gang plank. Afterward, one of them went back down to the dock and brought up his suitcases while the other brought up his baskets. The attendants stood beside Rocky and waited for their next instructions from the Captain.

The Captain told Rocky, "$30 to share the room with Mr. Hughes or $50 to have a private room." When Rocky stated that he'd share the room with Mr. Hughes "... if it was O.K. with him" and Langston said "Sure" Rocky felt so much better. He felt that things were beginning to look up for him. He realized though that the Captain was waiting to be paid and then Langston said, "Pay the man, Rocky." Rocky unbuttoned his shirt and then the top of his long underwear to get to his home made money belt. The Captain and Langston smiled at Rocky's security method. The two attendants looked at each other and with smiles, stifled laughs. Rocky peeled off $30 and gave it to the Captain and then buttoned himself up. He knew that he was coming off as a country bumpkin; he knew that in many ways, he was a country bumpkin; and he knew that he would be a dead country bumpkin if he spent another night in Charleston, so this appearance of a lack of sophistication had to be tolerated because only he and Langston knew the hell which he'd just experienced.

Rocky's first words on entering the room were, "Man, this is small."

"Yeah," Langston replied. "I've been sleeping in the bottom bunk, so I'll move up to the top. Why don't you take a shower and while you're in there why don't you wash your clothes? But first, count your money and then when you come out of the shower, count your money again; that way, we'll both know that nothing is missing."

"It's $380."

"You're not going to count it now?" replied Langston.

"No. I feel that you're an honest man."

"Thank you. I'll be reading and writing up on the deck for about the next two hours" and with that said, Langston left Rocky.

While sitting on the deck, Langston realized that Rocky would most likely have a hard time taking a shower without a deck chair to sit in. He got up and found the Captain and explained the problem. The Captain told Langston to go to the galley and tell the cook that he said that you're to have a milk crate. "That should be strong enough to support Mr. Johnson."

Rocky was sitting on his bunk feeling sorry for himself. He realized very quickly that he couldn't take a shower because he had to sit down for his safety. He realized that he couldn't wash his clothes for the same reason. He knew his mobility would be challenged even more once the boat took off from the dock. He thought of Brown's viciousness and of how anyone could treat him and his animals so cruelly. He knew that before he went to bed, that he had to pray for the souls of his pets. He thought about how Vanda Mae used to give him baths. How she would take the wash cloth and go all over his body. How her hands would replace the washcloth and how those soapy hands would drive him crazy with lust. He thought about how her lips would linger on his body as they descended down one side of his body and up the other. He had never dreamed that sex could be as exciting and as satisfying as it had been with Vanda Mae. Before she came along, he had dreamed of female partners but knew only self love. But he loved Vanda Mae for more than the physical thrills she brought to him. At night, they lay side by side talking to each other, hugging each other. During the day, she would gather sweet grass and clean it for him and he would make the grass into baskets. She was a helpmate to him. In keeping her sober and keeping her housed, he was her helpmate. He knew that they were made for each other but also, that there would be problems that they would have to face and conquer together. He knew that they could do it. He'd killed Big Jim, survived police torture, and set out on a journey of hundreds of miles, just to be with her. He knew that he would find her in that big city up north. He knew it and they would get back together. He didn't think that Smooth would present any problems as a rival for her affection; after all, he was Rocky, the hero. When she saw that he wasn't dead, she'd come back to him immediately. He smiled at the memory of how Big Jim was strangling him and how he was able to jab the knife into the murderer's neck. He smiled at the sudden uselessness of Big Jim's hands and at how quickly he became dead weight on top of him. Rocky's smile broadened when he reflected on Big Jim's facial expressions as they looked into each others' faces. Big Jim knew as his vision was fading, that the victor was Rocky and that his ass had been mutilated by a cripple. Rocky remembered all of the blood from Big Jim's stomach flowing over him. He remembered blood from Big Jim's neck, dripping on his face. Proudly, he considered this to be a baptism of himself. Shango and Eshu would have to be thanked during the evening prayers.

These were pleasant and painful memories which were jarred by the movement of the boat and the opening of the cabin door. Langston was standing there with a smile on his face and a milk crate in his hand.

———◆———

Rocky had finished showering and was sitting on his bunk in his underwear arranging his altar on top of his suitcases. The one chair in the room was positioned so that it would be facing him as he was sitting and praying on the bunk. The chair was for Langston. Langston came out of the shower with his underwear on and wanted to know what was going on and was told about the impending prayer. He was asked to join in. Langston stated that he would, out of curiosity concerning this ritual, but admitted that he had no idea as to what he could contribute to a prayer involving a cross and an African mask. Langston knew of Santeria and had witnessed ceremonies performed by Cuban priests of this faith, but was surprised to see that Rocky seemed to know something of this belief system. Rocky reassured Langston that his presence and attention were needed and that he would do the rest. "Also, 3 cups of water are needed, can you bring them to the altar?" Langston didn't answer, he just got them from the bathroom sink. Rocky placed one paper cup on the suitcase and to Langston's right. One cup was placed on the suitcase on Langston's left side and one cup in the center of the suitcase. Rocky asked Langston to turn off the cabin light and Langston complied. Rocky told Langston that, "We must be touching throughout this prayer. Either our feet are touching or our hands; always, skin on skin. Now put one foot on top of mine and I'll put one foot on top of yours." Rocky began by lighting the first of 3 candles and then ringing the bell 3 times. He bowed his head and held Langston's hands and prayed:

*"Dear Eleggua, you are one of the many angels of God. Your presence is needed at the beginning and ending of all prayers because you are the one who opens the door and closes the door to the land of the blessed departed and those that are yet to be born, to Olodumare, my forefathers' name for God, to the Holy Ghost, to Jesus, and those angels who will never be men, nor women, nor children; please Eleggua, be with us now."* Rocky struck the bell 3 times.

*"Dear God, some call you Jesus, some call you Jehovah, some call you the Holy Father, I press you to my heart as the Holy Ghost. In my motherland of Africa, you are known by many names. One of those names is Olodumare. Just as the Holy Ghost makes his presence known in the trees and birds, in the sea and in the mountains, and in the air that we breathe and in the smoke that we avoid; we acknowledge that Your presence, Olodumare, is everywhere and that You are the Master of all humans, animals, and forces of nature. Thank You for allowing me to get this far in my life. Thank You for allowing me to get out of Black Bottom and to still have all of my fingers and toes and eyes and teeth. Thank You for bringing the Angel Bell into my life. Only You could have protected me when my life was hanging by a thread. Thank You for Your divine intervention. Thank You also for giving my goat the strength to pull me all of the way to Charleston. You knew that they could go no further and that they could be of no more use to me on*

*my journey and so rather than have them suffer, You swiftly ended their lives. Thank You also oh great Olodumare for bringing Langston into my life. If he never were to help me again, he has helped me greatly.*

Rocky lets go of Langston's hand and strikes a match for another candle. When the flame has transferred itself to the wick, he rings the bell 3 times. "Langston, when I begin thanking our Guardian Angels, I want you to thank them also by saying Thank You and repeating the name of the Guardian Angel." Langston replied, "O.K."

*"Olodumare, You have surrounded us with Your angels, Your Guardian Angels. Yemoja and Olokun please watch over us while we are on this ocean. Many, many years ago, our forefathers and foremothers were received by you as they exited the boats during the Middle Passage. We are immeasurably stronger as a race today, because You chose our more fragile relatives. Thank You, Yemoja and Olokun for our lives today.*

"Thank You, Yemoja and Olokun for our lives today."

*"Obatala infuses our spines, our sinews, our blood, and our brains with moral uprightness. Thank You, Obatala for this gift and responsibility."*

"Thank You, Obatala for this gift and responsibility."

*"Shango, Angel of manhood, we feel Your presence in the flames between us. You give us the strength to go after what we want. You give us the strength to fight when we must fight. You give us the power to consummate our relationships. We look forward to consummated relationships. We look forward towards interlocking*

*relationships. Shango, oh Shango, infuse us with the Holy Spirit of the first man. Infuse us with the Holy Spirit of Adam. Help us to walk proudly as men, to accept each other as men, different though we may be, and to accomplish our missions as men here on this boat and in New York City. Thank You for joining us in this room, Shango."*

"Thank you for joining us in this room, Shango."

"Langston, I want you to be silent and keep your feet in place. I'm going to sprinkle water on you. The water will come from the middle cup. I'm going to say a prayer and I want you to say the last sentence in the prayer. I'll squeeze your hand to let you know that I've spoken the last sentence. When you're saying the last sentence, sprinkle me with water using one hand. Do it just as I have done you. Oh, after I've sprinkled water on your chest, I want you to bend forward so that I can sprinkle water on the top of your back. Remember, you're sprinkling water with one hand and holding my hand with your other hand. This is after I light the last candle and ring the bell."

*"Orunmila, Angel of foresight, Angel of wisdom, infuse yourself in us this night."*

Rocky dipped his fingers in the cup and flicked water at the face and chest and stomach of Langston. Langston bent forward and Rocky flicked water on the back of Langston's head, neck, and the top of his back. Rocky dipped his fingers in the cup again and flicked water up one leg, across Langston's crotch, and down the other leg.

*"Orunmila, Angel of foresight and wisdom, infuse yourself in us tonight."* He then squeezed Langston's hand.

"Orunmila, Angel of foresight and wisdom, infuse yourself in us tonight." Langston then dipped his fingers in the cup and flicked water on Rocky's face, chest, stomach, back, legs and crotch.

"*Ochosi, Angel of those who seek justice in particular and seekers in general, infuse yourself in us tonight.*" He then flicked water on Langston as before.

"*Ochosi, Angel of seekers of justice, infuse yourself in us tonight.*" He then squeezed Langston's hand.

"Ochosi, Angel of seekers of justice, infuse yourself in us tonight." Langston flicked water on Rocky.

"*Ozain, Angel of the forest and preparer of the healing herbal broth, please keep us well and protect Vanda Mae. We honor you with interlocking arms and by drinking these cups of water. In better times, we would honor you with a true herbal broth, for now though, please accept our humble offering.*"

The men took their cups, interlocked their arms, looked deeply in each other's eyes, and drank the water. After putting down the cups and holding both hands, Rocky said, "*Ozain, keep us well and protect Vanda Mae.*" Langston repeated this. "*Obatala, keep us morally upright and protect Vanda Mae.* Langston again repeated. *Orunmila, give us foresight and wisdom and protect Vanda Mae. Eshu, Angel of travelers, protect me, protect Langston, and protect Vanda Mae. Eleggua, thank you for entrance into the Holy Land.* After Langston had repeated sentence by sentence, that which Rocky said, Rocky blew out the candle on his right and directed Langston to do the same with the candle towards his right. He then said that they would blow out the middle candle together and they did. *"Ache', Amen."* Langston repeated, "Ache', Amen." They broke the skin to skin contact and got in their bunks. Both men were engorged.

Langston wondered to what extent Rocky was flirting with him or teasing him. He also wondered about the ceremony. How had Rocky learned such a ceremony? How did he know the names of the spirits which he called angels? Langston had seen Santeria ceremonies in Cuba, but even there he had to be brought to the ceremony by a Cuban mutual friend of the priest.

Rocky broke the silence, "How you feelin?"

"I feel hot Rocky and Shango is making me even hotter. In fact, I got the spirits of Adam and Shango flexing their muscles in my body right now and they're making me sweat. I think that I can get them to quiet down if I take a cold shower," and with that, Langston left his bunk and was in the shower. After a few minutes, he returned to his bunk and asked Rocky how he learned about Santeria? Rocky said, "What's Santeria?"

"Those angels," replied Langston, how did you learn about them?

"My grandfather and the root man, they taught me. My great great grandfather was captured in Africa when he was very young and he remembered some of the angels. He lived long enough to teach not only his son but also his grandson, my grandfather about the Orishas, our African angels. My great great grandfather was too young to have learned the proper way to conduct the religious ceremonies but he remembered some names and what they stood for. All of this was passed onto my grandfather and he passed it onto me. He lead me and my father in nightly prayer. The root man also knew about the African angels. He had learned of them from his father and grandfather. The root man, my grandfather, and me would get together and pray. It didn't have to be Sunday. Plenty of times we would get together on Wednesday nights and pray and eat and sing.

The root man was there when my grandfather was dying. Together, we prayed him into Heaven. We didn't think that Olodumare would mind if our ceremony was different. So that's how I know about the African angels and if I call them, "Angels," and the ladies in the neighborhood hear me call out Jehovah and Jesus, and the Holy Ghost; if they hear me recite The Lord's Prayer and say Amen; then they are relieved and think that I might be crippled, but I'm saved. Langston, I'm a Christian who believes that there are plenty of ways to realize God in your life. I ask my African angels for help, because that's why they're there. I also honor them through prayer, because I know that they have helped me many times and in many situations. Langston, I love my people and I keep them alive by praying for them through our ancestors and through our African angels."

"Thank you for your prayers, Rocky."

"Good night, Langston."

"Good night, Rocky."

# CHAPTER 11

# GETTING TO KNOW YOU

———◆———

*Wednesday, September 27 - Thursday, September 28, 1933*

BOTH MEN ROSE EARLY FOR breakfast. In the dining room they had scrambled eggs, sausage, grits, toast, and orange juice. After praying over their meal, Langston began the necessary conversation.

"Rocky, I've got some questions for you. I'm going to ask them in the order of importance. The boat docks tonight in New York City; so, where do you plan on spending the night and what will be your living arrangements for the near future? That's the first question. The second question is how do you plan on supporting yourself and the third question is who is Vanda Mae and why is she important to you?"

Rocky replied, "Well, now, you asked those questions in the order of importance but I'm going to answer them in the order of easiness. Vanda Mae is the lady that left me to come to New York. She left with a man by the name of Smooth. He has her hooked on Happy Dust, so she'll follow him anywhere and probably do anything for him just to get

Happy Dust. I want to get her away from him and off that Happy Dust."

"Now, with regards to living arrangements, I was hoping that I could stay with you or maybe that you would know of someplace where I could stay. And, with regards to supporting myself, I don't know. I got these baskets which I can sell if someone would buy them, but I know that my money would run out soon after they were sold. I got some money to support me for a little while. Do you think that I could live with you?

"Rocky, you're a nice fellow and I trust you, but I don't think that we could actually live together."

"We just spent the night together in a cabin that's got to be much smaller than your home. I know that it is smaller than mine. We did o.k. together, last night."

"Rocky, one night is just that, one night. People make adjustments when they know that a situation is temporary, but when a situation is long term, people act differently. I don't think that it would work out for us to live together. I think that the differences between us would cause friction."

"Differences, you're a man, I'm a man. We the same there. You're educated, I'm uneducated; so that's a difference; but I don't think that my lack of education is really what you're talking about. Langston, I could be wrong but I think that the difference that you're talking about is sweetness. I know that you got a little sugar. You got a surprised look on your face. Langston, we got sweet tea guys down in the islands. I might be country and crippled, but I ain't deaf, dumb, and blind. Langston, Olodumare made you just as you are and He don't make mistakes. It's man that messes things up and brings prejudices. That's why we got bad race relations; people hanging from trees. Langston, whether we live together or don't, you have helped me greatly and I am much appreciative of what you have done for me. I want you to relax and be yourself around me. I understand that we may not be able to live together but don't let sugar come between us. I bet that you know a whole lot of guys that are as sweet as peach cobblers, that you couldn't live with. You understand what I'm saying, Langston?

"Rocky, I don't think that we'll be able to live together. There is a basement to my building and I'm sure that the landlord won't mind renting it. There's a toilet in the basement, but there is no bathtub. Hell, there is no kitchen, but you will be dry and since the furnace is down there, you'll be warm in the winter. There is a problem though."

"What's that?" inquired Rocky.

"If you rent the basement, you will have to negotiate stairs."

"Negotiate, does that mean go up and down?"

"Negotiate means deal with. You'll have to deal with stairs."

Rocky was smiling when he heard this problem. "I can deal with stairs. I can negotiate stairs. I will negotiate them slowly if I have to. I can stay in that basement, Langston. Langston, everything is working out just fine. Come on, let's get out of here. Why don't we go to the lounge?"

"Rocky, we still got to talk about how you're going to make money. Your savings won't last you forever; particularly, if you plan on staying in New York.

"Langston, I'm not going back to Black Bottom. You saw that crazy cop kill my dog and my goat. He'll kill me if he gets the chance."

"You got crazy cops all over. A whole lot of them are the Klan dressed in blue. I don't blame you, Rocky for not wanting to go back." Then Langston remembered another question he had for Rocky. "Rocky, that cop, Brown, asked you about a killing down there in the islands. Why does he think that you know something about the killing?"

"Black Bottom is a small community. Like most small communities, people talk. Something like a killing of someone like Big Jim, a known murderer, the cops think that everyone in town knows, but no one is talking because Big Jim got what he deserved and no one trusts the cops anyway."

"Yeah, Rocky, we in New York don't trust the cops either, so, I'm not going to ask you anymore questions concerning Big Jim, but I do think that you know more than you're telling and let me be clear, I don't want to know anything; because something tells me, this Big Jim shit isn't over. Not by a long shot, is this Big Jim shit over."

"So, tell me Rocky, how are you going to make some money? Winter will be here before you know it. You don't have the proper clothing for New York. You are in no way prepared for New York. It's almost November. Christmas is coming. Do you think that people are going to be buying baskets in the snow? I'm serious Rocky, do you think that selling baskets will support you during the winter?"

"No. When you put it that way, it's like I'm doomed to be broke by living in New York City. I got over $300 and you talkin like that's not gonna be enough to buy some beans and rice and last through the winter." Rocky went on to say:

"Langston, I don't need sweet grass to make baskets. I can make baskets out of vines. I know you got all types of vines in New York City. It's not all tall buildings and no yards, no green areas. Not only can I make baskets, I can also draw pictures. I can draw fish, I can draw fishermen, I can draw trees and boats, and country scenes. With practice, I bet that I can draw the tall buildings in New York."

"Rocky, there is a term which is used in New York City and that term is 'starving artist.' I think that even if you stay in the basement of my building and even if you can sell some baskets and some art, that you will need more money coming in than you're going to make from your art. This is New York and it can be a very mean city where people don't care about you. Tell you what I'm going to do, I'm going to introduce you to my friend Carl; he's a writer for a newspaper and the publicity would be helpful to you. You should also have a vendor's license. That way the police won't hassle you. My friends Bruce and Aaron are artists, you should be able to buy paper and other types of art supplies from them. When I introduce you to Carl, I want you to have a portfolio ready to show to him."

Rocky wanted to know what a portfolio was. After being given an answer, he said, "Langston, sometimes you use words that I don't know the meanings of. I know that you're a real educated man, just by the way you talk. I ain't never been to school. Never, not one day in school. Colored kids got next to no schooling in the islands and crippled Colored kids got nothin. I learned how to write my name and there are a few words that I can read, but basically, I don't know how to read or write. I can count and I can make change, but that's it for math.

Langston let Rocky know that in order to get around New York, he would have to be able to read street signs, or become very familiar with a lot of landmarks. Langston told him that when the buses would be taken, that he'd have to use landmarks and quick reading to know when to get off of the bus. Langston also let him know that the subways would be more of a problem because most of them had the station names written on the walls and that sometimes he wouldn't be able to see the walls because so many people would be on the subway cars.

"Rocky, Father Divine has a school in his church. The school is for adults. He might be able to teach you how to read and write and I think that the people in my apartment house will help you learn to some extent; but I'm not going to promise you anything about how much help you will get from others.

"Langston," Rocky said, "give me your hand."

"Why?" replied Langston.

"We're gonna pray."

"Rocky, this is not the time, nor the place, for some long prayer. If you want to do some sort of long prayer, it needs to be done back in the cabin."

"Langston, this is a short prayer."

Langston placed his right palm on Rocky's left palm. Rocky stated, "Thank you Olodumare for this honest conversation and help us always to be honest with one another. Amen and Ache'."

Langston replied, "Amen and Ache'."

Langston convinced Rocky that this evening after leaving the boat, they should take a cab from the pier to Harlem. He wanted Rocky to know just how difficult it was going to be moving their luggage plus the baskets either down and up subway stairs or onto the buses. Langston also convinced Rocky since he had enough money to pay for both of them, that he should do this. Rocky told him that he would get the money out of his money belt before taking the suitcases out of the cabin.

———◆———

When the cab dropped the two off at Langston's apartment house, Langston had gotten all of the bags for himself and Rocky up the stoop stairs along with all of the baskets by the time that Rocky had reached the 5th stoop stair. Langston's friend, Bruce, was coming out of the front door as Rocky reached the top stair. Bruce was the first to speak.

"Langston, welcome home. How was Cuba? How was Javier?"

"Hi, Bruce. Cuba was great and it was nice spending time with Javier. I want you to meet my friend Rocky. He's here from South Carolina. He's an artist who works in basketry and drawing. I'm going to ask the landlord if he can stay in the basement." As Rocky reached the landing, Langston began the formal introductions. "Bruce, this is Rocky Johnson. Rocky, this is Richard Bruce Nugent." The two men shook hands and said that it was nice to meet each other. Langston stated, "Bruce, I thought that maybe you could sell a few supplies to Rocky so that he could get started creating his portfolio and also get some pieces ready for sale.

"I heard the word, 'sell,' in that sentence."

Langston continued, "Yeah, you can see that Rocky is going to have some problems with getting to art stores and carrying art supplies back to this house. Rocky can you give the money to Bruce, before he goes shopping? . . . I know that the two of you can work things out. I'm going to ask Aaron also if he'll help out in the same way." Bruce agreed and then walked on down the stairs.

After Langston got all of the luggage up to his second floor apartment, Rocky was invited to sit on Langston's couch and promptly sank low into the cushion. Next time, he knew that he would have to sit in a chair.

Rocky was uncomfortable with Langston's surroundings. He hadn't been with anyone, Colored or white, who had a couch, a table with chairs around it, a separate kitchen, running water, an indoor toilet, and electric lights. He saw something on a desk that looked like the same object he had seen while he was in the police station. He didn't know what it was and he made a note to himself, to ask Langston what it was and what it was used for. When Langston came back into the room, he asked if Rocky would like some vegetable soup.

"That's real nice of you Langston. Yeah, some vegetable soup would do me just fine."

"Well, the soup will take about fifteen minutes to fix; if you want to wash your hands or use the toilet, you're welcome to do so. The bathroom is right behind this door." Langston had his hand on the bathroom door knob before slipping back into the kitchen. Rocky struggled to get up from the couch. He had to place his crutch at such an angle that he could pull against it to raise himself to his feet. Rocky went into the bathroom, urinated, and washed his hands. All of those activities should have added up to two minutes at most, but Rocky was on the verge of tears. He knew that Colored folks existed that had homes and indoor plumbing and electricity; he just didn't personally know these people and he had not experienced their hospitality. In fact, the minister was the only person that he knew down in the islands that had more furniture and a bigger house than Langston and the minister didn't own that house, the church did. He had heard that Colored folks in the North had a better life than those who stayed in the South. Langston not only had more possessions than Rocky, he had more education. He had traveled outside of the United States, whereas Rocky rarely got outside of Black Bottom and even then, it was to come to Charleston. He knew that regardless of whatever happened with Vanda Mae, he had to stay here in New York City, even if it meant that he would have to sleep on pallets in the basement of this building and wash himself up in buckets. He knew that he had to thank his angels before going to sleep; he hadn't been robbed, he hadn't been killed, and he had made a friend who seemed to care about him and respect him as a man.

Rocky came to the dinner table and sat in a chair and waited for Langston to bring the soup to the table. Langston set the table with two place mats, two bowls, and two spoons. The salt and pepper shakers were already on the table. Langston served the soup in a very large bowl that had a notch in its edge and a dipper in the notch. Rocky looked upon these behaviors and possessions and was slightly perplexed. He knew that Langston could just as easily have dipped the soup from the pot directly into the bowls and placed them on the table. Rocky wondered to himself if all Colored folks in the North, lived like Langston. He thought that he should just keep his mouth quiet and observe how Langston lived. The soup was quite good and he complimented Langston on it. They both had two helpings.

"Langston, you made just enough soup. Thank you for sharing."

"Rocky, this is a special occasion; you're starting a new life. New York can be brutal just like the South, but you're not likely to see bodies suspended from trees. Tomorrow, you and I will spend some time, a few hours really, cleaning the basement and then you'll be cleaning it on your own because I have to work. Tonight is meant for the enjoyment of each other's company. Soup was all that I could share with you and I'm glad that you liked it. I wanted it to be a bit special, so I got my grandmother's tureen and ladle for this occasion."

"Langston, 'tureen and ladle,' I don't know those words. I think that I can guess what they mean though," stated Rocky.

"Go ahead, Rocky, guess."

"Well, I think that a tureen is a big soup bowl and a ladle is a dipper. Did I get 'em right?"

Langston was smiling as he said, "You sure did, Rocky."

"Langston, I want to learn things. I don't know how I'm going to go to school and make a living. I guess I'll be real busy for a long time; for a real long time."

After dinner, they washed the dishes and then the two of them talked and listened to records. Rocky learned the name of the black thing on Langston's desk that he had seen when he was in the police station. Langston called it a typewriter. He said that he used it to write down his thoughts. He said that he used it to write plays, poems, and essays. He had to define the meaning of the word 'essay' for Rocky and this he did. Around about 10:00 p.m., a man by the name of Wallace stopped by the apartment. Langston introduced his house guest to this visitor.

"Rocky, this is my friend Wallace Thurman. Wallace, this is my friend Rocky Johnson."

"Langston, Bruce told me that a friend of yours was moving into the basement and I wanted to stop by and welcome the gentleman to our abode. It's nice to meet you Mr. Johnson."

Rocky thought that 'abode' must be another word for 'home'. "It's nice to meet you Mr. Thurman."

Langston interjected that he and Rocky would be cleaning and straightening out the basement tomorrow morning. He said that he did not think that the landlord would mind renting the space since it could not be rented as an apartment. The money would be pure profit for him.

"Rocky, can I call you Rocky? Where are you from?" asked Wallace.

"I'm from the islands just off the coast of South Carolina. I'm from a little community called Black Bottom. How about you? Where you from?"

"I'm from Salt Lake City, Utah, but I've lived all over the western United States. Bruce said that you're an artist and that you work in basketry and paints."

"Yeah." Rocky was beginning to doubt his skills in either medium.

"Well, I look forward to seeing your work. You should come down and see what Bruce did with my apartment."

Wallace stated, "He put a strong black male theme into his painting of the walls. You get a 'back to Africa' feeling, a return to the motherland feeling when you see the murals which he placed on the walls."

Rocky thought, *"Another unfamiliar word. Mural, it sounded like they were talking about a painting on a wall. Why didn't these guys just call these paintings, wall paintings?"*

Langston turned to Rocky and said, "Rocky, you just may be inspired to create art regarding your African angels."

Wallace continued the thought and stated, "Yeah, Rocky, all the angels which we see are white. How come we don't see any black angels? Don't black folks go to heaven? You can be the one to create the black angels. Hell, you can do triptychs regarding lynchings where the African angel takes the soul back to the motherland. There can be a pantheon of martyrs. Yeah, I like that idea. I think that I'll try to play with that idea and turn it into a poem or maybe a short story. Langston has seen Bruce's work but you haven't. Would you like to see what Bruce has painted on my walls? My place is right down the hall; you don't have to do steps."

Rocky looked to Langston and said, "Langston, I'm your guest and I don't want to keep you up any later than you would normally stay up. If I spent a few minutes down there in Wallace's apartment, would that be an inconvenience for you?"

"No, Rocky. The door can remain unlocked. If you have never seen art work like Bruce's, it will probably make you think differently about the creation of art and the purpose of art. We here in this apartment house, are very political. We create with words or paintings. We show all sorts of things in our creations. We want to liberate ourselves and our people, our African brothers and sisters and when I use the term, African, I'm speaking of wherever we're born; here, there, the Caribbean or South America. So go on, view the murals, discuss them with Wallace and if Bruce stops by, discuss them with him. The door here will be shut but unlocked. I'll be typing for a little while. Wallace, I know that you're going to offer this man a beer or something harder so Rocky, remember, we have work to do in the morning." Looking directly into Wallace's eyes, Langston said, "That sofa over there, that's where Rocky's supposed to be sleeping. Don't get him so drunk that he can't walk down the hall to it."

"Langston, you don't have to be Rocky's big brother. Everything is going to be just fine. You know Langston, if you're worried, you can chaperone us. You can make sure that I don't ply Rocky with more than one beer."

"Good bye, Wallace."

Wallace and Rocky walked out the door and Langston got his pipe, sat at his typewriter and smoked and wrote for the next 40 minutes. When Rocky hadn't returned by that time, he went to the closet, got some sheets and a pillow, and placed them on the sofa. He then went to bed. At 6:00 a.m., he got up to check on Rocky and was happy to see that he was sleeping. Langston used the bathroom and then got dressed. After dressing, he woke up Rocky and asked him how he liked Bruce's art.

"I liked it just fine. I could feel Shango in the pictures. Bruce does very masculine art. If you look closely though at his art, you'll see a different picture than the one that you see at first. I like that. Bruce is very good. I'd like to learn how to do that type of painting. Wallace calls it fig-ure/ground painting."

Rocky stated that he felt that with the right training, he could make his art better. He didn't think that he could do murals with his bad leg, but he did think that he could get some pictures drawn which were just the right size for slipping into a tourist's shopping bag.

Langston cooked breakfast as Rocky got dressed. As breakfast ended, Rocky gave Langston a $10.00 bill. "Langston, you've helped me out mightily and I much appreciate what you have done for me. I have a new life because of you. I want you to have this $10.00 bill. Charity towards me is going to get tiring and I don't want you to feel that way towards me."

"Thank you, Rocky. This will help with the expenses. Let's get on down to that basement."

"Langston, don't you have to get permission for me to move into the basement? I could be denied access."

"That's not going to happen. You'll be making extra money for the landlord. That will be money which he won't report. The money will go straight into his pocket because you are not moving into an apartment. You aren't paying for a kitchen. You don't have a stove. You don't have a kitchen sink. You don't have a refrigerator nor an icebox. You don't have a bathtub. You aren't paying for your own private space. Anyone can go down there and get their articles that they've put down there. He'll be happy to rent to you; believe me. You can give him $20.00 a month. That will put a smile on his face and some pep in his step. You know how apple cobbler makes people happy? You'll make him apple cobbler happy! That's how much he'll like the idea of you renting the basement."

Rocky asked Langston for some twine and after getting it, tied it to the suitcase handles. He wanted to slide the suitcases down the steps to the first floor and then down into the basement. Rocky didn't want Langston to exhaust himself, helping him make this move.

Once in the basement, Rocky realized that the main light switch for the basement was at the top of the stairs. He asked Langston if he thought that the lights would have to stay on all of the time and Langston stated, "No. You're going to have to buy light bulb sockets which can screw into the light fixtures and also have a place for plugs so that you can run extension cords so that you can have more light. This was such a simple problem for Langston to solve but Rocky was still getting adjusted to the differences between Black Bottom and New York City, between his one room hut with no plumbing and nothing fancy and Langston's apartment with a kitchen and a bathroom and a bedroom. He didn't eat his soup from a pot, he ladled it from a tureen into a different bowl. Living in this basement would definitely be a step up from his dirt floor which was covered by his hand woven mats. It would be a step in the right direction. He saw himself as making progress and he was happy, but he knew that he had a great deal more to accomplish before he had attained the security that Langston and Wallace had.

Langston began pushing old furniture towards the walls. He saw a rolling office chair which he mentioned to Rocky, thinking that it would help him get around the base-ment quicker. There was a wash tub and a wash board, so Rocky would be able to clean his clothes and himself more easily. Langston warned Rocky not to ever push anything close to the furnace. He told him that it could cause an explosion which would kill him if the furnace were running and set the apartment house on fire. He said to Rocky that although the furnace was not on now, he couldn't predict when the furnace would come on since it was getting colder. He told him that the furnace would come on automatically and so it was better to never put anything in front of it. Langston next showed Rocky the coal bin and told him that if he put anything in the bin, that he would wake up one morning to find his possessions underneath a pile of coal.

Langston was thinking about the needs of Rocky and said to him, "Rocky, you need a card table down here and you need a bed and I don't see anything like those objects down here. Sleeping down here will be uncomfortable for the next few weeks but, you'll be safe and dry and after Thanksgiving, warm. We can ask the tenants in this building to save their newspapers for you, so you can make a bed out of them. I'll show you how to make a bed out of newspapers."

Langston and Rocky, but mostly Langston, cleaned the basement and moved the articles around so that there could be a living space for Rocky. After a few hours, Langston stated, "Rocky, I'm tired of moving dusty shit around. You do the best that you can down here. I'm going to need $40.00 to get you the items that I think that you're going to need. You're going to need soap, toilet paper, wash cloths, towels, cans of food, a hot plate, extension cords, light bulbs, light bulb sockets, glasses and cups and plates, and knives, forks, and spoons, and fuses; cause, you might blow one out. I'll tell you about fuses later. That may not be enough money, but it'll make a nice dent in the things that you need to make this basement comfortable. I'll bring you the receipt back."

Rocky got the money from his money belt and gave it to Langston.

"Rocky," Langston said, "I've got my own writing to do. This is how I make my money so, I won't begin to get these items until later today. O.K.?"

"O.K., Langston. You know I trust you."

Rocky looked around the basement after Langston went upstairs. Although the basement was large, he had only about twice as much useable space, as he had in his one room island home. There were three naked light bulbs which were glaring. He was sitting in an office chair with wheels. He had a utility sink to his left and a toilet behind him. There were doors exiting from the basement to which he did not have keys. Rocky thought of how quickly his life had drastically changed. Two mornings ago, he was hanging upside down screaming and now he found himself sitting here in this basement. Materially, it was one step up from what he had. Security wise, it was several steps up. Although he was several hundred miles from Black Bottom, he was still afraid that the police would blame him for the death of Big Jim. He thought that just as the police had tortured him, they could just as easily torture someone else and make that person talk. If they went easy on him for the death of Big Jim, they would give him the electric chair if they thought that he was involved with the death of O'Brien. He knew that he could never go back to South Carolina; not for a visit, nor anything else. His new home was New York City, at least for now.

Rocky went to a suitcase and took out a candle, a candle holder, and some matches and his bell. He rolled himself back to the sink and placed the candle and candle holder in the sink and then lit the candle. Off to the side, on a shelf, he saw a large mug; so, he placed the candle holder and candle in it. Rocky didn't want his future landlord to inspect the place and see wax in the sink. Rocky then rang the bell three times and prayed:

*"I am calling upon the Angel Eleggua to be with me now. Beloved Eleggua please place me in the presence of the great Olodumare, for it is through you, Eleggua, that I can ask Olodumare anything."*

The bell was rung three more times. Rocky waited about three minutes before continuing the prayer. Rocky was waiting for the spirit of Olodumare to radiate energy towards him.

*"Dear God, some people call you Jehovah, some people call you the Holy Father, some people call you Jesus. I call you by your African name, Olodumare. To me, you are the Holy Ghost. You take many forms. You are the trees, the earth beneath the trees through which roots grow, and the birds which live in the trees. You are the ocean, the shellfish, the jellyfish, the bass and the sharks. You are the thunder, the lightning, the wind, and the rain. You are the good humans who walk the Earth and the bad humans who walk this Earth. I am asking you to be with me now. Please have all of your angels with you. I need to be touched by your angels. Angels of Olodumare, come to me now and touch me. Come to me now and lay hands on me. Come to me now and enter me."*

Rocky rang the bell three times. He was quiet for the next ten minutes. With his eyes closed, he saw the Angels coming to him and laying hands on him. He saw them touching his face, his head, his chest, back, and legs and feet. Some Angels kissed him on the forehead, some Angels kissed him on the lips. Some Angels hugged him from the front and some from behind. After touching and kissing and hugging, all of the Angels slowly entered into him. Rocky whimpered and became teary eyed as the Angels entered him. He could feel tingling sensations as the Angels penetrated him. He also had a feeling of satiation as the Angels took up residence within him. Rocky spent the next twenty-five minutes allowing the Angels to caress and enter him. He felt much better, much stronger, and more determined to make a good life for himself here in New York City.

*"Thank you Olodumare. Thank you for allowing all of your different forms, all of your different Angels, to enter me. You have protected me so far and You have given me the strength to continue working to make a success of my life here in New York City. Ache'."*

Rocky knew that eventually he would run into Vanda Mae and that she would see how successful he had become. She would see that he was alive and she would come back to him. He knew that one day he would find Vanda Mae, the woman who would give him the love that a man needed. The woman who would make him feel complete.

### Vanda Mae Daniels & Robin *"Smooth"* Daniels

Vanda Mae was buxom and proud of her rack. It truly was an asset when it came to hooking up with men. Sometimes though, Vanda Mae was emotionally needy and at other times she was emotionally cold. She was a victim of incest and an orphan raised by an aunt and uncle. As a child, she captured small animals and buried them alive. She went to the fifth grade before being stopped by her uncle. He convinced her that she had to pay her way because they had been taking care of her for the last few years. Her job, he told her, was to make money for the family by being 'good' to men. Her uncle marketed her to 'good gentlemen' who took baths before having sex and they wore rubbers. At the age of 12, Vanda Mae met Smooth while working in a brothel. He also was 12 years old and was being marketed by his incestuous uncle. Vanda Mae knew that Smooth was truly the only male who fully empathized with her view of the world. They were like fraternal twins raised in the same house of ill repute by the same abusive care takers. She looked out for him and he looked out for her. She would later act as pimp and protector for him and he would pimp and protect her when she was with a john. At the age of 16, when they had run away and were on their own, she had shot a john who was being too rough with him. At the age of 17, he had done the same for her. Both bodies were left in the various woods where the sex acts were being performed. The johns never suspected that they carried weapons. The two of them traveled from town to town as brother and sister looking for day work. At the age of 18, they joined an African Methodist Episcopal church in Charleston. They both got jobs cleaning the inside and outside of the church and they both soon found themselves to be the paramours of the minister and his brother, the deacon. Vanda Mae (Daniels) and Smooth (Robin Daniels) played along with the 'Holy Men' since the church offered them a free place to stay and a food allowance and a small salary. The pretend siblings worried about their looks eventually fading and then not being looked upon favorably by the 'Holy Men' or by future johns. When Big Jim came along, Vanda Mae felt that this was her chance to have a much more stable life with someone who would and could protect her.

As Big Jim was making his presence known to Vanda Mae, Jacob Snyder was making himself known to Robin Smooth Daniels. Jacob liked Smooth because he was street smart and because Smooth knew how to satisfy him as a man and be discreet about it. Jacob paid more than Smooth asked and as such, their bond strengthened. Jacob introduced Smooth to Happy Dust and to its potential for generating income. Smooth knew that he was being recruited as a salesman and knew that it could be dangerous for him, but he was ready for something different in his life. When it came time for him and Vanda Mae to go their separate ways, they hugged and kissed on the lips. They swore that they would stay in contact with one another and they did. When Big Jim saw the letters, he thought that a loving brother was writing to his sister. He never suspected that Vanda Mae and Smooth had no common relatives.

That morning as Rocky was deep in prayer and was being filled with the Angels of Olodumare, Vanda Mae was lying in bed. She too was being filled with the joy and security and passion generated by her man, Smooth. Smooth's tongue had left her neck and ear and had moved down to her left breast. His left hand moved down her body with a gentleness none of her Johns had ever given to her. The fingers of Smooth's right hand gently hooked into her hair. Smooth's tongue on her nipple sent electric charges through her body and she heaved. Smooth liked this in her, this abandonment to the moment. He placed both of his hands on her left breast and used his tongue to make love to it. As he licked and nibbled on her, he rubbed himself against the sheet. He changed positions so that he was over top of her and slowly brought his tongue down from her navel to her nub of love. His tongue made her see colored lights. His tongue made her hear bells and horns and traffic and trains. His tongue made her heave and scream. Smooth was a master at making love. In anticipation of Vanda Mae's locking of her thighs around his head, he had already cupped his hands around her love triangle; this allowed him to breathe while his tongue was nudging her into an ecstatic euphoria. After the screaming and heaving had stopped, Smooth crawled up beside her and they held each other tightly. He whispered into her ear, "I want you to use the glove."

Although Smooth had taught Vanda Mae the right way to orally satisfy a man, he didn't want that now. He wanted a long slow ride to heaven which would end for him in a tidal wave of pleasure.

Vanda Mae rolled over and opened the nightstand draw. She took out a latex glove and a small squeeze bottle of mineral oil. She liberally coated her gloved thumb and made a fist with her thumb sticking up. She held this fist in place with her other hand. Both hands rested on top of her crotch. Smooth got on his knees over top of her and pulled his cheeks apart. As he lowered himself onto her thumb, she pushed it up into him. She flexed her thumb as he had taught her to do. Smooth was in the saddle now. This was a ride that he loved. As much time as he had spent lapping at her love zones, she spent in pleasuring him. His rocking back and forth on his knees, looking at the ceiling and then at her, breathing heavily, made her feel content; it made her feel whole. She had shown love to this man and he had shown love to her. They complemented each other. Smooth was getting close to a climax and he started growling while he was bouncing. He got the bottle of mineral oil and squeezed a small amount into his hand and then applied it to his manhood. He was now riding through the clouds on Pegasus. Breathing hard and looking down at his love, he used the squeeze bottle to make an oily dollar sign on her stomach. Leaning forward, he began biting Vanda Mae's neck while rubbing his engorged shaft over her stomach. He bit and growled and rubbed and she wiggled her thumb inside him. His mythical horse was now a biplane zooming through the clouds and she was supplying the motor spirits for his engine. He started screaming and grunting and yelping and shaking and humping her stomach. Just as he was beginning to shoot his love across her stomach, she removed her hands from between the two of them and squeezed his butt cheeks as hard as she could. She pulled him to her and they lay there in the bed, sticking to each other. He inserted his tongue into her mouth and pushed it over hers. His tongue played with hers and he said, "Vanda Mae, I love you." Vanda Mae replied, "Smooth, I love you too and I don't want us to part again." They slept until noon.

———◆———

After his prayers were said, Rocky wanted to bathe, but he also wanted to catch Bruce and give him money for the art supplies that he hoped to get from him and he wanted to pay him to get more supplies. When he saw Bruce, he wanted to have his money ready to give to him. He figured that he'd get it out of his money belt now and have it ready for when someone came down the stairs. Hopefully, it would be Bruce coming down the stairs. He felt silly though, knowing that he was going to have to wait around for someone to do him a favor. He wanted to constructively use his time. He knew that everyone moved faster than he did and so, he decided to go up to the first floor and to wait for Bruce to come down the stairs. It was a struggle getting up to the first floor but, between his crutch, his good leg, and the banister, he was able to get up the stairs. After about forty minutes, Bruce came down the stairs with a fellow in tow. Bruce had a shoebox along with some rolled up white paper in his hand. Rocky spoke first.

"Good morning, Mr. Nugent."

"It's Bruce, Rocky. There is no need to be formal around here. This is my friend, Billy. I'm giving you some paper, some pencils, and some paints. When these run out, you'll have to buy your supplies."

"Thank you, Bruce. I've got money for you. I hope that $20.00 will get me enough to use through the winter." Rocky handed him the money.

Billy spoke up immediately, "Good morning, Rocky."

"Good morning, Billy. It's nice to meet you." Rocky knew that he didn't know everyone in the building, but this Billy guy impressed him as having his bedroom somewhere other than in this apartment house. He decided that he would not satisfy his curiosity and so he redirected his conversation to Bruce.

"Bruce, you do really good art work. You make me feel the Motherland when I see your art. You make me feel all of my African relatives when I see your work. You know, we're a African people. We been in this country a long time, but we still a African people. I'd like to learn how to paint as good as you."

Bruce was impressed. Rocky might have been "country," but he knew about Africa and best of all, he was not ashamed of his heritage. He thought that it was going to be really interesting having Rocky so nearby.

Bruce said to Rocky that he'd put the shoebox and paper down in the basement and then he and Billy would be off. He wasn't sure when he'd return, but when he did, he'd have the rest of the art supplies.

Rocky walked with them out onto the stoop and then bid them a nice day as they were walking down to the street. As he turned around to re-enter the apartment house, he read the apartment house number, 267, and he wondered, what street he was on.

Rocky was standing at the top of the stairs leading into the basement when a feeling of despair came over him. He didn't want to live in a basement even though he knew that it was the best that he could do during this time in his life. Rocky thought of his home in Black Bottom and how he was friends with everyone there. He had three friends here in New York City. In Black Bottom he could go fishing and catch his meals, but here in New York City he had to open up a can of something and eat it. In Black Bottom, he could take a bath once a week right after washing his clothes in the wash tub and someone would tilt over the washtub for him. Here, he was not sure how he would get someone to come down to the basement and drag the tub to the door for which he had no key and empty the washtub outside. He had been gone from Black Bottom for three days now and he was homesick. He then saw himself hanging upside down from the tree branch and he knew that his Black Bottom days were over for good. He thought that eventually someone would tell Brown that he was the one that killed Big Jim. He knew that someone would tell Brown that he had gone to New York City. He figured that he'd eventually be blamed for two deaths. No, he couldn't go back there and staying in New York City might not be that safe either. Still, he didn't feel like going into the basement. He didn't want to draw anything on the rolls of paper which were given to him by Bruce. He thought that his art work would look funny if he had to negotiate getting down on the floor and then moving around on it with pencils in his hand while dragging his leg. It would be better to wait until he had a card table on which he could draw. Rocky thought that if bathing was going to be cumbersome and if drawing was out of the picture for him, then there was nothing left for him to do but explore his new surroundings. He thought that walking until he got just a little tired would be o.k., after which he would turn around and come back home.

As Rocky was about to close the front door behind him, a wave of fear came over him. He had no key, he hadn't gone to the bathroom. He knew that he lived at 267 on some unknown street. Still, he pulled the front door shut and heard it lock. He held onto the banister and steadied himself with his crutch and eased himself down the stairs to the street. He turned to his left and started walking. He had never seen so many buildings before. They were all so close together. He had never seen so many Colored folks before. They seemed to have a different way of walking here in New York City. He figured that if he could find a bench, then he could observe these Colored New Yorkers better and maybe have a better understanding of them. Bruce and Langston were two guys who seemed to be go-getters, people that wanted to work, people that were concerned about the race; but Rocky didn't believe that all Colored New Yorkers were like Bruce and Langston. As he walked, he thought of Wallace; this man seemed to be in a class all by himself. Rocky knew that Wallace was as smart, if not smarter than Bruce and Langston, but Wallace seemed to be more fragile than his friends. Wallace also seemed to have more money at his disposal than they had. His apartment had more furniture than Langston's. Rocky thought that Wallace probably had a job which paid more than Langston's. Upon reaching the corner of the block, Rocky saw a lamppost with "7th Ave." and "W 136th Street" plaques attached to it. From the position of the plaques, he guessed that he lived on W 136th Street and that the word after the numbers was "street." He didn't know what the letter in front of the numbers meant and he didn't know what to make of the 7 and the "A" word after it. He understood right then and there that he could not live well in New York City without learning how to read and write. Also, he would have to pay more attention when people around him talked. He had been distracted by all of the people, noise, and tall buildings when he and Langston got a taxi to the apartment house. He should have paid attention when Langston gave the address of their destination. He knew that he had to try not to be so taken by the differences in how these Colored New Yorkers lived. He did see though why Smooth liked New York City. He couldn't see why Smooth would ever want to go back south for anything.

Rocky was wondering if he should proceed directly across the street or if he should stay on the block and again, turn to his left and go to the next corner. He decided, to be daring and then turned to his right and crossed 136th Street. He was slowly making his way down 7th Ave. Looking in the windows he saw Colored folks talking with white store keepers. The way that they stood when talking to whites seemed to be different from the way Coloreds stood back in South Carolina.

Arriving at the corner, he was happy to see "135th Street" on the street plaque along with "7th Ave." on the other plaque. His happiness was due to his realization that there was a logic to these numbered streets. *"Now,"* he thought, *"what to do?"* He could cross 135th Street, he could cross 7th Ave., or he could head back to the apartment house and wait for someone to let him in. *"Hell,"* he thought, he'd *"turn left and cross 7th Ave."*

On the other side of the street, he noticed that the numbers on the buildings were getting smaller. He wondered what happened when they got down to zero. Could you have an address with only a zero? As he walked, he saw Colored men entering and exiting a building on his side of the street. He stopped and supported himself with his crutch and continued to observe. Most of the men looked like they were about something serious; about something important; about something that might make them some money. He thought that he might as well investigate and so he proceeded on to the interesting building. Upon entering it, he found that it was the Harlem YMCA; a hotel for Colored men. This was when Rocky momentarily became speechless. A hotel for Colored men in New York City! The thought that Colored men could have something so nice as a hotel for themselves, stunned Rocky. No matter what Langston said about the problems with the police in this city, this place was better than South Carolina. Rocky had started speaking to the desk clerk, a Colored fellow, when his mind drifted off; when he realized that he was supposed to be paying attention he apologized to the man immediately.

"Sir, I'm sorry but I was kind of surprised when you said a hotel for Colored men. Back where I come from, we don't have anything like this. In fact, I've never heard of anything like this. "

"Where do you come from?" the man inquired.

"South Carolina."

"Yeah, well there is a lot in New York City that you won't find in South Carolina. In this hotel, we have a theater and we have Colored actors performing. We have music recitals. We have art lessons and we have education classes for adults."

"No," Rocky said. "It's hard to believe that all of this is available to Colored men. This is what I need. I am 23 years old and I have never spent one day in a school house. I have never learned how to read. I can write my name and I know a little bit about how to do numbers but I know that there is so much more that I could learn."

"Well, we have a sliding pay scale here so you probably can afford the reading, writing, and math lessons."

"What's that mean, sliding pay scale?"

"Some people will pay a little bit, some people will pay a little bit more, and some people will pay nothing."

"Sir, I don't have a job. I've got a bare bones place to live in, close by and the rent is cheap but, I've got just enough to cover the rent for a few more months and eat. I'm going to have to sell my art to make money and I've already seen the work of a really good artist. I've met someone who takes art way beyond where I am. My abilities are nothing when compared to his. I need art classes and reading and writing classes. I need to learn more with numbers and I don't have the money to pay for the classes. Can this hotel help me?"

"What's your name sir?"

"Rocky Johnson."

"Mr. Johnson, I think that you came to the right place. I think that the "Y" will be a place of comfort, culture, and learning for you. I want you to feel that this is your second home. All classes begin at 5:00 p.m. The art classes are on Tuesdays and Thursdays and the education classes are on Mondays and Wednesdays. Why don't you sign up now for the courses? And maybe, you can pay a very small amount. Maybe $5.00? Maybe $5.00 per course?"

"Yeah, I'd like to sign up, but what seems like a small amount to you, seems to me that much closer to homelessness. I have to pray on this." Rocky lost the smile that he had on his face.

"Well, Mr. Johnson, we'll see if you can take the courses for free. I'll fill out the form for you but I'm not making any guarantees about the cost of the courses. What's your address?"

Rocky proudly said, "267 136th Street."

"Mr. Johnson, you're at 267 West 136th Street. It is important to state the West part of the street. You must give the exact address if you are to get mail in this city. You may still get your mail, but it might take longer to get it. I know that your address is on the West side because we are close to the Harlem River and East 267 would be in it, unless you live on a houseboat. Do you live on a house boat?"

Rocky chuckled and said, "No. What's your name sir?"

"Alexander, Michael Alexander. I think the "Y" will help you make a good transition from the South to New York City. You don't know it but we get a whole lot of Colored fellows coming here from the South and they're all glad to be out of there. There's an art class tonight, but it probably would be better to start on Monday; that way the teachers can plan for your arrival. I'll tell them that you need a lot of help with academics and some help with your drawing skills. There's something else that you should know Mr. Johnson." Rocky wondered what else could this nice Colored fellow have to say. "If you become a member of the YMCA, then you get to use the swimming pool and the showers. If you took classes here every day, you could take a shower every day before going to class. The cost is $25.00 for one year. You would also have a reduced price on your courses." Rocky knew that this was a really kind way for Alexander to tell him that he looked like he needed a bath.

"Thank you, Mr. Alexander. I'll take everything that you said, into consideration. You've been real kind to me. It would really be a change for me to take a bath four days a week. I've never bathed that often before."

"Rocky," Alexander interrupted, "the "Y" is open every day of the year. If you're a member, you can come in here every day and take a bath."

Rocky looked Alexander in the eyes and said, "I'll be here on Monday. This is a blessing on me. God made me come here. I was feeling bad and God made me leave my apartment house and come down the street. God made me turn towards my right and cross the street. God made me walk to the end of the block. God made me look towards my left and then cross the street. God wanted me to find this hotel. God wanted me to find this Balm in Gilead. I feel blessed. I can now go back to my apartment building and wait for someone to open the door."

"Why do you have to wait for someone to open the door? You're paying rent so you should have a key!"

"Well," Rocky stated, "I get approved to move into the basement today. I've been told that there will be no objections since I won't be in a real apartment and it will be extra money for the landlord."

"Mr. Johnson, I hope that you get your living arrangements worked out today. Why don't you use the restroom here, just in case there is no one at the apartment house when you get there."

"Thank you, Mr. Alexander. . . Mr. Alexander, if I took showers here, could a stool or small chair be placed near the shower so that I could sit on it while bathing?"

"Sure, Mr. Johnson. Just make sure that you join the "Y."

<hr>

After leaving the restroom, Rocky walked back to his hoped-for home and found Langston and a white guy talking on the stoop. Noticing him, they started walking down the stairs. The white guy greeted Rocky on the sidewalk.

"Hi. Mr. Hughes tells me that you're Rocky Johnson and that you want to rent the basement, right?"

"Yeah."

Fine with me. Just don't push anything up against the furnace. Also, don't put anything in the coal bin. The rent will be $20.00 a month. I'm going to give you a key to the apartment building front door and a key which opens both of the basement doors. If you don't keep those basement doors locked, except when you're exiting, I'm going to throw you out. You got it? Here are the keys. You got the $20.00 on you?"

"No, but if you wait, I can get it and ..."

"I don't feel like waiting. I'll be back here at 9:00 a.m. tomorrow. Have the money ready for me by then. O.K.?"

"O.K."

The white guy turned around and started walking away when Rocky called out, "What's your name?"

"Saperstein, Julius Saperstein."

As Saperstein was walking away, Rocky turned to Langston and said, "You know Langston, things are working out for me."

"That's good, Rocky. I'm glad to hear that and I think that I got some more good news for you. Guess what I found in an alley?"

Rocky wondered what would be thrown out and into an alley. What do these Colored New Yorkers consider trash?

"Langston, I can't guess. What did you find?"

"A card table. It's got a few bullet holes in it and some blood stains on it, so I guess that it was unlucky for its owner or someone."

"And you're giving it to me?" Rocky was looking very stressed.

"It's in the basement right now, Rocky." Noticing the expression on Rocky's face, he asked, "Rocky, you're not superstitious are you?"

Looking into Langston's eyes Rocky said, "Langston, I am superstitious. I'm not one to believe in seven years of bad luck for breaking a mirror, but I do believe that bad luck is associated with that table."

"Rocky, you need something to write on. You need something to draw your art on. You need something to set your hot plate and your dinner plate on. I walked with this table for three blocks to help you and now you're getting all scared? To me, you sound ungrateful. You don't realize how much went into getting that table to the basement. I had seen the table after getting you all of the things which you need to turn that basement from a refuge, into a home. I saw that table when I was walking here. I had to go back to get the table after leaving the items which I bought for you, in the basement. Now, you come up all scared. This is New York City! It is not unusual to see homeless people sleeping outdoors during the winter with nothing but newspaper over them. They don't have hot plates; they don't have extension cords, they don't have toilets and they don't have tables and you just got here. Be thankful Rocky for all the things that you have and have experienced. Things will be all right."

"Langston, I'm sorry, but I am scared. I was happy when I was coming down the street and happy when Mr. Saperstein agreed to rent to me. I stopped in at the "Y" and things went well for me there; but the thought of bullets and blood made me think of Bell, my goat, my life dangling by a string, my run-ins with the law, and the hundreds of black men with mutilated bodies dangling from tree branches. That's what the bullets and blood mean to me. I know that I need a table. Thank you for helping me Langston. I'll get over these feelings that I have and these pictures that I see in my mind."

"Rocky, I know that you're seeing all this death and pain. Hell, I'm still rattled by the killings of the dog and the goat. Remember, Rocky, I was standing right beside you when both of those animals were killed. I also know that you're feeling sad and glad about what you left when you left the South. You're not fully adjusted to New York City. Rocky, I've visited cities in Europe, Africa, Cuba, and Mexico as well as a bunch of cities here in the United States and I can tell you that they are all different from one another and they differ in small ways and sometimes in big ways. It takes time to get adjusted to a new city."

Rocky responded that "All those cities that you been too, they're all different from Black Bottom in big ways. They got indoor plumbing; they got toilets; and they got electricity. Thank you, Langston. You've done so much for me. Thank you. I'll be O.K." They started walking to the basement entrance when Rocky said, "Langston, do you know of a root man here in Harlem? The root man down in the islands had a son up here in Harlem. I'd like to find him and get him to bless my home."

"Rocky, there are herb shops here in Harlem but off the top of my head, I can't think of where one is. Zora may know though. You'll meet her and you'll like her. She's a close friend of mine and she's close with everyone in the house. She'll be a good friend to you. She can help you. Now let's get down in that basement and get that table set up and the extension cords run. We've got to turn that basement into a home." Rocky slowly descended into his new home and he wondered what the future held for him.

As Rocky was entering the basement, he heard the front door open. He looked up the basement stairwell and saw someone that he did not recognize. When their eyes met, the gentleman said, "Hi, you must be Rocky Johnson. I'm Aaron Douglas. It's nice to meet you. Is Langston down in the basement?"

"I'm Rocky and Langston is in the basement. I've heard that you're a painter, maybe one day I could see your work. I want to improve on my drawing skills and your ways of drawing maybe could make my art better."

"Rocky, I don't have any problem with you watching me while I work. If you want to ask some questions, that's O.K., too, as long as it's not so many questions that I can't get my own work done. Anyway, man, welcome to the Manor.

"Thank you." Rocky thought that "manor" must mean house or apartment house or rooming house.

Aaron yelled into the basement, "Langston!!!!"

"Come down the stairs, Aaron. You sound like my grand-mother calling me to dinner."

Aaron passed Rocky on the steps and said when he hit the bottom step, "Guess who I saw today and guess where we've been invited?"

Rocky was descending the steps when Langston said, "I'm not up for 'Twenty Questions.' Whom did you see today?"

"I saw Zora coming out of A'Lelia's house this morning. A'Lelia's giving a party Saturday night for Pushkin's grand-daughter, the Countess Alexandra von Merenberg. It's going to be a high class affair. Half of the people attending, you don't like, or won't like, but it will still be a very differ-ent experience to be around someone like her. I've never met real royalty."

"Everything that Wallace talks about, will be played out at that party," noted Langston. Langston looked to Rocky and stated that, "Wallace believed that Colored folks were color struck and that lighter skin was valued over darker skin."

Rocky replied, "If you're black, get back. If you're brown, stick around. If you're light, bright, damn near white, you're all right. We are color struck. It's a sickness we got in our heads and we carry that sickness from one generation to the next. We all came out of Africa. We need to see each other as brothers and sisters. We all the same. I seen men whose bodies were charred, hanging from trees. They used to be light skinned, but their skin color didn't save them. It's a false way of looking at the world, being color struck. You got to deal in reality."

"Damn, Rocky," Langston stated. "You fit in just fine here in this house. I love to hear you talk that way. Everyone in this house thinks the same way and Zora also thinks the same."

Rocky continued, "So, are you two going to this fancy dress party and who is this Pushkin person and why is his granddaughter being made over?"

Aaron spoke up first. "Pushkin was a poet in Russia. Russia is the largest country in the world. Pushkin was the greatest poet that they've produced and he was descended from an African man from Ethiopia who was taken to Russia as a slave. The slave eventually gained his freedom and his son excelled in the Russian military. It was the grandson of the Ethiopian who became the great poet. The poet is named Alexander Pushkin and it is Alexander's granddaughter who married a royal, a Count, who died a few years ago. She goes by the name of Countess Alexandra von Merenberg."

Langston added that even though the Countess was a royal, she didn't really have a lot of money. "She has more money than all of us in this house, but she doesn't have great wealth. She is most likely staying with A'Lelia because A'Lelia can treat her the way that she is accustomed to being treated. Servants will wait on her. In fact, A'Lelia is probably the only person in this country who would treat the Countess so nicely."

Aaron added that it was A'Lelia's mama who had the money and that A'Lelia was a rich working girl who had to keep working to keep the money rolling in.

Rocky asked, "Whose A'Lelia's mother?"

Langston said, "Oh, you've heard of her. Even down in Black Bottom, you've heard of A'Lelia Walker's mother."

"Who is the woman?" asked Rocky.

In unison, Aaron and Langston said, "Madam C. J. Walker."

"Oh - My - God!" Rocky could not utter any other words. When he regained his composure he said, "You mean that there was a real person named Madam Walker?"

"Yeah," replied Aaron. "She's been dead for more than a decade. A'Lelia runs the business but she also loves to throw fabulous parties and entertaining 'royalty,' especially royalty whose larder is lacking, is just up her alley."

"She'll be in rare form Saturday night," said Langston.

Looking towards Rocky, Aaron let it be known that "Zora said that everyone in the house is invited. I know that you don't know A'Lelia, but you might as well come."

"Aaron, I don't have fancy clothes. I don't have college degrees. I don't even have a job. I wouldn't fit in with all of the high class people at that party."

"Rocky," Langston said, "you need to expand your list of contacts. You're an artist, you need people with extra money to buy your art. Those types of people will be at this affair. That's why you need to attend it."

"Between me, Langston, Bruce, and Wallace, we should be able to get you properly dressed and Langston's right, you need to make money, as soon as possible." Aaron added, "Rocky, all artists live on the edge of society. You need to get out and mingle. You need relationships with people who have a more stable life than you have, people who can keep you from going over that edge." Aaron added, "Why don't you and Langston make this basement look inviting?" With a smile, he continued, "Maybe you can find a girlfriend at the party and when you have more furniture, have her over for conversation and other things." Aaron paused, "Rocky, are you into women?"

"Aaron!" Langston shouted, "That's a rude question."

"Langston, this house is so sweet, we could open up a candy factory right here in Harlem." Rocky started chuckling at this description. "If I run across a nice lady, I need to know if she can be more than a friend with Rocky. The same goes for a man, if Rocky favors men."

"Aaron, no one has asked you to play matchmaker," interjected Langston.

"You're right, Mother Dear. I've delivered the message and I'll make sure that Wallace and Bruce are informed. But Rocky, which is it, roosters or hens?"

"Hens. The reason that I came North was to find a hen. A hen that is hooked up with a no good rooster."

"You hear that, Mama?"

"Three's a crowd, Aaron." Langston added, "Besides, don't you need to get to your paintings?"

## Thursday Evening, September 28, 1933

Vanda Mae and Smooth were riding the subway down to lower Manhattan. Vanda Mae had on a light weight dark gray cotton skirt, white blouse, and dark gray jacket. Her dark gray patent leather shoes had one and one-half inch heels. She was perfectly attired and looked as though she could be a model for the New York Amsterdam News. Smooth had gotten this outfit for her. He figured, if the outfit looked good on the mannequin, it would look good on her. He bought her six outfits based on what he saw mannequins wearing. He bought extra cotton blouses so that Vanda Mae could have variety. He wanted her to look nice wherever they happened to go. Vanda Mae was his woman. Vanda Mae was the person for whom he cared. He and Vanda Mae had been looking out for each other and they would always look out for each other. Those dalliances with Rocky and Big Jim didn't bother him. In the end, she chose him, the one that had always been there for her. They got off the boat from Charleston ten days ago and they had made love and snorted Happy Dust every day. Vanda Mae though didn't want to stay home and cook for Smooth and wait for him to come home from his deliveries of dust. She also wanted to be out in the world doing things. She had made a decision that if she had to, she would rent her body out. She had this in her history and so this wasn't so bad; but she wanted more. Vanda Mae saw all of the Colored women working as maids and charwomen and she thought that she could do those jobs; if she had to. She wanted something different though. She wasn't sure what that job was which would be different, but it was out there. Smooth was accompanying her on a job interview this evening. She was happy to have the company and happy to have Smooth make the introduction. Smooth said that the man wanted a female model and that he would pay her well if she were just the right person; if she had just the right look. Vanda Mae pictured in her mind how she would be dressed when her picture was taken. In her mind's eye she envisioned herself in the Colored newspapers around the country. There would be pictures of her modeling dresses, modeling shoes and probably doing house work. There would be pictures of her with children. She could do this type of work. She thought of all of these things as she and Smooth were riding to the studio in the Village.

They got off the subway at 14th street and walked the two blocks to 12th and then around the corner. Vanda Mae saw a closed sign on the door and wondered if this was the place where the interview would take place. Had they gotten there too late? Smooth rang the doorbell and after a few seconds, a white male opened the curtain and then opened the door. "Hey, Smooth; it's good to see you and I see that you brought a very beautiful lady with you."

"Carl, I want to introduce you to Vanda Mae." Turning to Vanda Mae, Smooth continued, "Vanda Mae, this is Carl." Turning back to Carl, he said, "Carl, I want you to understand that Vanda Mae is a very good friend and a friend that I have known for a real long time. She is like my sister. That's how close we are." Turning back to Vanda Mae, Smooth continued, "Vanda Mae, Carl is my best client. I treat him differently than my other clients. Carl and I relax together. I'm learning photography from him. I can't always be the purveyor of dust. Dust sales are going to have to stop at sometime and I need to be able to earn some money doing something legit. I come here every Thursday night and learn something new regarding photography. Carl pays for the dust and he gets a little something extra with it and I get a little something extra with it also. It's a great relationship that Carl and I share. It is a relationship which is mutually satisfying to both of us and we are inviting you to be a part of it with us."

Vanda Mae looked at the two men, one a Colored long time friend and the other, a white man who was dressed professionally except that he didn't have on shoes. This white man, this good friend of Smooth's, came to the door without any shoes. He greeted them in his socks. She thought that his feet must hurt awful badly. "Smooth," Vanda Mae said, "I'm not sure what you are getting at. I thought that I would be photographed in these clothes that you bought me. Am I going to be photographed?"

Smooth replied, "Vanda Mae, you are going to be photographed, but not necessarily in those clothes. Those are your street clothes. I bought them for you, just because I love you. O. K., Vanda Mae?" Smooth didn't wait for her to respond. "Now we're going to share some dust." Smooth extended his hand to Carl and received in it, several bills. These were placed in his wallet and they all sat down around a table and proceeded to inhale dust through their nostrils. After all six nostrils had been innervated, Carl stepped away from them and brought back a tray of crackers and something that looked like black jam, but smelled fishy. "I'll get the spumante, Carl" and Smooth brought back some fancy glasses and a bottle of wine. Vanda Mae realized that there was more to this relationship than she originally thought.

Here was a Colored man who felt comfortable going into the kitchen of a white man and bringing him a drink, after the white man had served him smelly jam and crackers. They were indeed, very close men.

Vanda Mae soon learned that they were snacking on fish roe, something which she discarded when in Black Bottom. "Yeah, Vanda Mae, different fish produce different colored eggs; just like different birds produce different colored eggs," Smooth expounded. "The name for these black eggs is, caviar. The sturgeon produces these eggs." He said this as he was taking off his shoes. Vanda Mae was wondering if the 'job interview' was going to go in a different direction? Would the three of them end up nude in this studio having sex, taking pictures, eating caviar, and drinking spumante? Smooth got paid, would she get paid?

Carl invited Vanda Mae to dust one of her nostrils. He unbuttoned his shirt as she inhaled. He then invited Smooth to dust a nostril. The unbuttoned shirt was now being slipped off. Carl was sitting there in his undershirt with the button at the top of his pants, undone. Smooth leaned backwards and sighed, "This is some fuckin' good shit." He then stood up, dropped his pants and took off his shirt. He looked at Vanda Mae and said, "We're going to tell a story in pictures. Carl is going to take some of the pictures and I'm going to take some of the pictures. We'll be photographed nearly nude or in the nude." Smooth continued, "Vanda Mae, let me help you out of those nice clothes. Let me hang them up for you." As Smooth approached Vanda Mae, in his underwear, undershirt, and socks, Carl took more dust up his left nostril. He started swaying to a tune he heard in his head and then got up and dropped his pants.

He placed them on a nearby chair and then slipped off his socks. He then poured more spumante. Smooth came up behind Vanda Mae and helped her slip out of her jacket. He unbuttoned her blouse. She loved this rear buttoning long sleeve blouse; it made her feel so cultured, so sophisticated. He eased her skirt down from her waist. Smooth hung all of her clothes neatly on a hanger. After Carl placed his glass on the cocktail table, he went to the camera and adjusted the lens. Afterward, he focused a spotlight towards Vanda Mae and Smooth. He then made another adjustment to the camera and went over to Smooth and Vanda Mae. With him on the left of Vanda Mae and Smooth on the right he said, "Smooth, place your right hand on Vanda Mae's belly." Carl then placed his left hand on top of Smooth's hand. He commanded, "No one look at the camera" and then the flash went off. Carl was clearly in charge now.

"Smooth, we've got about a minute before the next flash. You need to take off the undershirt and the socks and turn your back to the camera. Smooth complied. Carl was in only his underwear also when he said, "O.K. now, place your right hand on top of Vanda Mae's crotch. Carl then turned his back to the camera and placed his left hand on top of Smooth's hand and the flash went off. "O.K. now, we're going to drop our drawers and press our crotches into Vanda Mae's hips and lean backwards. Vanda Mae, you're going to grasp and squeeze Smooth's right butt cheek and your other hand will do the same to my left butt cheek. Lean back some more, Smooth." They were captured in the next flash. Carl went to the camera and moved a button and announced that the flash would not go off now. He invited Smooth up to see the button which tripped the flash and the shutter. "Vanda Mae, come on up here. You're also going to take some pictures. When I tell you to take the picture, you're going to push this button right here. O.K.?"

"I got it, Carl" Vanda Mae said.

"Vanda Mae, what's been going on is that I've been loosening you up. I want you to relax in front of the camera. You're going to come out of that slip, panties and bra. You're going to take off the garter belt and stockings. You're going to drape that cloth over there, over yourself like in this picture." With that, Carl opened a book to a picture of a white woman with cloth coming over one shoulder and descending down between her breasts. The cloth was wrapped around the woman's hips to form a skirt. We're going to reshoot the pictures we just took, with you dressed this way and with Smooth and me nude. O.K.?"

Vanda Mae replied, "Am I gonna get paid for these pictures?"

Smooth said, "Vanda Mae, you're getting $25.00."

"Well, Carl, let's reshoot those pictures," Vanda Mae said with a smile. She knew that she was not going to be in an advertisement appearing in the Amsterdam News. She reasoned that taking money this way was a cleaner and safer way of selling her body than she had been used to.

They must have taken 100 photographs that night. There were wrestling poses involving the nude guys, which Vanda Mae took. There were poses involving bows and arrows and quivers with Vanda Mae and Smooth in loin cloths. There were pictures of Carl and Vanda Mae drinking from leather bags while resting on fallen fake tree trunks and Smooth took these pictures. Vanda Mae noticed that none of the poses in any of the pictures involved the guys having sex with one another nor them having sex with her. Still, she believed that Carl and Smooth had shared their bodies with each other. In the past, she was the protector when he was getting intimate with a male, just like he protected her when she was on her back for a john. Yes, they had gone their separate ways, she with Big Jim and then with Rocky, but she didn't think that Smooth would develop such an intimate relationship with a male; especially a white male; a white male who was his customer and his teacher.

Carl went to his pants and took out some cash. He then handed it to Vanda Mae. He started kissing Vanda Mae and then Smooth joined in. He kissed Carl on the right side of his face and Vanda Mae on the left shoulder. Carl stopped his passionate romancing of the couple long enough to pull the sofa out and into a bed. Vanda Mae was on the bed between the two men. Their mouths were working in tandem. Both tongues were stimulating both breasts. Both tongues were easing down the sides of her body. Both tongues met up at the innermost part of her triangle and both tongues licked and massaged her. Vanda Mae whimpered and then screamed while all of the time bucking on the bed. As she was coming down off of her 'high,' she noticed that the two men were smiling toward each other. She guessed that they liked bringing her to this climax. She watched the guys as their right hands extended across her body and around each other's neck. She watched as they gently and simultaneously pulled each other closer until their lips and tongues were touching. They all changed positions and Vanda Mae was sitting on the bed providing fellatio to a standing Carl while he was licking Smooth's nipple. She used two hands when giving oral love. One hand held the penis shaft while her lips and tongue focused on the corona and the other hand supported the man's testicles while her fingers massaged his perineum. Previous men loved the techniques she employed and Carl was no exception. Smooth pulled himself away from Carl and went to his pants. He retrieved from the pocket a handkerchief. Inside the handkerchief were rubber gloves and rubbers. Vanda Mae saw that he then went to a drawer in the studio kitchen and got out something and brought it back to the bed. When there, she could see that it was a small squeeze bottle of mineral oil. Smooth knew where Carl kept his mineral oil! Smooth placed his hand in one glove and then placed oil on its thumb. Lying on his back on the sofa bed, he placed this hand between his legs and on top of his thighs, just below his scrotum. He held his gloved fist in place with his ungloved hand. He then extended his sheathed and liberally lubricated thumb. Carl got down on his knees and straddled Smooth's reclining body. He then eased himself down on Smooth's extended thumb. Smooth flexed that thumb and Carl rocked back and forth. Vanda Mae now knew where Smooth had learned this love position.

———◆———

The sun was setting on Black Bottom. The folks were sitting outside of their homes. Some men were playing checkers and some were playing cards. Some young ladies were bathing their siblings while their mothers cooked the evening meal. Bobby had been working on the fishing boat all day and he smelled of fish. He had fish scales and fish blood on his skin, on his clothes, and on his shoes; and even his bandana had blood and scales on it. Melissa, Bobby's wife, was waiting for him to come home. She had two pitchers of lemonade sitting in the icebox. She liked to serve him this when he arrived. Upon entering the home, Melissa blew her husband a kiss and went to the icebox and got the lemonade. There were a few things which this man wanted in his wife. He wanted a wife who would help in making a better life for themselves. He wanted a reliable and fun loving sexual partner; after all, he was 23 and ready to rut at anytime. He wanted a wife who would cook and sew and take care of the babies if the Good Lord blessed them with babies. His wife also had to understand that he liked his solitude after work and that taking a bath and getting the smell of fish off of him was important to him. He had to bathe before he could kiss and embrace her; he didn't want her to have the smell he was trying to rid of himself. Bathing was so important to Bobby that he had created a special gutter system for his home. Rain water was directed into a series of barrels which were connected by pipes. The barrels were on cinder block pads and were 2 feet, 3 feet, and 4 feet above the ground. The lowest barrel had a faucet on it through which water would go into a washtub through a 20 foot hose. Bobby built a room around his bath tub and furnished it with a small table, two chairs, and three lanterns. He grew lavender all around his house so that the leaves could be used to scent the water. Bobby knew that he was good with his hands. He knew that he could see possibilities for buildings that others didn't see. He wanted to go to Tuskegee Institute and better himself in carpentry and plumbing, but he was scared of leaving Black Bottom. The Klan was everywhere and it was just waiting for a Colored man to step out of his place and so for the last seven years, he had been designing and building items first, around his parents' home, then around his and Melissa's home. A few neighbors commissioned his skills at building cabinets and rain collection systems for them. In his spare time, he built what they wanted and saved the money which they gave him. He thought that one day, he and Melissa would have to leave Black Bottom and go North, like so many other Colored folks did. Somewhere up North, they could have better lives. Bobby thought about all of these things as he prepared to step into his tub. He was waiting for Melissa to enter the bathroom. When she came there, she poured a glass of lemonade and then went back to the stove and brought a pot of water in which a poultice of lavender leaves had been simmering. This scented water was poured into the washtub and cooled by the water from the barrel. Bobby kneeled in the tub and began washing his hair with Madame Walker's shampoo. He then rinsed it with this clean scented bath water. Only after his hair was washed would he apply soap and water to the rest of his body. By the end of this bathing routine, Bobby had sufficiently let his mind contemplate a better life and how to bring it about. By the end of this routine, he was ready to grab his sixteen year old wife and kiss her with all of the love that he had in him. By the end of this routine, he was also ready to eat dinner.

———◆———

Ofc. Brown was preparing to leave the Police Station when he saw the Captain working at his desk. He hoped that the Captain would approve his request for promotion. He had passed the test and so, it should have been a done deal, but he had not heard that he would be promoted. He decided to ask what was going on.

"Excuse me, Captain Rodham, can I speak with you for a minute?"

"Yeah," replied Rodham. ". . . go on and speak."

"Sir, I know that I passed the test, but I haven't heard anything regarding my promotion. Can you explain the delay?"

"Sure, I can explain the delay. I haven't signed off on your promotion."

"But Sir, Captain, I need that promotion; I've got a pregnant wife to support."

"Listen Brown, you've got a pregnant wife that you beat. I've seen her. She didn't tell me; shit, she didn't have to. One of these days, she's gonna take that gun of yours and do you in. Keep whipping her ass and see what happens; especially, when she finds out about your mistress and how nice you treat her."

"Captain, you ain't got no business delving into my private life. I'm a cop and I should be judged on my work."

"Yeah, yeah, yeah. Have you caught Big Jim's killer yet? . . . Well, have you? Why are you silent? Cat got your tongue? You seem to be a little deficient in your ability to solve a capital crime. It ain't all book learnin' Brown."

"I brought Rocky in, but I couldn't get him to talk. I even shot his dog and his goat in an effort to get him to talk, but he disappeared after that."

"Brown, do you have cotton for brains? Do you think that I have cotton for brains? I heard Rocky's screams. All you did was get us written up in a northern newspaper as being a bunch of barbarians. You shot the man's dog in front of a crowd of people. That action made you look like you were deranged and you confirmed your derangement when you came back and shot the goat. Brown, I can look the other way on the animals. I am looking the other way regarding Rocky's false imprisonment and torture. Hell, nothing's documented and so nothing happened. But I'm having a hard time looking the other way when you talk about drinking on duty."

"What are you talking about, Captain? I haven't been drunk on duty."

"Bullshit! Weren't you talking about alcohol when you went on your animal killing spree? Didn't you say something about alcohol in your veins? That's what six dog lovers came to me and said, you said. Six of them, Brown. Six witnesses to your animal-hating drunken behavior. Two of the witnesses go to the same church as my wife. I've heard the crazy cop at the station story every day since the killing spree. I'm the one in charge of the crazy drunken cop. By the way Brown, have you found O'Brien? Have you found his car? Missing persons falls under the category of police work. Try to earn the paycheck that you receive. I don't want my budget reduced because of a drunken incompetent crazy ass policeman. Now, do you have any other questions of me?"

"No, Sir."

"Well then, have a nice evening, Brown and please close the door behind you."

Brown had walked out onto the station parking lot when he decided to turn around. He went back to the Captain's office and knocked on the door. When the Captain said,

"Enter" he opened the door and said, "If I can find out who killed Big Jim and get that person arrested and if I can find O'Brien, can you sign my promotion papers?"

"Yeah. Any more questions?"

"No."

"Then, good evening, Ofc. Brown."

———◆———

It was 9:00 p.m. and Langston and Rocky had long since finished turning the basement into a home. It would never be as nice as what the guys upstairs had, but it was dry and now had more useable space than his home in Black Bottom. He had the harsh light from the naked bulbs, he had a toilet, and Langston had bought toilet paper. He had a bed made out of stacked newspapers. His bed was 30 inches wide by 72 inches long and 3 inches deep. Over this, two Salvation Army sheets and a blanket, were placed. He knew that he had to add newspaper to the bed to get its height to a level which would eventually be comfortable for quickly and easily getting in and out of it.

Rocky had some pots and pans and some canned food and a can opener and a hot plate. He had his art supplies and he had a table on which he could create art. He knew that the reason which he had these things was because he had made some friends in this apartment house. He reflected that he had saved his money and when the time was right, he gathered his courage and left Black Bottom. He reflected on how he had been treated by the police and by his own people; brutalized by the police; sometimes laughed at by his people and sometimes pitied by them because he wasn't a whole man. He was a deformed man; he was a crippled man. He knew that the common belief among the people of Black Bottom was that he was a man who really wouldn't amount to much; not in comparison to other men, in their twenties, in Black Bottom. The thinking was, "What good woman would want to take for a husband, a crippled basket weaver?! Better to let Vanda Mae have him." Rocky heard all of the snipes which were said behind his back. Their pity hurt him, even when they knew he was going to fight Big Jim, they thought him foolish. He thought back to the fight and how no one helped him against Big Jim. Bobby and Hattie gave him weapons, but neither was actually there when the fight occurred. No one came up behind Big Jim and hit him, no one took a knife and cut him, no one took a baling hook and stabbed him. If Big Jim had killed Rocky, the community thinking would have been, *"Better to sacrifice Rocky and have Vanda Mae snatched from the village than to have Big Jim walking around and killing other residents of Black Bottom."* Rocky knew, that was how they thought. Well, Rocky had earned their respect by killing Big Jim, but he hated that such an extreme action had to take place before some dignity could be bestowed on him. He was thankful that no one had turned him into the police, but wondered how long they would hold out. Rocky was sitting at his table with his bell and candles. He lit a candle and then struck the bell three times. He prayed:

*"Eleggua, I am asking that you visit me now. Eleggua, I am asking that you take my hand and lead me to my*

*ancestors and my protective angels. Eleggua, the angel who
moves between humans and the divine world, please visit
me and stay with me and place me in the presence of the
protective spirits."* Rocky began breathing deeply and
after waiting a few minutes, he rang the bell again.
*"Some people call you Jesus, some people call you Jehovah,
to me you are the Holy Ghost and your name is Olodumare.
You are the all powerful protector. You are the all knowing one who sees my future, who plans my challenges, who
trips me up and helps me over the hurdles. Thank you for
the blessings which you have bestowed on me. Thank you
for the Guardian Angels Bell and my goat. Thank you for
putting the root man in my life and please help me locate
his son up here in New York City. Thank you, Olodumare
for my friends here in New York City. Please bless and protect Langston and Bruce, and Wallace, and Aaron. Please
bless Mr. Alexander, he helped give me hope when I was
feeling low. Ololdumare, I am asking you to also bless
Mr. Saperstein, he didn't have to rent this space to me. Please
give to me the wisdom to make the best decisions while I am
living in this basement. Please give to me the wisdom to
make the best decisions about the people who will be coming
into my life. Please protect Vanda Mae and when you think
that it is the right time for me to find her, please help me
to be ready to help her ease herself off of dust and back into
my heart. Please let her heart accept my love. Please help us
to forge a path together in this city or in some other place.
Please let us live in love and harmony. Olodumare, I am
praying that you will help me to be a man who has a gentle*

*nature and also has a good character. I ask this of you, the Holy Ghost. Amen. Ache'."* Rocky rang the bell three times and then blew out the candle. He sat there quietly and slowly breathed for the next twenty minutes and then went to bed.

## CHAPTER 12

# HE'D NEVER HAD IT SO GOOD

---

### Friday Morning, September 29, 1933

ROCKY WOKE UP AT 5:15 a.m. He was used to getting up early like the rest of the adult males in Black Bottom, even though he did not go out on the boats. He knew that he would not be making a lot of baskets here in New York City and so he thought that he should start drawing pictures. This seemed like the logical thing to do, since he was supposed to be making money as an artist. He hadn't painted a picture before, due to not having had paints nor paint brushes, but he thought that he still should be able to produce a decent painting, if he could make a decent drawing of something. He wasn't sure of what to draw. He thought fish, he could draw fish. Then he thought about a scene involving fishermen, nets, rods, reels, and knives. He then thought of doing a portrait. The portrait would be of Langston. It would be done in pencil and presented to him as a gift.

It took 20 minutes to do the portrait. He thought that it looked close enough for someone to say, "That looks like Langston." He wasn't fully satisfied with the portrait, but he wasn't sure how to make it more lifelike, more a mirror of the man. He wanted anyone who viewed the portrait to feel that Langston was a trustworthy, positive gentleman, a man worthy of admiration. He was hoping that his art class would help him with these problems.

Rocky wanted to do another drawing before breakfast and before going to pay for his membership at the YMCA. He started sketching a tree. In this first picture, he wanted to capture the peacefulness of a grove of peach trees. The colored pencils which Bruce gave him were coming in handy. The peach grove was seen at a distance. In the next picture, there was a focus on a tree with a double trunk. In the third picture, the double trunk was displayed as a burned body suspended by a rope which was tied around its neck. There was a slightly burned peach in the man's mouth and the peach was kept in place by barbed wire tied behind the head. Rocky didn't know if the picture would sell; it was quite disturbing. He wasn't even sure that he had finished the picture. He felt that Olodumare had entered him and had guided his hand. He thought that the picture spoke of what he had seen. The picture had presented a truth. Rocky had been filled by the Holy Ghost.

———◆———

At 9:00 a.m., there was knocking on the front basement door. Rocky was surprised by the sound and wondered about it. Who would be knocking on the front basement door?

"Mr. Johnson, you in there?"

It was Mr. Saperstein knocking on the door. He yelled to the door, "Coming, Mr. Saperstein." He rolled the office chair to the door and reached into his pocket and unlocked the front door. "Come on in, Mr. Saperstein. Look around and see what has been done with the place." Saperstein entered, looked around, tried the back door and commented, "You got the money?" Rocky had taken it out the night before and placed it underneath one of his candle sticks. He retrieved it and gave it to the landlord.

"Mr. Johnson, you've made a good start. Remember nothing goes in the coal bin and nothing goes in front of the furnace. I'll return November 1st for November's rent. I'm not giving you a receipt because we're keeping this between ourselves. As far as I'm concerned, you're staying with Mr. Hughes. Got it?"

"Yeah, Mr. Saperstein, I got it."

"Mr. Johnson, this ain't the country. You are in New York City, the largest city in the United States. People lock doors in this city. Just like you had that front door locked when I was knocking on it, keep the door locked at all times. Unlock it only if you are leaving through it and then immediately lock the door. Don't go to sleep with either the front door or the back door unlocked. Understand? You don't need to get any cross breezes by having the doors ajar. Understand? I don't care how stuffy it gets down here. When you open one of these doors, immediately lock it as you exit. I tell you these things for your own safety. People will enter and rob you and hurt you. You're already crippled and you don't need to have anything else happening to you." With that said, Saperstein left via the front basement door.

"I don't hear you locking the door!"

Rocky rolled towards the door and locked it.

"Good. See you November 1st."

Rocky was concerned about thieves here in New York City. What type of place had he moved to? He then realized that in Black Bottom, he hid his money from everyone. Disappointment came over him as he realized that people were the same wherever you went. New York was not Heaven for Colored folks, it was just better than Black Bottom.

———◆———

Capt. Rodham was sitting at his desk talking to his cousin Ronnie. Ronnie Rodham was an instructor at the state police academy. The Captain told his cousin that he had a missing policeman and a missing police car. He said that he would like to get both of them back, but if not both, then he wanted the car retrieved. Ronnie said that he would talk it over with the superintendent of the academy and see if the freshman class could be sent out to scout the back roads around Charleston. He said that he would call him back before the end of the day with the superintendent's answer.

———◆———

Byron Tolliver had the week off. He wanted to rest, listen to his records, read up on herbs and their properties, and hang out (a little bit) with his girlfriend, Zora, and these things, he did. His herb shop though, was the most important thing to him. He wanted to provide natural remedies for the ailments of people. He had a two bedroom apartment with one of those rooms dedicated to the storage, cataloging, pricing, and preparation of herbs for sale. If someone needed something and he was home and he had it, he met that person's need, for a price. He stressed that his products were not to be used only when something bad happened. They were to be used daily to keep the person healthy. That was how the herbs worked best. He talked about a healthy life style, but most people didn't follow his advice.

Byron was a third generation Root Man, as far as he knew. He took pride in his work; but the money derived from his herbal prescriptions did not pay the bills. No, working as a conductor on the railroad supplied those funds. His herbal enterprise though, was a labor of love and a way of demonstrating his acceptance of his role in nature. He considered himself to be a vessel for the earthly works of Ozain, the Orisha of herbs and natural healing. Most of his customers didn't understand him when his conversation veered away from mundane events or the specific use of herbs; that's why he rarely discussed his religious beliefs with anyone. The one exception was Zora. She accepted him as he was. She wanted to learn of his religion. She'd talk politics with him and argue with him and still be his friend. They disagreed regarding Booker T's legacy and the path in which Du Bois was moving the NAACP. They agreed on the necessity of a strong positive cultural identity which was inclusive of the religious and sexual minorities within the African Diaspora. They were free spirits who liked to share love from time to time with no strings attached. They both made their careers primary in their lives, which was why they knew that they could never marry each other. Byron "Babatunji" Tolliver and Zora Neale Hurston, were like vinegar and olive oil. You could shake them up real good and they could be great together, but they would always eventually separate. When Zora mentioned A'Lelia's party to Tunji, his reply was predictable. He suggested that one of her poet friends should accompany her. He was not in awe of faded royalty, well to do royalty, mustifino royalty, coal black royalty, nor snow white royalty. Haile Selassie was a good guy, but one man, one vote, with minority rights, was better. After that comment, she finished her scrambled eggs and coffee, kissed him, and told him that she would catch up with him next month. As she was walking out of the door he said, "I bet you're going to hook up with one of your artsy buddies this morning." Her reply was, "You got it."

———◆———

Rocky was hobbling up the street. He knew that he would make better time if he used two crutches but he didn't like the impression that, that picture presented. One crutch presented a more hopeful picture, at least in his mind.

He would soon be at the "Y". He brought his towel with him and his soap. He was looking forward to a long relaxing shower. He was hoping that a chair or stool or crate would be near the shower or at least quickly obtainable. When Mr. Alexander saw him with a towel around his neck, he let Rocky know that the "Y" provided towels and soap. He also let him know that he could lock his clothes in a locker and place the locker key on his wrist. Rocky paid him $25.00 for the "Y" membership and because he was now a member, he got the reduced class fee of $4.00 each for a reading class, a math class, and an art class. When he got to the shower area, he saw a wooden and cloth folding chair. He positioned the chair a few feet from the wall and then adjusted the water stream so that it fell gently onto the chair. Once in the chair, he let the warm water caress his body. He soaped this area and that area while under the shower, but mostly, he enjoyed relaxing in a warm supportive affirming environment. He'd never had it so good. As the water poured over his body, he clasped the soap between his folded hands, closed his eyes, and quietly thanked Olodumare.

———◆———

Smooth was beating eggs and cutting up vegetables for an omelet and Vanda Mae was cooking bacon and boiling grits. He was reflecting on how profitable last night had been for him and Vanda Mae. He had made $200 from dust plus he got more training in how to work a professional's camera. Vanda Mae got $25 for posing for a bunch of pictures. She was naked in the pictures, but it was still $25. They were 23 and lucky. Neither of them had any diseases and neither of them had been placed in jail. They'd both killed johns in protection of the other. It was a fast life based on shallow good times. Could they live this way when they were 40? He knew the good times couldn't last. He knew that he was not jail material. That's why this apprenticeship with Carl was so important. He had to learn everything he could so that he and Vanda Mae could start a new life, maybe in a new town. He also knew that his new life could not have dust in it. It would be an expense which would be too great unless he was extremely successful as a photographer or unless he was pushing it on the side.

He told his thoughts to Vanda Mae and she agreed that they could not sustain the life they were currently living. She just wasn't sure how they could achieve financial stability. They enjoyed a higher standard of living than many Coloreds in New York City and most Coloreds in the United States. A Depression had gripped the nation. Jobs were scarce and there were plenty of white folks that didn't have the good lives that they had. Giving up dust sales would take a major commitment to making his photography profitable. She wanted to know if he stopped pushing dust, would he or both of them, stop turning tricks? She let him know that she liked modeling as long as it paid $25 a day. He told her that the police would still charge her with prostitution if they got wind of what was going on. He told her that Carl was important in New York and that was why the police did not bother him. When she looked at him quizzically he said, "He makes his money writing for a newspaper. The photography is like a side business. It's more than his hobby, but it's definitely not his main source of income. If the shop closed today, he'd do just fine."

"I'll ask him this evening if I can get more on-the-job experience. I'll propose that we split whatever profits are made, down the middle."

"So, does that mean that you are going to tell him that you are going to cut back, I mean cut out his dust supply? Are you going to tell him that you're going to hold back on the nooky?"

"First, I've got to get more experience. When that's in place, when I'm ready to start out on my own, I can cut out the dust. The nooky is different. He knows high class Coloreds and some of them are going to want to have their pictures taken. Some of the sweet ones are going to want more than photographs and they'll keep their mouths shut because half of them are married."

"Smooth . . .," said Vanda Mae.

He interrupted her and said, "I ain't in no sportin' house now. That part of me has got to fade away. Vanda Mae, I got to become Robin Daniels and I want you to become Vanda Mae Daniels. I don't want us to pretend to be sister and brother; I want us to be husband and wife."

"Smooth, O.K., I'll call you Robin, but how we going to be married if you turning up your ass to high class Colored men and also to Carl? I like money. We haven't talked about my bringing in cash. If half of the high class Colored guys want you, the other half might want me. We been living this way for a long time, why stop? We still got our looks. We can slowly go legit. All we got to do is change our customers. We don't have to stop working."

"You're making sense Vanda Mae. . . . I mean, Mrs. Daniels. I'll speak with Carl this evening. But Vanda Mae, you know that trickin' is for the young. . . One other thing, Vanda Mae, I think that we're going to have to begin going to church."

"Robin, what's with all of these changes? Why we got to go to church? Are you losing your mind? You grew up in a whorehouse. We turned tricks before we turned 13. Tricks and dust have been in our lives for a long time and now you want to go and change everything. We ain't church people."

"Vanda Mae, it makes good business sense. Think about it, we're around people who got money to give away. They're going to want pictures of their children and grandchildren. They're going to want wedding pictures and so, they'll turn to us. We'll be members of the congregation. We'll be advertising in the church bulletin. You can wear the nice clothes I bought."

"I can wear those clothes when I'm picking up married school teachers also. Smooth, Robin, you haven't convinced me that I should begin going to church. You should be true to yourself when you're a church going person. If you're in the House of the Lord, how you gonna advertise love for sale? Cause that's what I'd be doing. Mr. Daniels would be pushing photographs while Mrs. Daniels would be humming "Love for Sale." The church ladies would ban both of us from the building and the minister wouldn't say a word cause it's the church ladies who put money in the plate."

Robin wasn't ready to discard this idea. "I got to think this through some more," was his reply.

———————

Rocky was hobbling past the front desk when Mr. Alexander said, "How'd you like your first shower at the "Y," Rocky?"

"It was a blessing, Mr. Alexander. I feel real good. I can't wait to start my classes, although I'm kinda nervous. It's something new for me. Little kids, they just go to school and don't think anything of it. They learn their numbers and their words and then they go outside to play. The next day, they pick up where they left off."

"Rocky, it's the same with adults. Don't let the newness of the situation get to you. You'll learn what you need to learn. You'll build on your learning from one day to the next. Believe me Rocky, there are a lot of guys like you coming up here from the South with only 2 or 3 years of schooling. You are not the only one who has never been to school. Miss Stapleton teaches the guys who haven't had any schooling. She's nice, you'll like her. She's from North Carolina.

She came up from Raleigh to go to Miner Teachers College in D. C. and she got her Master's Degree in History from Howard University. She's been teaching here in New York City for 3 years. She's 27 and she's cute. You'll like being in Miss Stapleton's class. Remember, the classes start at 5:00 p.m. and repeat themselves at 6:30 p.m."

"Thanks, Mr. Alexander. Have a nice day." With that information and his bath out of the way, Rocky hobbled back to his home. He set as his goal, the drawing of 3 more pictures before going to bed that evening.

———◆———

At 3:00 p.m., Capt. Rodham received word that 45 police cadets would be utilized in the search for Ofc. O'Brien and for the lost police car. They would be combing the back roads of Charleston in 15 groups with 3 persons to each group. Nine of the 45 cadets would be searching the road he most likely took from his home in order to get to work. They would leave from the academy at 8:00 a.m. tomorrow and return at 4:00 p.m.

———◆———

At 8:00 p.m. that evening, Rocky heard footsteps coming down the stairs from the second floor and then he heard them descending from the first into the basement. At the top of the basement stairs Wallace announced, "I got something for you Rocky!" Rocky was being handed a black suit, white shirt, and a red tie. He mentioned to Rocky that since they were close in size, he would loan Rocky clothing for the party. He said though that he was concerned with Rocky's leg brace; specifically, he wondered if it would fit inside the pant leg and would it rip the material? He told Rocky not to force the brace in the pant leg. If it were to get stuck, then he shouldn't try to force it. Bruce had multiple pairs of black pants and he was the largest person in the house. Bruce would have to loan him a pair of black pants to go with his black jacket.

# CHAPTER 13

# THE END OF THE WOODLAND FEAST

---

### *Saturday Afternoon, September 30, 1933*

THE FINDING OF O'BRIEN'S BODY was radioed to the superintendent and the superintendent telephoned Capt. Rodham. It was a grisly scene according to the Superintendent. Animals had started eating O'Brien. When Rodham arrived on the scene, he noticed that more than the group of three cadets were combing the scene. It looked as though there were nine cadets on the scene. "Good," he thought, maybe they will find some useable evidence. He asked a cadet where the body was and the cadet answered by pointing. Rodham was finding fault with this freshman class. Pointing was unacceptable; they were to respond verbally. He'd let the Superintendent know. Just then T. J. and his assistant drove up in the morgue's van. They stepped out of it and started walking in his direction. When the three of them got about thirty feet into the woods, they noticed that there were no cadets congregating around the body. The Superintendent would have to be told about this also. His cadets had not protected the "crime scene." Rodham stopped walking when he saw a tree full of crows. He thought that the birds symbolized death. As he, T.

J., and the assistant drew nearer to that tree, they saw a fox tugging at something. Moving a few feet closer, they could see that the fox was ripping out pieces of O'Brien's throat. First the fox growled at them, then it barked at them, and then it ran off. They gazed on O'Brien's mutilated body and Rodham understood why the cadets didn't want to be around it. O'Brien's eyes had been gouged out by birds. Two pools of bloody pulp greeted the onlookers. His nose had been bitten off by some creature. An onlooker would clearly see the hard palette of O'Brien's mouth through this enlarged opening. His fingers had various sized bite marks indicating that a variety of animals had found him to be a tasty meal. Rodham understood the cadets' feelings of disgust, but they were still supposed to follow standard operating procedures. Revulsion for a crime scene was one thing, but doing your job correctly and fully was another; particularly if the crime was high profile in nature; particularly if the crime involved a fellow cop.

They heard someone approaching them and turned around and saw the police photographer walking toward them. Cory D. Ackerson, the cops called him Kodak, was doing a job which he loved. In high school, he got his first camera and started taking pictures of the students and the teachers. He would develop the pictures in a dark room which he built in the basement of his home. During his senior year, some of his pictures made it into the yearbook. The first job which he got out of high school was as a photographer for the weekly paper. When the opening came along for a police photographer, he had the prerequisite amount of experience and as such, he was a shoo-in for the position. The mayor, his grandfather, made sure of that.

Kodak let them know that he had photographed a rope near the road as well as the inside of the police car. He said that the driver's seat had dirt in it; small bits of leaves and grass, soil and twigs. Like the person sitting behind the wheel had been playing in the dirt or dragged through the dirt. He said that a guy from the lab was trying to get prints off of the car. Kodak asked the guys, "What do you think was going on out here? Why was O'Brien in these woods? Did you notice that O'Brien's gun is still in his holster? Isn't that odd?"

Rodham's reply was, "Those are good questions, but before I jump to a conclusion, I want to read what T.J. has to say." Turning to the medical examiner he continued, "You got your work cut out for you this weekend. I hope that you can come to some conclusions, in spite of the animal contamination."

"We'll see," said T.J. He ordered his assistant to bring two cadets, a blanket, a body bag, and the stretcher back here and tell them that the order came from Captain Rodham.

Kodak had finished taking pictures by the time the cadets and the assistant arrived. The assistant placed the stretcher on the ground near O'Brien and the cadet placed the bag on the stretcher and opened it. The cadets and the assistant put on latex gloves and breathing masks before getting closer to the body. They understood that O'Brien's body might have picked up something contagious from the animals feasting on him.

The cadets were stooped down and facing each other. One was at O'Brien's head and the other was at his feet. They had the blanket pulled tightly between them and lying on the ground. The assistant was on O'Brien's left side grabbing the corpse by the right shoulder and hip and pulling the body toward him. The cadets pushed the blanket towards the middle of O'Brien's body then the assistant let the body down and raised the left side of O'Brien's body and the cadets pulled the blanket completely under it. T. J. told them that they would move the body into the bag on "Three."

"One . . . Two . . . Three . . .Lift."

As they lifted the body, a rat covered in blood ran out of the pant leg and up the arm of one of the cadets. The cadet's screams drowned out the laughter of the group. Needless to say, O'Brien had been dropped. Rodham followed the cadet to the assembled group, got a different "volunteer" and got the body lifted into the bag and then onto the stretcher and into the van. All he needed now was the autopsy report.

———◆———

Rodham was feeling good. He could check off two more things on his "To Do" list. His report combined with T. J.'s report, would give an explanation of what happened to O'Brien. Best of all though, he got the police car back. He wouldn't have to use police funds to buy another car. Of course, the police car wouldn't be useable while the crime lab was inspecting it, but it should be back in service soon.

Rodham thought that the Big Jim murder needed to be wrapped up in some way. Recording it as "unknown assailant" left an opening for some future political opponent to attack his investigation skills. He didn't think much of Brown's abilities as a police officer and really, he didn't think much of him as a man. It was one thing to cheat on one's wife, but it was another to beat her. Wife beating was an accepted practice that he didn't like and hadn't engaged in; but since he wanted to be mayor, he wouldn't rock the boat and let it be known that he was against the practice. Still, Brown was the weakest link on his police force and his investigation of Big Jim's murder had turned up nothing. The drunk would not be getting a promotion this year and it was kind of a shame since he had that baby coming. He thought that Brown should shadow him for a few days, just to see how a detective gathers information. It was Saturday afternoon, a day that he normally did not work. It was time for him to go home, change into civilian clothes, and then take the wife out to dinner at the Blind Tiger Restaurant. He thought about T. J. most likely feeling the same way. He would probably place O'Brien on ice and then do the autopsy on Monday. That meant that his official report might not be ready until the 8th or 9th of October. He really didn't want to wait that long. Rodham went to the phone and dialed. T. J. picked up on his end.

"Hello."

"Hi, T. J."

"Well, if it isn't the Captain. You caught me just in time. I was about to head on home and get cleaned up and take my wife out to The Blind Tiger. I haven't taken her out to dinner in a month. So, make it quick Captain, cause I got homework waiting for me." This was the story he always told Rodham when he was asked to work on his day off. Rodham knew what he'd have to do.

"T. J., it sure would be helpful for my investigation if I could get your idea about how O'Brien died. That is, if

I could get, this evening, some idea of what caused his death. You think that you could work a few more hours on O'Brien? I could treat you and the wife to dinner. In fact, why don't you call her up and tell her I'll pick her up and bring her, along with my wife, to The Blind Tiger. You can meet us there. How about that?"

"What you're saying is that if I could squeeze in a few more hours of work on my day off, that you would buy me and my lovely wife dinner this evening, and then I could come in late to work on Monday, right? Is that how I should interpret what you're saying?"

"You left out the part where you give me information over dinner."

"But, the rest is right?"

"It's right," said Rodham.

"What time will you be picking up my wife?"

"7:00 p.m."

"I'll be at the Tiger at 7:30." T. J. hung up and resumed his inspection of the body but, his mind kept drifting to the top shelf liquor he'd be ordering this evening, at the Captain's expense.

# CHAPTER 14

# A ROYAL MESS

———————

*Saturday Evening, September 30, 1933*

T. J. WAS THE FIRST to arrive at the restaurant. After he was shown to a table, he ordered a double Canadian Mist with a sweet tea chaser. The Captain and the two wives arrived a few minutes later. The Captain let the wives know that this was a business dinner and that if they heard something that sounded sensational, they were to keep their mouths shut. The women had heard this announcement before from him. They hadn't talked in the past and they were not likely to talk this evening about anything related to a crime. T. J. asked the Captain to step outside for a minute. They excused themselves from their wives and when out on the street, T. J. said that it looked as though O'Brien's neck had been broken and that his spinal cord had been severed most likely by a large dog. The bite on the back of the neck looked like a dog bite. He also thought that the same dog had ripped out the Adam's Apple. He thought that the woodland critters' bite marks were much smaller. He asked the Captain, "Is any of this making any sense to you?"

"No," Rodham answered.

T. J. continued, "I wonder if the rope which was found had anything to do with O'Brien's death. You think he was trying to be a one man lynching party and the dog surprised him?"

"That's possible," answered Rodham.

"Who do you think he was trying to lynch?"

"It would have been someone who he thought to be fairly weak, since his gun wasn't taken from its holster. If it was an attempted lynching, then the person to be lynched was someone who was unarmed and who couldn't fight back; either a fairly weak adult or a teenager who couldn't run away, or a child."

"You got any suspects?"

"Yeah, I got a suspect. Brown shot Rocky Johnson's dog. Maybe, Rocky Johnson's dog killed O'Brien earlier in the day. O'Brien was the type to string Rocky up to make him talk about who killed Big Jim. O'Brien had been torturing him in a cell, so seeing him on the road alone, he would have been the type to try and make him talk. O'Brien definitely had sadistic and bullying aspects to his personality."

The wives came outside and announced that they had ordered dinner for their husbands and that the salad was waiting to be consumed.

———◆———

Saturday evening, at A'Lelia's townhome, Rocky was very slowly ascending the steps. He was going from the first floor where there were many party goers to the second floor where the Countess was seated and talking to those around her. When Rocky entered the room, he saw that several women were seated and he wondered which one was the Countess. Most of the guests were standing, talking, walking around, and drinking out of fancy glasses. There were Colored folks at this party and as Aaron had predicted, a good number of them were light-skinned. Some of the folks even looked white.

Rocky was getting tired of standing with the support of his crutch, so he looked around for the closest empty chair. Spotting one, he hobbled over to it and took a seat. As soon as he sat down, a young copper colored man with a tray full of snacks appeared in front of him and offered them to him.

"Canapés, sir?" said the waiter.

"Thank you. How many can I take?" Rocky thought that he should remember this new word. He said it over and over in his head. *"Little snacks are canapés."*

"Most people take one or two, sir. You can fill up the napkin though, if you like."

"Thanks." Rocky placed his crutch between the back of his chair and the wall. He took a napkin from the tray and placed five canapés on it. Soon after that, a man came by with a tray full of fancy glasses. Beside him was a waiter with a bottle which was wrapped in a towel. The one with the bottle said, "Champagne, sir?"

Rocky replied, "Thank you" and took a glass and then extended his arm toward the waiter with the bottle. He had never had champagne. He thought that fancy educated people drank champagne. The bubbles tickled his nose. He was hoping that he wouldn't cough and then spill the canapés and his liquor. He was determined not to be known as the country cripple who took one sip of wine, got drunk, and ruined Miss Walker's fancy carpet. He thought that he should exhale through his nose while pouring a little wine into his mouth. He tried that and it worked. He was relieved.

A lady in the best looking dress he'd seen so far, approached him. She was accompanied by a waiter who was holding a small chair in front of himself. The waiter placed the chair beside Rocky and the lady sat down.

"Hello, sir. My name is A'Lelia Walker. I don't recognize you. What's your name?"

Rocky's mouth was full. He held two fingers to his lips and swallowed.

"It's a pleasure to meet you Miss Walker. You have a beautiful house."

"Your name, sir. What's your name?"

"Miss Walker, my name is Rocky. Rocky Johnson." Rocky extended his hand to shake hers. She shook his hand though she wasn't as enthusiastic as he was.

"Mr. Johnson, how did you hear about this party?"

Oh no, had he done something wrong? Was it that obvious that he didn't fit in with these sophisticated people. He heard in his mind the saying, *'You can take them out of the country, but you can't take the country out of them.'* "Aaron mentioned the party to me, Miss Walker."

"Aaron Douglas?"

"Yes'm."

A'Lelia looked towards the waiter beside her and said, "Ramone, see that a small table is placed beside Mr. Johnson. Also see that he gets a small plate, some napkins, a coaster, and more canapés. Lastly, Ramone, make sure that Mr. Johnson's glass is filled up with that special ginger ale that I bought. Do I need to repeat anything, Ramone?"

"No, Miss Walker. A small table, a small plate, some napkins, a coaster, more canapés, and the special ginger ale."

"Ramone, also go to my office and get a sheet of paper, fold it in fourths, and write on the outside of it, Reserved Seat." Turning to Rocky she said, "That way Mr. Johnson, you can come back to this seat, if you have to use the bathroom. Any of the waiters can tell you where the nearest bathroom is. Enjoy the party, Mr. Johnson. Ramone, I want you to follow me." When they were out of earshot A'Lelia said, "Ramone, make sure that the bathroom is clean after he uses it."

"Yes, Miss Walker."


Langston walked up to Rocky and asked, "I hope that you are enjoying yourself."

"I am, Langston. I'm glad that I came. I figured out which of the ladies on the other side of the room was the Countess, just by watching how people acted around her... Tell me Langston, who are the light-skinned guys that are talking to the Countess?"

"The shorter one is Walter White. He's head of the NAACP and the other one is not light-skinned, he's white. That's Carl Van Vechten. He's a writer for a newspaper."

"Langston, does Vechten have two photographers following him around?"

"He probably does Rocky. One of the guys, the white one, is the newspaper photographer and the other guy, the Colored one is Van Vechten's personal photographer. Van Vechten told me earlier that he was training him. He's an apprentice photographer. It looks like they're headed this way."

As they approached, Rocky's words were, "Oh shit."

"What's wrong, Rocky?"

Before Rocky could get the words out, Carl was standing with them and asked, "Introduce me to your friend, Langston."

"Rocky Johnson, this is Carl Van Vechten. Carl is a writer. Carl Van Vechten, this is Rocky Johnson. Rocky is an artist who works in basketry as well as drawing."

From behind Carl, the Colored photographer asked, "When did you start drawing, Rocky?"

"Smooth, I been drawing all my life. I just haven't had an exhibition. When did you get a legit job?"

Carl's head swiveled from one to the other. "The two of you know each other?"

"Where's Vanda Mae, Smooth?"

Carl looked at Smooth and said, "He knows Vanda Mae?"

Langston stated, "Carl, it appears as though they have some unresolved issues. Let's let them talk in private."

"Yeah, I agree," said Carl. "Robin, remember, you're representing me while you're here. I don't want my name associated with anything scandalous. Don't forget, there are other reporters and other photographers from other newspapers covering this party for the Countess. They're just waiting for a scoop. I can see the headline now, in block letters, ! ! ! **A Royal Mess** ! ! ! Do you understand what I'm saying, Robin?"

Smooth replied, "Yeah, I understand."

"Come on Langston, let's let them talk."

As they were walking off, Carl turned to the other photographer and said, "You need to follow me."

He replied as he started to follow, "I'd rather see the Royal Mess."

Smooth sat in the chair left by A'Lelia. Rocky spoke first. "Where's Vanda Mae?"

"She's around here, somewhere. This is a real big house. She'll turn up. You know we thought that you'd still be in jail if not dead by now."

"Pushing dust is going to land your ass in jail," replied Rocky.

"Rocky, I'm trying to go legit. That's why I got this photographer's job. I'm an apprentice to Van Vechten."

"Admit it, you got Vanda Mae turning tricks for you. You taking the money and giving her dust."

"Rocky, you don't know Vanda Mae like I know her. Vanda Mae and I have been friends ever since we were children. Yes, Vanda Mae has turned tricks; but you want to know something, so have I. We've worked johns together. We were tricking when we were children. That's what I mean when I say that you don't know her the way I know her. We got a whole lot of history together. There's something else you should know. . . yesterday, I asked her to marry me."

"What was the answer?" demanded Rocky.

"She didn't say yes and she didn't say no. She's thinking about how we'll make money as husband and wife."

"I risked my life for her not once, not twice, but four times between Big Jim's death and today." Rocky added, "I want to see her and tell her that I love her. Then she might choose me as her husband."

"Well, Rocky, here's your chance to do that, cause she's walking this way."

"Rocky, I'm glad to see you." She bent down to hug him and kiss him on the cheek.

"You used to kiss me on the lips. What's wrong?" said Rocky.

"Rocky, things have changed" she said.

"Vanda Mae, I killed Big Jim, the man that raped you and knocked you out cold! I have survived being tortured by the police. One of the policemen caught me alone in the woods and strung me up. I'm talking about a lynching, Vanda Mae. An angel in the form of a dog attacked the policeman and killed him. Later that same day, another policeman pointed a gun at me and then shot the dog that protected me and also shot my goat. I got Big Jim's blood on me, dog blood on me, and goat blood on me; all because I want to be your man. Marry me, Vanda Mae. Don't marry this drug dealer who's putting you out on the street."

Vanda Mae let him know that she had not made up her mind about marrying 'Robin' but that he was changing his life for the better. She added that his understanding of her goes back many years, long before Big Jim came along. She stated that she appreciated Rocky's getting Big Jim out of the picture and that she appreciated the efforts he expended in getting from Black Bottom to New York City. She told him that it was too soon to consider him as a husband when this morning she thought of him as either dead or in prison for life. "Rocky, we're going to have to go soon. We're riding with Carl. Where are you staying and do you have a phone?"

"267 West 136th Street and no, I don't have a phone."

"We're at 288 West 139th Street. We're just a few blocks away from you. . . Rocky, Carl is looking this way, it's time to go. We'll be talking." Vanda Mae got up quickly and walked away with Smooth following.

A tuxedo clad Bruce came by and sat with Rocky. "Man, I'm sorry about the way this night has gone for you. The one good thing is that you're out of the South."

"Bruce," said Rocky, "a lot of good things have happened to me since leaving Black Bottom and you're one of them. Thank you for helping me out."

"You know Rocky, I said that you fit in well in our house. We're here for you."

"Yeah," he said through water filled eyes. "Thank you."

A lady left the Countess and came over to Bruce.

"Introduce me to your friend, Bruce."

"Zora Neale Hurston," he said, "this is Rocky Johnson. Rocky Johnson, this is Zora Neale Hurston. Rocky is an artist working in basketry and drawing. Zora is a writer. She writes about real people and how they live and she also writes from her imagination."

Rocky was shaking Zora's hand and stating that he was pleased to make her acquaintance. He stated that he'd heard that she might know a root man and if so, he'd like to get him to bless his home. Zora mentioned that most root men don't bless homes but that she did know of a root man that might bless a home. She wrote Rocky's address on a napkin and stated that she would speak with Tunji about this request. Rocky interrupted her and stated, "Tunji is his nickname. That's exactly the root man that I'm looking for. Please tell him that I need him immediately. Tell him Rocky Johnson from Black Bottom." Zora assured Rocky that she would contact Tunji.

"Thank you, Miss Hurston."

"Call me Zora."

"Thank you, Zora. Tunji is much more than someone who passes out dried plants for ailments. He is a very spiritual man. He's just like his father. Tunji is living his religion by dealing with plants and people. Tunji is honest and he's not caught up in stuff that doesn't really matter. That's why I want to talk to him. That's why I want him to bless my home."

"You've definitely described the Tunji that I know. I'll tell him, Rocky. You can see that I'm putting your address in my purse. I'll contact him first thing tomorrow morning."

"Thank you, Zora."

Zora rose from the chair saying, "Rocky, Harold Jackman is over there. I want to go and say 'Hello' to him. It was nice speaking with you." As she walked away, she was concerned with the neediness and urgency which Rocky expressed. She would call Tunji before she went to sleep.

Wallace's eyes connected with Rocky's from across the room. Rocky watched him take a bottle of champagne from the waiter and walk towards him.

"I've been watching you Rocky. That chair beside you hasn't had a chance to get cold. What you got going on here? You know this is the Countess's party, not the welcome to New York party for Rocky."

Rocky smiled and said, "I met several people that I wanted to meet this evening. It has been a sad and a hopeful evening."

"Let me hit that glass for you."

Rocky took his glass off the coaster and extended his arm toward Wallace. The glass was filled almost to the brim. Wallace then did the same for his own glass. "Welcome to New York City, Rocky. May your stay in this great city, be beneficial to you." They toasted one another several more times and ate canapés the rest of the evening.

"Uh – oh," said Wallace, "Here comes Mama. Doesn't she look stern?" Rocky looked towards his left and saw Langston marching toward them.

"If Rocky falls down the steps, it will be your fault Wallace." Langston continued, "You know better than to get Rocky soused."

"I'm sorry, Mama" said Wallace, mockingly; "he made me do it. I didn't want to, but he forced me. He's bad, Mama. Rocky's a bad influence on me."

"Don't call me Mama," said Langston. "I want you to walk in front of Rocky while he's going down the steps so if he falls, he can use you as a cushion."

"Hear that Rocky? You'd be bouncing off of me. Sounds like fun to me. Let's drink to that!"

"It's time to go. Bruce is down stairs waiting for us. Aaron has already left. He's probably home by now," said Langston.

"Ooh, ooh, I got to go to the bathroom," said Wallace to Langston. Acting like a six year old in the first grade squirming in his seat he said, "Can I go? Can I go? Please. Please. Don't leave until I go, O.K.?"

"Go."

"Yes, mam, I mean Mother Dear." With that said, Wallace was up and headed toward the restroom.

Looking towards Rocky, Langston said, "If I had a son, I'd want him to have Wallace's brains. His insolence though, would be thrown in the Harlem River."

"You'd make a great father, Langston."

"Thank you, Rocky. That's a nice thing to say. I like children, but I don't think that they're in my future."

"Yeah, well, you would and here's something to think about, how come the very best people to be fathers or mothers don't become fathers and mothers? Do you think that the work that they are to do on the Earth, is not to be hampered by children? Do you think that the work that those people do is to improve the lives of all people and not just a handful of children?"

"That may be, Rocky; but it sounds kind of close to a person's life being predetermined for him or her and that really isn't where my head is. I am an artist. Creating with words is what I do. I look at the world and try to put what I see into beautiful appropriate words. I love being black. I want to raise the awareness and self-pride of our people, more so than raise children. Wallace is that way and Zora is that way. We're word artists. Bruce is that way also, but he works in words and pictures. . . . Here comes Wallace. Come on, it's time to go."

The guys left the party and walked back to their apartment building. When they arrived at the apartment house, Langston said to Rocky, "We need to talk. Can we do that inside your home?"

"Yeah, sure." Rocky limped toward the basement entrance and Langston and Bruce followed him. Wallace went up the steps to the front door. Rocky figured that Wallace already knew what Langston and Bruce would be saying.

When inside, Langston noticed that Rocky needed a lamp near the entrance, so that he wouldn't trip in the dark. He also needed more chairs. He certainly couldn't have company down here if he had only one chair. He told himself that this would change with time.

"Rocky," Langston started, "one of the goals which you set for yourself has been accomplished. You found Vanda Mae and you got her address. You know that she is going to have to move in your direction if she wants to be with you and you know you can't force someone to love you. You know that you can't get love from someone, who feels obligated to love you."

"Yeah, Langston, I know these things."

"Well, Rocky, you got to begin making a better life for yourself here in New York City. To put it bluntly Rocky, you got to seriously concentrate on making money."

"I know that also."

"I spoke with Carl, Rocky. I told him that you work in basketry and drawing. I asked him if he could look at your portfolio once you developed one and he said that he would. He also said that if you wanted to model for him, you'd get paid $25. That's November's rent, Rocky."

"What do you mean, 'Model for him?'"

Bruce let Rocky know that, "Carl takes pictures of men and women in classic poses, with no clothes or very few clothes on."

"Is Carl a pimp? What does he do with all of these pictures of naked people? Would I be having sex in front of his camera?"

"You wouldn't be having sex and it's his hobby," replied Bruce. "It's something to think about."

"I'm thinking about it right now. I'm thinking Smooth is taking the pictures of me naked. I'm thinking that he is using me the way he is using Vanda Mae."

Langston replied, "I brought that up to Carl and he told me that Smooth would not be there the evening that the pictures would be taken."

"I'll have to think about it, Langston. The $25 sounds good but taking naked pictures, doesn't."

"Rocky, a lot of artists have modeled for Carl. Some of them have been quite famous. You won't be the first and you certainly won't be the last. Remember, the November rent will be due in 32 days. Also, this is a legitimate way to make money. Artists have been using nude models for hundreds of years. Also, you're pretty much guaranteed work at the colleges in the city. Your club foot is different. It will be something that the students normally don't draw or paint. You may be requested to pose nude wearing your brace and also without the brace. Rocky, if Carl puts in a good word for you at the colleges, you may be able to make December's rent and January's rent."

"Langston, it's something for me to consider. I certainly like the idea of easily making my rent money."

Bruce let it be known that Rocky couldn't take a long time to make up his mind. The college art classes had already started and the sooner his name was placed on their modeling lists, the more likely he would be to get the jobs, particularly if he had a recommendation from Carl. "This is not the time to tarry. You can turn that bad foot of yours into a moneymaker."

"O.K., Bruce, you and Langston have convinced me to model for Carl. When do I begin and where will I work?"

"5:00 p.m., tomorrow, in the Village." Langston continued, "I'll have to come with you to help you with the subway system and in negotiating the streets to get to his studio."

Rocky was feeling slightly better about the outcome of this evening. "Damn," he said, "I lost Vanda Mae and I got a job, all in the same night."

# CHAPTER 15

## NOMINAL CONSEQUENCES

————◆————

### *Sunday Morning, October 1, 1933*

SLEEPING WAS HARD. HE LOOKED at Vanda Mae and held her but he couldn't relax. Coffee, maybe that was what he needed? Maybe bacon? Maybe eggs? Letting go of Vanda Mae and rolling onto his side, he hopped up and out of bed. Sitting down on the toilet with his elbows on his knees, he peed and reflected on the events of the last few days. What was wrong this morning? Was he hungry? After washing his hands and walking into the kitchen, he gazed at the frying pan and the coffee can full of bacon grease. Opening the refrigerator door, he stared inside but none of the cold contents beckoned him. He decided that it was too much work to fix eggs and way too much work to fix bacon. He really didn't want breakfast; he wasn't hungry. If he wasn't hungry and he couldn't sleep, what was the problem? Why did he have this unpleasant feeling? It was like he was worrying and like he was mildly pissed off. "No," he told himself, "if I'm not hungry, then what's wrong?"

He got a glass of water and sat at the table. His reflections kept bringing him back to Vanda Mae. He didn't like what she had said to him about church. His goal was to make money, legally. He needed constructive criticism, not a roadblock, not a dashing of his dream.

The kitchen table was where he had left The Amsterdam News. Turning the page he saw:

| | |
|---|---|
| **St. Philip's Episcopal Church** | **Abyssinian Baptist Church** |
| **204 West 134th Street** | **132 West 138th Street** |
| **New York, New York** | **New York, New York** |
| **Services: 9:00 a.m.** | **Services: 9:00 a.m.** |
| **11:30 a.m.** | **11:00 a.m.** |

The churches were calling to him. This would be a big step for someone who was raised in a house of ill repute, a sportin' house. Smooth, the drug pushing pimp had to "die" if Robin Daniels, the photographer and businessman, were going to live. All of the energy which was put into acquiring, paying for, and then reselling dust, had to be directed towards acquiring a new customer base. He needed Colored folks who would decorate their coffee tables and side tables with photographs; Colored folks with some extra money.

The church was an overstocked fishing pond full of ladies who had a few extra dollars at the end of each month. Their ends met. Vanda Mae was right, she couldn't come onto the men in church without the women immediately recognizing that she was trolling in their pond. Vanda Mae would be thrown out the building and since he was her "husband," he also would be thrown out and there would be no sales. So, Vanda Mae had to stay at home. Sunday would become a work day for him. It would be a day devoted to advertising his business in a tasteful manner to those ladies who had middle class aspirations and to those who were already living the dream.

Robin Daniels, photographer and businessman, understood that he had to effortlessly project that he was upwardly mobile, ambitious, and clean living, just like they were. He may be new to their place of worship, but he was cut from the same cloth as they. They shared the same values. They had the same aspirations. He knew that it would be difficult to fake a church history because too many of the ministers knew other ministers in different states. Better to tell the truth; he hadn't been raised in the church and it was time for him to make a change. That would be the story told to all who wanted to know. He lived in the neighborhood; he was up from the South; his wife did not attend church (she wasn't raised in the church either); and he was a photographer in the Village trying to get his business started. He would always put a dollar in the collection plate. They could relax around him, because Robin Daniels was their kind of people.

Daydreaming, he saw his advertisement in the church bulletin. A private and personal marker of his financial success would be his photographs on church fans; which of course, would have been donated by him. His trendy suits would have to do for now but as he prospered, they would be replaced with more conservative attire. His wide brim hat would not be worn again. After gaining the trust of the church ladies, he'd suggest to the choir director that the choir be photographed and that the sale of the photograph, minus the reproduction costs, could benefit the choir. He would suggest 100 reproductions of the photograph.

Coming out of the dream, the question was which church to join? The Episcopalians generally had more education and more disposable income. The Baptists had the larger congregation. He was looking for a church home. He was exploring. That would be the rationale for attending both churches. He knew the church ladies would talk. He knew that they would soon know that he attended both churches. He planned a 3 months period of exploration. This would be 3 months of alternating between 9:00 o'clock services and 11:00/11:30 services, between the two churches. Then, he would join both churches. It would be odd, but not audacious. If he kept this "job" up, he believed he'd seamlessly move from trolling to trawling. This was his plan to build his customer base.

It was 7:50 a.m. A quick shower and shave and he could begin testing his plan. He'd tell Vanda Mae that he was going to church plus he would leave her a note on the kitchen table.

---

The warm water was cascading down Rocky's body. He had gotten to the "Y" at 8:00 a.m. He wanted solitude. He wanted the warm water to wash away his drunken grogginess. He sat in the chair and soaped himself and rested and contemplated his future. He knew that he had to get himself together quickly. He realized the truth of what Aaron had previously said, "Artists live on the edge." They were all the same. All of them were just getting by, just making ends meet. Wallace was the exception though, he had a steady job, a good paying job. Rocky thought that he needed the same. Modeling was o.k. for now, but it should eventually supplement his income. He felt the same for his art. He needed a job that he could do with his bad foot and his lack of education. He would keep his eyes and ears open for the right opportunity.

Rocky didn't think that he would be sharing the shower so early on a Sunday morning. He nodded to the guy and kept on soaping and rinsing himself. He really didn't want anyone else in the shower distracting him from his thoughts.

"How are you doing?" said the stranger. "My name is Mike. What's yours?"

Good Lord, thought Rocky; conversation with a stranger was not what he wanted this morning. "My name is Rocky."

"That's an odd name for a Colored fellow," said the stranger. "Is it your nickname?"

"No," said Rocky.

"Rocky is usually an Italian fellow's nickname. . . Well what's the name on your birth certificate?"

"Michael, I really don't feel like having this conversation. My name is none of your concern. If you cannot accept 'Rocky,' then that's fine. Please don't talk to me." Rocky grabbed his crutch which was leaning against the wall and limped out of the shower and into the locker room.

On the walk back to his home, he saw two little girls dressed in their Sunday clothes apparently waiting for an adult to come out of the house and take them to church. The girls were playing a clapping game and saying,

> *"Poor poor Rocky, didn't have a home.*
> *And old lady Montgomery was always alone.*
> *So old lady Montgomery put food in a bag*
> *And poor poor Rocky made his tail wag.*
> *Now Rocky and Montgomery are never alone."*

Rocky thought that it wasn't until he got up here in New York City, that anyone questioned his name. Now he was feeling unsure about it. He knew that some unusual names were taken from the Bible but he also knew that was not the case with his name. When he was born and his parents saw his club foot, they agreed that they'd put a positive spin on the challenge of raising a lame child by naming him after the fish they most love, the Rockfish. He would be raised in love. After reflecting on his childhood, he resolved that there were more pressing things to think about than the 'oddity' of his name or how much his parents loved him.

As he approached his apartment building, he saw some-one sitting on the steps. Who was this fellow? As he got closer he could see a familiar face. Tunji. Their eyes locked and he speeded up his limp. They embraced on the side-walk. It was good to see a familiar face from the past.

"Tunji, come on down to my home. I got about as much now as I had back in Black Bottom, but I got a chance now to make something out of myself. I got a chance now to get an education and I'm going to get it. Tunji, I got to tell you everything. I don't know how much you heard from your father but you gonna get the full story from me."

Rocky told him of the rape of Vanda Mae, the hurricane, the killing of Big Jim with a knife (he left out Bobby and Hattie's names), the torture in jail, and the healing that Big Tunji had facilitated. He told him about Bell and how Bell rescued him. He told him about Bell's death and his goat's death. He told him about Langston, Bruce, Wallace, and Aaron. Tunji called them Zora's poet and painter friends. Rocky told Tunji about Mr. Alexander and the YMCA, his showers and his upcoming classes. Rocky also told Tunji about Robin "Smooth" Daniels's new name and his legit job. He then mentioned his nude modeling job this evening. Rocky finally said to Tunji, "If they tortured me, they'll do the same to someone else. I think that it's only a matter of time before the police are looking for me up here."

"Tunji, I don't know what to do. I don't know which way to turn. I told Zora that I needed a house blessing, but I really needed to talk to someone who knew Black Bottom and knew New York City. Can you help me? I don't want to go to jail and I definitely don't want the electric chair because my dog saved my life."

"Rocky, if I were you, I'd change my name and get out of town. I'd tell the people at the "Y" that you decided to get rid of your "country" name and go with a more citified name; like the way immigrants on Ellis Island change their names and start new lives, that's what you're doing. You are no longer Rocky Johnson, you are Roland K. Johnson. Get the card on which 'Rocky' was written and tear it up. Hopefully, when the police come to investigate the records, they won't be talking to Mr. Alexander. Was he on duty this morning?"

"No," replied Rocky.

"O.K., maybe we can get the card. Did you identify yourself to the attendant as Rocky Johnson?"

"No, I just showed my pass and went on in."

"O.K., you're going to tell the desk clerk that you put your nickname on the card and that you want to correct the card because you are moving to a new address tomorrow and you want the card to have the correct information. Got it, nickname and you're moving. You want to write your name on the old card and when you get the old card, you mess up your name, tear up the card and ask for a new one. Then you ask me to do it for you, because my handwriting is better and I'll write your alias, that's your false name and I'll give a false address. You ready to do this?"

"Yeah, Tunji, I'm ready."

"Let's walk back there."

When they got to the "Y," they went over the plan again. They then entered and executed the plan and the Rocky card was torn up and the Roland K. Johnson card was substituted and since Roland K. Johnson moved to 555 East 111th Street, the poets and the painters wouldn't be harboring a fugitive from the law. His friends should be safe.

Tunji's plan worked beautifully. The only down side was that he could no longer go to the "Y." He could no longer take those long showers which he loved. He wouldn't get a chance to get an education. Tunji had saved his life it seemed, but the price was giving up a chance to advance himself in New York City. Tunji was saying that he should start over in a new city such as Washington, D. C. It was a southern segregated city, but it was much more friendly towards Coloreds. Rocky didn't want to move to D. C. He didn't know anyone in that city. He didn't think that he could find a cheap place to live there and certainly, he would not find such a place as quickly as he had found this home, this abode, this manor. His friends were rubbing off on him. He didn't know how to spell those words, but he knew what they meant. He liked being around smart people. He would miss them, but he knew Tunji was right. The question at hand was, when should he leave New York?

Tunji also told him that he could never use his alias. The alias was to throw off any investigators. He said that

Rocky needed a second alias, an entirely new name, one that he could easily remember; a name of which he would be proud. He then asked Rocky if he'd like to have Langston's last name, since he thought so highly of him.

Rocky replied, "Yeah."

"O. K., who else do you think very highly of?"

"Paul Laurence Dunbar."

O. K., Dunbar will be your middle name." Tunji continued, "John is a common first name and that's what you need. John Dunbar Hughes, that will be your new name."

Rocky said, "I like Jonathan better."

"Jonathan Dunbar Hughes, I like the sound of it. O. K., I'm going to write it down on this paper and you practice writing it and saying it." Tunji reached for some drawing paper, folded it into 1/8 sections and wrote his address in ink on one section. No name was written. He then tore this 8th from the rest of the paper. He said, "Jonathan, take your shoe off please." When Jonathan had complied, he was told to take the laces out of the shoe. He was then told to hand the shoe to Tunji. Tunji pushed the shoe's tongue back as far as it would go and then took out a pocket knife and started peeling back the top layer of the inner sole. He peeled from the toe of the shoe 1/3 of the way back. Tunji asked Jonathan if he had Scotch Tape. When it was given to him, he placed it over the small addressed piece of paper. Both sides of the paper were taped. The paper easily slipped underneath the inner sole of Jonathan's shoe. "Rocky, I mean, Jonathan, when you get yourself settled in D. C., send me your new address. Now, we're going to look around this basement for a small paperback book. We want one that looks like a dusty dime store novel." Rocky pushed some boxes to the side and revealed a small bookcase containing dusty paperbacks. Lifting a book from the bottom shelf, he handed *Ivanhoe* to Tunji. Tunji printed on the inside of the cover, Byron Tolliver. "Never lose this book. When you write to me, always use that name. The church ladies will write letters for you. You can hand them a piece of paper with my name and address on it, but they're the only ones. You need to get to the point where you can write names and addresses from memory. Schooling is important. You got to learn as much as you can, particularly living in Washington. You'll be around a lot of high school and college graduates. They'll be working in the city government and the federal government. They'll also be working as maids, busboys, and porters. They're the ones who are trying to get government jobs. So, you've had my education talk. Remember, always keep my name separated from my address. That's a safety precaution, in case the police stop you. When you start your new life, you are Jonathan Dunbar Hughes not Roland K. Johnson.

"I got it, Tunji. I'm Jonathan Dunbar Hughes and I got to learn how to read and write and do math and I got to keep your name and address separated."

"What about the church ladies?"

"Use them to write letters for me until I can write them on my own."

"Jonathan, I want you to join Daddy Grace's church. Daddy will shelter you and feed you and there are loads of single ladies in his church. Neither one of us is a "high up in the holy sanctified Christian," but I'm telling you, you're going to have to play along with them. You're going to have to go to church every Sunday and put something in the collection plate. Daddy likes silent collections, but you put at least a quarter in the plate until you can get steady work. Keep working with and socializing with the church ladies and before you know it, you'll be able to get a low level government job. Oh, there is one more thing that's very important to know; you cannot join the Communist Party nor can you associate with Communists."

"What are Communists?"

"Communists believe that the mines, the oil wells, the fishing industry, the farms, the railroads, and all sorts of other ways of making money should be owned by the government and not by rich people. You can be fired from a job if you're a Communist."

"Seek out Daddy Grace's Church and don't hang around Communists," Rocky said.

"Jonathan?"

"Yeah, Tunji."

"You need a background."

"What do you mean?"

Tunji explained that everyone has a history. When people ask you about yours, say that you moved around a lot in the South. "Tell them that children with clubfeet couldn't go to school and so you never got an education. Tell them that your father did odd jobs and that he was constantly on the move. Tell them that your mother died when you were young. That's enough history to keep most people from prying any further into your past."

"One more thing," said Tunji. "You're going to need a Bible. The older, the better. The Bible should have a family tree chart inside it and preferably, the chart will be blank. You want to have Jonathan Dunbar Hughes listed on that family tree with your birthday. If that's not done before you leave New York, then the folks at Daddy Grace's church will have to help you with that. . . There's talk about something called Social Security and you're going to need to record a birth date. The government will accept Bibles with birth dates in them."

"Jonathan, there is an entrance to St. Nicholas Park near here. Let's get something to eat on the way there and then pray underneath the shade of the trees. How's that sound to you?"

"Yeah, Tunji. Everything is moving so quickly now. My head is spinning. I just need to relax. The park sounds good."

Tunji had never been in St. Nicholas Park and was unaware of the steepness of the hills. The friends went to the first shady spot created by several trees, just past the entrance. The coolness beneath the canopy was refreshing as they sat on the ground. They had gotten 3 sandwiches and 2 Cokes a piece at a nearby deli. A bottle opener and 2 apples were also purchased. Tunji paid for everything.

Underneath the canopy they prayed. Tunji was tapping a Coke bottle with the opener. After a minute of silence, he tapped 3 more times. They were relaxing themselves, preparing their bodies for visitation by the angels. Tunji led the prayer and at times Rocky repeated after him.

*"We call upon the Holy Angel Eleggua to be with us now and to open us up to the divine world."*

Rocky repeated, *"We call upon the Holy Angel Eleggua to be with us now and to open us up to the divine world."*

In unison, *"We call upon the Holy Angel Eleggua to be with us now and to open us to the divine world."*

Tunji continued, *"We wish to honor the Angel Ozain, in whose home we deliver this prayer. Thank you Ozain for giving us the forest, the herbs, and the healing waters. Please help me to be your good and faithful servant. We honor you by partaking of this slice of apple."*

*"Thank you Ozain for giving us the forest, the herbs, and the healing waters. Please help Tunji to be your good and faithful servant. We honor you by partaking of this slice of apple."*

Tunji sliced a wedge for Rocky and then for himself. They were quiet as they ate.

*"Ozain and Eleggua, you know of the hard times which have fallen on Rocky. You know of the blessings which have come his way. Thank you for the blessings."*

Rocky repeated, *"Thank you for the blessings."*

*"Obatala, Father of Humankind, fill us with moral uprightness and spiritual purity. Infuse every cell of our bodies with spiritual purity. Orunmila, Angel of Wisdom and Foresight, enter us and infuse wisdom into every cell in our bodies."*

Tunji continued after tapping the coke bottle 3 times.

*"Ochosi, Angel of the Accused, the Angel Who Looks out for Us when we are in treacherous situations, we need you to be with us now. Olodumare, God, the One who keeps the planets in orbit, God the one who keeps life on this planet no matter how often man destroys it. God, the one who accepts our souls when our work on this planet is finished, please be with us now. Some call You The Holy Father, Some call You Jesus, some call You The Holy Ghost, we call You by Your African name Olodumare, the Supreme Being. Please help us in ways big and small as you see Your divine plan being carried out. Eleggua, Ozain, Obatala, Orunmila, and Ochosi are all aspects of your Divine Love. They are the angels which bring about your desires for our futures. We give ourselves*

*to you. Rocky has needed You dearly in the past and Rocky has honored You dearly in the past and in the present. Right now, he is in desperate need of your guidance. You know that his life is in danger. He rode a dangerous road to get to this metropolis and You gave him Guardian Angels along the way. You put Bell in his life. You put Langston in his life. It was because of Langston that he found Vanda Mae and he found me. He accomplished tasks due to Your intervention, which would seem impossible to most men. We are grateful for all that You have done for him."*

Rocky took over the Prayer. *"Olodumare, I need your angels Ochosi and Orunmila. I need their protective cloaks as I venture onto another city. I need to be ever aware of my surroundings and alert to the opportunities which come my way. I need wisdom and foresight to distinguish heartfelt honest actions and words from those actions and words which are veiled in honesty but, have lies and trickery at their core. Olodumare, please enter us and make us a beacon of love for mankind. Olodumare please use Shango to intensify and diminish our glow of love. Obatala and Ochosi, Orunmila and Shango, I need you to link your arms and form a stretcher for me and to carry me over the modeling waters this evening."*

Tunji continued, *"Orunmila infusion. Ochosi infusion. Obatala infusion. Shango infusion. Ozain infusion. Olodumare, infuse us with grace. We ask Olodumare because You exist to be asked."*

In unison:

*Our Father, who art in heaven,*
*hallowed be thy Name,*
*thy kingdom come, thy will be done,*
*on Earth as it is in Heaven.*

*Give us this day our daily bread.*
*And forgive us our trespasses,*
*as we forgive those*
*who trespass against us.*

*And lead us not into temptation,*
*but deliver us from evil.*

*For thine is the kingdom,*
*and the power, and the glory,*
*for ever and ever. Amen. Ache'.*

The men rested under the trees and ate their apples and sandwiches and drank their Cokes. It was a good afternoon. Rocky didn't think that it would be a Last Supper.

———◆———

### Sunday, October 1, 1933
### 12:30 p.m.

Her arm was reaching for that comfortable form, those curves and muscles, those hard spots, soft spots, those rough spots, those "Smooth" spots. Her anticipation was left wanting. Opening her eyes, Vanda Mae saw that Smooth or Robin, as he wanted to be called, was not in the bed. A vague memory regarding church bubbled into her consciousness. Getting out of bed, she quickly surmised, from her position in the bathroom, that he wasn't in the apartment. Wandering into the kitchen, she saw a tented sheet of paper resting on top of a loaf of Wonder Bread. Reading it revealed what she already had figured out, he'd gone to church. She thought that it was a bit much though, to attend two different churches. Looking at the clock, she deduced that he must be at the second church by now. She thought that she could shower and then make lunch for him. She also thought that making lunch for him encouraged him to think of her as wife material; as someone in the position of being obedient to the man of the house. Vanda Mae fully understood that obedience meant inequality and she wasn't about to give Smooth the idea that he was her superior.

While showering, previous questions regarding their economic future kept surfacing. How quickly would Smooth transition out of dust sales? Was he becoming soft? Thinking that if he got caught, would she have to become the bread winner for this "family?" As she was toweling herself, visions of twenty dollar bills stuffed in her bra were before her. Definitely, the hell with lunch; Smooth could have lunch waiting for her when she got back from a few hours on the street. While he was trying to prime the sanctified pump for future business, she would be bringing home the bacon. She might even buy two pounds of bacon tomorrow.

The decision was made; she didn't need Smooth's protection. Millions of women worked without pimps and she could do the same, at least for this one time. If he could be a choirboy, then she could be a working girl and Sunday afternoon was as good a time as any to turn a trick.

Walking down St. Nicholas Avenue with the top three buttons on the front of her blouse undone, was her test to see how much attention she could generate. She'd stop walking when she got down to 136th Street. She had planned to stand near the entrance to the park. She was going to negotiate with the customers; blow jobs only. She had rubbers and the customers had to wear them. She was prepared to give a false name. She would be "Tina" to the johns.

A cutie in a CCNY t-shirt was eyeing her from across the street. He was keeping his eyes on her as he crossed the thoroughfare, oblivious to the traffic. He looked kind of simple walking towards her with a smile on his face. She liked them young and dumb. This kid didn't look like he'd even started shaving. She laid down the rules and the price, which had to be paid in advance, and they entered into the park. As they were ascending the path, he began squeezing her backside. He told her that he liked the way she felt and she told him that he was good looking.

Looking to the left of the path, she saw two men relaxing in the shade sitting on the bare ground, paper bags and sodas separating them. Watching them from the rear she thought of how strong the bond must be between the men since they were deep in conversation and obviously not worried about grass stains. Walking a little further, she noticed some trees, a bench, and a boulder, on her right, a natural blind spot. Walking up to the back of the bench, the john leaned against it and started kissing and fondling Vanda Mae. "Oh, hell no," she thought and pulled away. Cutie pie wanted to know what was wrong and she informed him that he hadn't given her $20.00 nor did he have on a rubber, which she handed to him. The john quickly went inside his wallet and gave her the money and then put on the rubber. Vanda Mae immediately stooped down and started servicing the young buck. Her right hand lightly held the penis shaft while her mouth went in circles around the penis head. She was visualizing putting chalk on a pool stick. Vanda Mae's left palm was applying a light upward pressure to the guy's balls while the fingers on her left hand massaged the skin between the balls and the bottom of his cheeks. She was driving him crazy. His naked butt was bouncing off the back of the bench. He was grunting and grabbing her head and then he started moaning. Vanda Mae immediately pushed four fingers into his flesh with the index finger twitching just inside the bottom of his cleft and the pinky lightly tapping the back of his balls. The young buck held her head tightly and moaned in a low voice; hips thrusting reflexively.

Messy hair was a byproduct of her job. She was combing her hair as he was removing the rubber and tucking himself back into his pants. She was happy; mission accomplished, and then he said the golden words.

"I have two friends. Can I bring them to you?"

"Are they college boys?"

"Yeah."

"$20.00 a piece plus they have to wear rubbers. I'll wait right here."

Vanda Mae was watching Cutie Pie run across the park to get his friends. Sixty dollars was more than she made with Carl. She liked this gig. The college was on the other side of the park. The park was near her home and the young bucks were much safer than the older johns. She smiled at how well things were going for her.

After a half hour, she saw three guys running towards her. Cutie Pie had brought a friend with a pimply complexion and a friend who was chunky in stature. The prerequisite money was exchanged and the rubbers were placed on the penises. Chunky was slowly stroking himself while Pimples was getting his mind blown. When Pimples pulled out, Chunky immediately filled Vanda Mae's mouth. Vanda Mae had become a machine, she was prodding, palming, and poking perineums in this secluded part of the park. Her fingers were twitching and tapping testicles and the bottoms of ass cheeks.

Cutie Pie called out, "Tina, I got money. I wanna go again. I'm gonna get a rubber out of your purse." He then slipped $20.00 into her brassiere.

Vanda Mae could say nothing with Chunky still in her mouth; but, she could count. Another twenty dollars meant $80.00. She didn't care what her hair would look like when she finished with this crew. If she could just get these three once a week, she'd be sitting pretty. Chunky was taking a long time to climax so Vanda Mae let go of his equipment, went to her purse and pulled out the squeeze bottle of mineral oil and with a teaspoon size pool of it in her palm, she told Chunky to take off his rubber. She would get him off by hand. Standing behind him, she stroked his penis with one hand and massaged his balls with the other. He started shooting in less than a minute.

It was Cutie Pie's turn and she stooped down again. Her mouth was ready to latch onto his manhood.

"Tina, I want you on your back on the bench."

She had gotten the word, "No," out when Pimples pulled a rope out of his pocket and had it around her neck. When she screamed, Cutie Pie punched her in the jaw, then the stomach, and then the jaw again. Chunky pulled off his shoe, then his sock, and then stuffed it in her mouth. He then took off his belt and tied it around her mouth. Getting behind Pimples, he pulled her arms backward while Cutie Pie pushed her onto the bench. The good looking guy then pushed her skirt up and pulled her panties down and took his prize face to face. Vanda Mae knew that it was useless to fight in this situation. She had resigned herself to take this rape and always have Smooth nearby in the future. When Cutie Pie had finished, he switched places with Pimples and held the rope tightly around Vanda Mae's neck. After Pimples, it was Chunky's turn, but he was different. He didn't want sloppy thirds. He told Tina to turn on her stomach cause he was going to be a real 'backdoor man.' When she started fighting back, he and Pimples grabbed her, lifted her body, and forced her to bend over the back of the bench. Chunky got a rubber from her purse and then rammed his gloved shaft past her sphincter. She was fighting as best she could but her legs were being held off the ground by Pimples and Cutie Pie was pulling her head down on the front side of the bench. She struggled and struggled and then stopped. Chunky still couldn't climax with a rubber on and so he took it off and massaged himself until he came on her backside. Pimples dropped her legs and Cutie Pie let go of the rope.

The guys felt good. Tina had serviced them well. Sunday afternoon sex outdoors made all three freshmen feel real good. Cutie Pie reminded them that they each owed Tina $20.00. He told them that it was the right thing to do. She deserved to get paid for all that she had been through. He ended his speech by saying that she would feel much better when she woke up and found $120.00 stuffed in her brassiere. Pimples placed his twenty in her brassiere. Chunky took a $20 bill out of his wallet and wrapped it around his finger. He then pushed his finger into her vagina and left the bill there. After putting his shoe back on, the three of them started walking toward the path. Once on the path, Chunky said that he had to get his belt and that they should wait for him. When he returned, he had the belt in his hands, and he was threading it through the loops. He left it unbuckled and he purposefully left his fly open. The three friends walked down St. Nicholas Avenue until they came to a nondescript basement door which was generally known to the CCNY students as an unlicensed bar. They entered and proceeded to consume pitcher after pitcher of beer. By 5:00 p.m., they had killed the 6th pitcher and had discussed in exquisite detail Tina's titties, her snatch, her ass, her hands, and her mouth. They talked about how good it felt to get some, while a breeze was blowing across their nuts. The owner of the speakeasy let the group know that he ran a respectable establishment and that loud vulgar talk was unacceptable. The young bucks ignored the owner and continued their conversation; this time talking about places to stuff twenty dollar bills. They also talked about moist greenbacks and how Chunky had left his presents in two moist places. The guys were young, they were strong, they were virile, they were sexually liberated, they were free, and they were in control. They were in heaven. The world was their oyster and Tina had been their prized pearl. Tina was the woman who had removed the yoke of virginity and had dashed it on the rocks of St. Nicholas Park.

Pimples proposed a toast and the guys filled their glasses in anticipation.

"Hands on dicks," he commanded. "Here's to Tina, the best damn whore working St. Nicholas Park. May she service us every Sunday for the next four years."

Cutie Pie added, "May she service us throughout Graduate School."

Chunky threw in, "Jesus, don't ever let Tina into your places of worship on Sundays. Always have her on her knees with her hands and her mouth ready to do our bidding."

In unison, they said, "Amen," clinked their glasses and downed their beers.

The owner approached their table again. "It's time for you boys to leave. I can't have the Lord blasphemed in my establishment."

"O. K., Pop," said Chunky, hand still in his pants. "Let me go take a leak and I'll be out of here."

The three of them rose and walked to the one stall restroom. Together they unzipped and let loose streams of urine on the stall sides, the toilet seat, the toilet paper, the restroom walls, and the floor.

Before exiting, Chunky took off his remaining sock and pulled it back and forth between his exposed ass cheeks. The sock was left on the sink. He said to his friends, "He ought to be nicer to us. We're paying customers."

---

### Sunday, October 1, 1933
### 3:30 p.m.

Rocky and Tunji watched the 3 guys come down the path and then go off to a spot on the other side of it. They also saw the same three leaving the spot, fixing their zippers and threading a belt through the loops. They thought that things didn't look right.

Rocky wanted to investigate. Tunji said that New Yorkers don't get involved. They say, "That's too bad" and turn their heads. Then Tunji said that in his head, he could hear Olodumare saying, *"Go and see what took place over there."*

From the path, they saw a Colored lady with her skirt pushed up over her hips, draped over the back of a bench. Going toward the bench to get a closer look, they saw five rubbers on the ground. The victim's face was facing the back of the bench and her arms were obscuring the sides of her face. The woman's hair was a wild mess. The woman's high heels were a few feet behind her body.

Tunji said to Rocky, that "Raped women will sometimes accuse the persons that find them, of rape." He said that Rocky will most likely be charged with a crime in one state and that he did not need to be known to the police in this city for any reason, even for doing a good deed. Tunji told Rocky to go across the street and watch from the corner of the block and that he would assist the lady. Rocky knew that Tunji was making sense and so he did as he was told.

Tunji stood above the victim and called to her. While circling her and calling to her, he was careful not to step on the rubbers. He noticed that the body was not moving like it was breathing. He saw that a rope was loosely around her neck. He shook her head and again called out to her. Pulling the woman's hair up, he raised her head and saw a battered face and the toe of a sock sticking out of the woman's mouth. Placing his fingers near her nose, he felt no movement of air. Touching her wrist, he felt no pulse.

Tunji started running to the park entrance where he found a pedestrian walking in the direction of the subway station. He asked the stranger to alert the subway attendant that there was a dead woman in the park. He was not surprised to hear, "I don't want to get involved" while the person never slowed down. Tunji ran to the subway station and told the attendant of the location of the body. He then ran across the street and told Rocky what he had found. He let him know that the police would soon arrive and that it was best if they laid low for now.

As they were walking toward Rocky's apartment, they heard sirens approaching the park. Turning around, they viewed the police cars stopping near the park entrance. Once inside Rocky's apartment, Tunji recounted how he felt for a pulse and how he placed his fingers near the woman's nose. He spoke of how he raised the woman's head and how he had seen her battered face. He mentioned the sock which was stuffed in her mouth. He told Rocky that the woman was definitely dead when they had come upon her.

Langston was coming down the steps into the basement, announcing as he walked, that they needed to leave soon for Carl's studio. On the bottom step, Rocky introduced Tunji as his root man friend and then Langston was told what happened in the park.

"Damn, that's a shame," was Langston's reply, "but we still have to go."

The three of them left through the basement door. When they got to the sidewalk, they saw Bruce and Wallace standing there watching the commotion going on at the park.

Rocky said that they saw the guys that did the killing after they were leaving the scene of the crime. He then introduced Tunji. Wallace let it be known that Tunji was welcome to rest upstairs in his place and that liquid refreshment was available to him, if he so desired. Tunji took Wallace up on his offer and Bruce joined them as Langston and Rocky were walking to the bus stop.

While drinking, Bruce got his sketch pad and began sketching the scene as described by Tunji. They talked of what happened as an urban lynching; '. . . after all, there was a rope, something was stuffed in the victim's mouth, the victim was sexually abused, and the victim died.' They agreed that regardless of whether or not she was a whore, she did not deserve to be raped nor killed.

Bruce was sitting at the dining room table, sketchbook in front of him, drink to his side. Wallace had placed a bottle of Old Fitzgerald on the table and had given each of his guests a cold bottle of Coke. A general crime scene picture had almost been completed. Tunji was asked, "Where in the picture, should the discarded rubbers be placed?" Bruce placed them where Tunji was pointing.

Flipping to another page, Bruce said, "Let's do her face."

After 15 minutes of descriptions, Wallace announced that he thought that he knew the woman. Bruce agreed and started drawing without input from Tunji. When the picture was finished, Tunji said, "That's her. How do you guys know her?"

They said, "That's Vanda Mae."

"Rocky's Vanda Mae?"

"Yeah," said Bruce, "Rocky's Vanda Mae."

———————

All day Langston had been trying to decide whether taking the bus to the Village would be better than taking the subway. It was Sunday afternoon and the buses wouldn't be crowded. It would take longer than the subway but it would be much easier on Rocky. He reasoned that if the subway were to be used, then Rocky would have to negotiate going down steps twice and then up steps twice. Langston thought that for this afternoon, it would be easier on Rocky and on himself, to take the bus to Greenwich Village. Taking the bus would allow Rocky to get a better feel for the size of Manhattan. He could see meaningful landmarks along the bus route. So, the decision was made, they would leave at about 3:30 p.m. and take the city bus to make their 5:00 p.m. modeling appointment.

On the ride to the Village, Langston pointed out landmarks to help orient Rocky. He mentioned that the bus was slower than the subway, and that the subway speaker system was not always understandable. He said that one has to be able to read if the speakers aren't working. So he wanted Rocky to first, get use to the buses and then later on, to the subways.

Rocky was thinking that this was a good time to let Langston know that a detailed knowledge of the New York City bus system was not going to be necessary since he would soon be leaving for Washington, D. C. He told him that since he left the South, he would be doing what the immigrants on Ellis Island did, he would change his name. He told him that his last name was going to be Hughes, in honor of him. He then explained his first and middle names. He said that he appreciated all that he had done to help him, but that he had to work towards the potential of his new name. He had to learn to read down in Washington and he had to get a job down there.

"Rocky, I mean Jonathan, does your leaving have anything to do with the death of Big Jim?"

"Yes, Langston. It's easier to tell you the truth. I hope that you won't spill my new name to the police if they come by looking for me. Let me tell you what happened." After telling the full story to Langston, minus Bobby and Hattie's input, Rocky summarized it by saying that he stopped a kidnapping of Vanda Mae by the killer, Big Jim. He then added that the dog which Ofc. Brown killed, had killed Ofc. O'Brien when he had strung him up. He said that if the police thought that he was somehow involved with O'Brien's death, he'd be looking at the electric chair. That was why he was changing his name and leaving town. He asked Langston not to reveal his new name nor where he was going to anyone and Langston said that he would keep the secret.

As they were getting off of the bus and walking, Rocky reminded Langston that he was now Jonathan Dunbar Hughes. Carl would only need to know that Rocky was following in the footsteps of the Ellis Island immigrants.

In the studio, there were no problems with inappropriate behaviors. No pictures which could be construed as blatantly sexual in nature were taken. All of the shots were replications of classical drawings or photographs taken from murals or pottery scenes or variations on these works of art. Carl mentioned to Jonathan that part of becoming a really good artist involved the ability to draw the naked body. Jonathan mentioned that as he improved in his art skills, he would keep that point in mind. Langston asked Carl if he could write a general letter of recommendation for Jonathan so that he might earn some money from modeling? While Rocky was getting dressed, Carl typed out the letter. Rocky left the studio with $25.00 and the letter of recommendation in the name of Jonathan Dunbar Hughes. Langston was happy that Carl had typed the letter on his studio stationary. It not only was more professional, it was more artsy. This recommendation would carry weight with the art schools in D. C.

———

The service at St. Philip's ended at 1:00 p.m. After a little bit of socializing, Robin was back home by 1:30. Vanda Mae had always been there when he returned. He wondered if he had been taking her for granted. Had she gone sightseeing? He ruled that out. She was still fairly new to the city and did not know the buses and subways that well. Had she struck out on her own? Robin thought about their night time conversation. Might she be looking for guys? He hoped not. She knew that could be quite dangerous. He decided that he would wait for her to return. Sitting down at the kitchen table, he felt lost. He couldn't just sit and wait. He had to do something. He decided to make coffee. That would distract his mind. While it was brewing, he placed a cup and saucer and spoon on the table. He again sat down and waited, this time for the aroma in the air to announce that the coffee was ready. His mind was wondering about the possible situations in which Vanda Mae could find herself. He told himself that maybe Vanda Mae had a change of heart and that maybe she was going to try out a church. That was a comforting thought. She would be safe in a church. She could sit in the back and maybe begin drumming up photography business in a third church. They could really begin making money if that was made their plan. Even though she had come out against going to church, the thought of it comforted him and so he kept that thought in his mind; besides St. Mark's Methodist was close by, she just might be there.

Smooth's stomach was still turning, though. He felt as though something was wrong. He told himself that Vanda Mae was most likely all right, but that feeling wouldn't go away. He thought that he should go out and walk the streets. He hoped that she wasn't street walking. He hoped that she hadn't decided to solicit in the park. It then dawned on him that she had probably been arrested for solicitation in the park. That was what explained everything for him; that was why she wasn't home. He'd have to go to the police station or court house and pay the fine. He knew that it would take several hours before she would be arraigned and so he decided to get the money from his chest of drawers and rest for a while. In two hours, he would contact the police station to see if a Vanda Mae Daniels had been arrested and if so, was she in jail there or at the court house. There was nothing else which could be done at this point.

———◆———

Capt. Rodham was sitting in the bleachers watching the teenagers sing praises to God. He was happy that he was attending a 50 minutes long Catholic service and not his own 2 hours and 50 minutes long Baptist service. Still he was antsy waiting for the service to end. But he wouldn't be able to leave when the service ended. No, he had agreed to throw out the first pitch for the softball game that afternoon. He had also agreed to judge the hotdog eating contest. He was paying Kodak $50.00 to take pictures of him with this group of likely voters. His plan was to have his picture taken with numerous families and individuals. After the photos were developed, he would write a generic but still slightly personal note on the backs of them. "The Roberts family and Capt. Rodham at St. Pius's Church picnic, Sunday, October 1, 1933." He definitely had to get the priest's picture. He'd then use the priest to identify the families in the pictures. Election Day was 13 months away, so this was the perfect time to quietly, in a nondescript manner, begin his unannounced campaign for the Mayor's office. Always thinking a few steps ahead with his eyes focused on his goal, he knew that any political opponent would say that the police camera and police film were being utilized for these pictures which was why he bought the film himself from the drugstore and had the store enlarge the pictures to 8 X 10 at his own expense. The camera being used was purchased by him also. Kodak's role was to focus the camera and he would take the pictures on his days off. If there were any accusations of a misappropriation of police funds, he'd be able to immediately refute them. He kept all of his receipts in a notebook labeled PCOA (Personal Community Outreach Activities).

It was going to be a long day. After glad handing, he'd have to get to the office and type his report naming Rocky as a person of interest in the death of O'Brien. He had planned to be in the office for no more than 20 minutes and he had planned to eat a light dinner when he got home. His plans also included cuddling with his wife while they listened to The Lone Ranger. This was his homework.

This was what he had to do to keep his home a harmonious place to lay his head.

He had a cooking timer in his office just for these short duration occasions. When the bell was struck after 20 minutes, he was already placing his chair underneath his desk when his eyes fell on the autopsy report for Big Jim. He had not had the time to read it during the week. Big Jim got what he deserved and Rodham was only going through the necessary motions to appropriately close the case. But, a time management conflict was arising for him. He was exceeding his 20 minutes and wifey needed some homework. He set the timer for 5 minutes and started skimming the report. T. J. had noted that Big Jim had sustained a massive puncture wound just above the diaphragm. The wound was made by an unknown very sharp instrument such as a spear or a dagger. The weapon had left a fish hook in the body. Microscopic inspection of the fish hook revealed that the shaft of the hook had been bent and given an edge so that it would easily slice through skin and muscle. Extracting the hook would increase the size of the hole in the victim. T. J. posited that the weapon most likely had multiple hooks and their extraction was the reason Big Jim's wound was so large and so ragged.

"Ding." The second sounding of the timer meant there was to be no compromising regarding time; no good excuses for lingering. Dinner would be waiting and homework needed to be done. Driving home he tried to visualize a spear with multiple fish hooks. He wondered if such an instrument could be bought. He wondered if the weapon had been made especially for Big Jim.

———◆———

Robin left the police station after being told that no one by the name of Vanda Daniels or Mae Daniels had been incarcerated. When he said that she might have used a different name and could he see the female prisoners picked up for solicitation, he was told, "No" and that he needed to get out of the station before he was considered a pimp.

Robin decided he would walk the streets of Harlem looking for Vanda Mae. He would begin at 140th Street and walk down to 130th Street. He would walk between St. Nicholas Avenue and Lennox Avenue. Back and forth he walked. He called out her name. People came up to him and asked if his dog were missing and he would correct them and say his wife. When he got to 136th Street, he remembered Rocky. He had momentarily considered that she had left him for Rocky. He told himself 'No,' but since she wasn't at home, maybe she was spending time with him. It was worth a visit.

Robin was reaching for the door bell when the door opened. Bruce had been periodically looking out the front door for Rocky and Langston when he saw Robin and said, "Mr. Daniels, come in. My name is Bruce Nugent and I'm one of the residents here. We briefly met last night at the party. I guess you're here about Vanda Mae?"

"Yeah, can I speak with her?"

"Mister. . . Mr. Daniels . . . ," it hurt Bruce to say, "Vanda Mae . . . Vanda Mae . . . is dead. Come upstairs and let's talk about what happened."

After Bruce introduced Robin to Tunji and Wallace, Tunji began telling what he had seen and done. Vanda Mae was already dead when he and Rocky came across the body. He expressed his condolences to Robin.

Looking at the picture of Vanda Mae, an emotionally drained Robin wanted to know who drew it and could he have one drawn of her which was more artistic and without the bruises? Something that he could frame? Bruce agreed to do another drawing. Robin could get it in a few days.

Tunji wanted to know, "If you could draw Vanda Mae, could you draw one of the killers?"

"Sure," said Bruce.

"I got a quick look at the stocky one who was putting on his belt as he was leaving the crime scene."

Bruce told him to relax and to close his eyes. He told Tunji to let the killer's face appear to him. He should let it stick in his memory and when he was ready, he should open his eyes and answer the questions posed to him regarding the shape of the head, the position of the cheek bones, the shape of the ears, the shape of the chin, the way the eyebrows were shaped, and the way the hair was cut. After 25 minutes, Tunji said, "That's him. The only thing missing is the CCNY t-shirt." Bruce then drew a slightly pudgy body beneath the face and onto that body, he drew a CCNY t-shirt.

Wallace wanted to know what Robin was planning on doing now that he had a picture of one of the killers? "Before you answer," said Wallace, "I want you to know that you cannot use this apartment to plan killings nor maimings of the killers."

Tunji let it be known that his shift began Tuesday morning at 6:00 a.m. and that he would be riding the rails for the next few days. He said that he wouldn't be participating in any revenge killings.

"So it's up to me," said Robin. "I'm going to have to do this by myself. Vanda Mae and I looked out for one another for years and just because she's dead don't mean that I'm gonna stop. You want me to work within the law; but you know how the cops are. Vanda Mae is Colored. The cops don't care about a Colored woman, particularly one who they suspect was soliciting in the park."

"Robin," said Bruce, ". . . the first thing you got to do is claim the body. Then you got to have a funeral or a memorial service. Focus on those things first."

"Then," said Wallace, ". . . you got to think like a teenager. What would a teenage boy do after he probably got his first piece? What would three teenage boys do after they participated in a gang bang in a park on a Sunday afternoon? What do you think that they would do, Robin?"

"They'd probably brag about it over beer. They probably got pissy drunk this afternoon. The glow won't wear off after they're sober, though. They'll continue to brag about it for the next few days."

"Yeah, so you got to go to the speakeasies near the park and see what you can find out." Wallace continued, "If you do all the prep work for the police, they may do something. They may arrest this one in the drawing and he may lead them to the others."

There was a knocking on the door. "Come in," shouted Wallace. Rocky and Langston walked into the room. Rocky immediately said, "Smooth, what are you doing here?" Before he could answer, he hurled the next question, "Where's Vanda Mae?"

Everyone was quiet.

"Tunji, what's going on?" Rocky limped closer to the table and saw the pictures of Vanda Mae and the pudgy killer. "Tunji, tell me it's not what I'm thinking. Tell me that wasn't Vanda Mae in the park. Tunji. Tell me, Tunji."

"It was Vanda Mae, Rocky."

Rocky went to the table and put his head in his hands. He didn't cry. Crying would come later, when he went to bed. He was dumbstruck. How could this have happened to Vanda Mae? Out of all of the women in New York City, why did it happen to her? He felt as though his life was draining from his body. He felt weaker with each breath that he took. Someone was saying something to him, but he couldn't hear him. It was just like when he was being burned by O'Brien and his screams were sounding muffled to himself.

Langston was talking to him, "Rocky . . . Rocky, hold hands, we're going to pray."

Langston, had gotten a Bible from Wallace.

*"The LORD is my shepherd; I shall not want.*

*He maketh me to lie down in green pastures: he leadeth me beside the still waters.*

*He restoreth my soul: he leadeth me in the paths of righteousness for his name's sake.*

*Yea, though I walk through the valley of the shadow of death, I will fear no evil: for thou art with me; thy rod and thy staff they comfort me.*

*Thou preparest a table before me in the presence of mine enemies: thou anointest my head with oil; my cup runneth over.*

*Surely goodness and mercy shall follow me all the days of my life and I will dwell in the house of the LORD forever."*

Langston immediately followed that prayer with:

*"Our Father, Who art in heaven,*
*hallowed be thy Name,*
*thy kingdom come,*
*thy will be done,*
*on Earth as it is in Heaven.*

*Give us this day our daily bread.*
*And forgive us our trespasses,*
*as we forgive those*
*who trespass against us.*

*And lead us not into temptation,*
*but deliver us from evil.*

*For thine is the kingdom,*
*and the power, and the glory,*
*forever and ever. Amen."*

He then read Psalm 143.

*"Hear my prayer, O LORD, give ear to my supplications: in thy*
*faithfulness answer me, and in thy righteousness.*

*And enter not into judgment with thy servant: for in thy sight*
*shall no man living be justified.*

*For the enemy hath persecuted my soul; he hath smitten my life*
*down to the ground; he hath made me to dwell in darkness, as those*
*that have been long dead.*

*Therefore is my spirit overwhelmed within me; my heart within*
*me is desolate.*

*I remember the days of old; I meditate on all thy works; I muse*
*on the work of thy hands.*

*I stretch forth my hands unto thee: my soul thirsteth after thee, as a thirsty land. Selah.*

*Hear me speedily, O LORD: my spirit faileth: hide not thy face from me, lest I be like unto them that go down into the pit.*

*Cause me to hear thy loving kindness in the morning; for in thee do I trust: cause me to know the way wherein I should walk; for I lift up my soul unto thee.*

*Deliver me, O LORD, from mine enemies: I flee unto thee to hide me.*

*Teach me to do thy will; for thou art my God: thy spirit is good; lead me into the land of uprightness.*

*Quicken me, O LORD, for thy name's sake: for thy righteousness' sake bring my soul out of trouble.*

*And of thy mercy cut off mine enemies, and destroy all them that afflict my soul: for I am thy servant."*

## Psalm 142

*"I cried unto the LORD with my voice; with my voice unto the LORD did I make my supplication.*

*I poured out my complaint before him; I shewed before him my trouble.*

*When my spirit was overwhelmed within me, then thou knewest my path. In the way wherein I walked have they privily laid a snare for me.*

*I looked on my right hand, and beheld, but there was no man that would know me: refuge failed me; no man cared for my soul.*

*I cried unto thee, O LORD: I said, Thou art my refuge and my portion in the land of the living.*

*Attend unto my cry; for I am brought very low: deliver me from my persecutors; for they are stronger than I.*

*Bring my soul out of prison, that I may praise thy name: the righteous shall compass me about; for thou shalt deal bountifully with me."*

## Psalm 141

*"Lord, I cry unto thee: make haste unto me; give ear unto my voice, when I cry unto thee.*

*Let my prayer be set forth before thee as incense; and the lifting up of my hands as the evening sacrifice.*

*Set a watch, O LORD, before my mouth; keep the door of my lips.*

*Incline not my heart to any evil thing, to practice wicked works with men that work iniquity: and let me not eat of their dainties.*

*Let the righteous smite me; it shall be a kindness: and let him reprove me; it shall be an excellent oil, which shall not break my head: for yet my prayer also shall be in their calamities.*

*When their judges are overthrown in stony places, they shall hear my words; for they are sweet.*

*Our bones are scattered at the grave's mouth, as when one cutteth and cleaveth wood upon the earth.*

*But mine eyes are unto thee, O GOD the Lord: in thee is my trust; leave not my soul destitute.*

*Keep me from the snares which they have laid for me, and the gins of the workers of iniquity.*

*Let the wicked fall into their own nets, whilst that I withal escape."*

Langston closed with Psalm 116.

*"I love the LORD, because he hath heard my voice and my supplications.*

*Because he hath inclined his ear unto me, therefore will I call upon him as long as I live.*

*The sorrows of death compassed me, and the pains of hell gat hold upon me: I found trouble and sorrow.*

*Then called I upon the name of the LORD; O LORD, I beseech thee, deliver my soul.*

*Gracious is the LORD, and righteous; yea, our God is merciful.*

*The LORD preserveth the simple: I was brought low, and he helped me.*

*Return unto thy rest, O my soul; for the LORD hath dealt bountifully with thee.*

*For thou hast delivered my soul from death, mine eyes from tears, and my feet from falling.*

*I will walk before the LORD in the land of the living.*

*I believed, therefore have I spoken: I was greatly afflicted:*

*I said in my haste, All men are liars.*

*What shall I render unto the LORD for all his benefits toward me?*

*I will take the cup of salvation, and call upon the name of the LORD.*

*I will pay my vows unto the LORD now in the presence of all his people.*

*Precious in the sight of the LORD is the death of his saints.*

*O LORD, truly I am thy servant; I am thy servant, and the son of thine handmaid: thou hast loosed my bonds.*

*I will offer to thee the sacrifice of thanksgiving, and will call upon the name of the LORD.*

*I will pay my vows unto the LORD now in the presence of all his people.*

*In the courts of the LORD's house, in the midst of thee, O Jerusalem. Praise ye the LORD."*

"Thank you, Langston. I needed those prayers because, there is nothing else that I can do. I am going to go downstairs now. Today has been very rough and I need to be alone to get myself back together. Tunji, I know that you're going to have to leave, but can you walk with me?"

"Thanks for the hospitality Wallace. I wish that it could have involved a better circumstance." Tunji then waved and said, "Bless all of you," and then followed Rocky down to the basement.

In the basement, they held hands and bowed their heads. They were seated opposite each other, one in the chair and one on the bed. A candle was lit and the bell was rung.

Tunji lead the prayer.

*"Eleggua."* Tapping the bell, *"Eleggua, please be with us now and show us the way to Ochossi. . . . Ochossi, Vanda Mae needs your divine intervention at this time. Please help Robin to make good decisions. Please let his actions bear fruit."*

Tunji dipped his fingers into the bowl of water and flicked it over the shoulders of Rocky. Rocky reciprocated. Rocky took his thumb and dipped it in the bowl and then pressed it against Tunji's forehead and Tunji did the same for his friend. They both said, *"Ache'."*

"Tunji, what did you mean about Smooth making good decisions and his actions bearing fruit?"

"Rocky, he's trying to change his ways. Just like you're trying to make something different of yourself, he's trying to do the same. He's going by Robin now and you're going by Jonathan. When he goes back to acting like Smooth, the drug pushing pimp, then call him by that name. You said the man had a legit job. Let's respect him for that. Nobody's perfect. . . Anyway, Robin will be going to the morgue to claim Vanda Mae's body. Also, he's going to begin walking around trying to find out if the killers went to a bar this afternoon."

"Tunji, I wanna help Robin. I feel useless letting him do all of the work to find the killers. You and I saw the killers. You and I found Vanda Mae. You notified the authorities."

"We each have our parts to play, Jonathan. This investigation is his part. You told the folks in Black Bottom that you were going to New York. The police know that your goat was shot, so they know that you are not traveling by goat cart. It won't take long for them to figure out that you took a boat to the city. If you're a suspect in the killing of Big Jim, the New York City police are going to be told. That means that this city isn't safe for you. If the police get their hands on you, you're going to be returned to the South. Are you ready to be strung up? You've already said that you'll fry if the police think that you're involved with the death of O'Brien. So, Jonathan, which is it? You gonna look for Vanda Mae's killers or are you gonna save your own ass?"

"You're right, Tunji. I gotta get out of here, but I don't like this move. It's like I 'm being forced out. I came here on my own terms and I'd like to leave the same way."

"Yeah . . . I'm leaving Tuesday morning at 6:00 a.m. You gonna be on my train?"

"Yeah, Tunji."

"Bags packed."

"Bags packed."

"No sweet grass baskets."
"No sweet grass baskets."
"I'll be here by 4:00 to help you with your bags."
"Thank you."
"I'm going home. I'll see you then."

# CHAPTER 16

# MOVING ON

———◆———

## Monday, October 2, 1933

VANDA MAE'S PICTURE WAS STARING at Robin as he made coffee that morning. There would be toast with butter and jelly to be consumed with the brew. Robin thought about the gun which was kept in the apartment. It had been used to protect each other in the past. It could now be used to avenge the death of his "wife," his "sister," his friend. His friend, that was all that she was in reality; a childhood friend that had been similarly exploited by family and abused by society. Juveniles who should have been showered with love and given educations and not turned into sex slaves.

Vanda Mae was young, as was he; just 23 years old. They had been on their own for only 7 years. Now he was going to claim her body. Bruce had warned him to tell the truth to the morgue clerk. If he said that they were married, information regarding her parents' names would be asked of him. The city in which he married Vanda Mae would also be asked of him. Since Vanda Mae had been murdered, the police might be coming around him for the next few months. He said that husbands were always suspects when women had been murdered. Bruce had told him to think carefully about claiming the body, particularly if he were still pushing dust.

At the morgue, he told the clerk he was Nelson McDonald and that the murdered Jane Doe was his sister, Nellie McDonald. After showing the clerk the fake driver's license he'd created in the studio for this occasion, he designated a funeral home with an attached crematorium to pick up the body. The clerk stated that the police had as evidence, $100 taken from the brassiere of the victim and $20 which was removed from the victim's vagina. If his sister didn't have any other children or a husband, he as the brother, could claim the money "... once Miss McDonald's estate had gone through probate."

The clerk had spoken so matter-of-factly, so nonchalantly, so casually, that the real meaning of his words almost slipped by. Robin wasn't even sure that he had heard the clerk correctly. Now was the time for clarification.

"Sir, what do you mean by any other children?"

"Mr. McDonald, your sister was pregnant."

It was at that point that Robin started coughing. His stomach was heaving as though he would throw up but, nothing was coming. He was doubled over by the convulsions when he gave in to them and fell onto the floor and placed his head between his knees, this was when the tears started. He was unable to stop. The clerk inquired if he could be of help, but Robin said that he would be all right.

Tears were still falling on his cheeks as he took the subway to the funeral parlor. He knew that there was more paperwork to fill out, an urn to choose, and a cremation bill to pay. He had brought $400 and the total bill came to $250. He was told to return in three days to pick up the cremains.

Back at the apartment, there were more tears, more buttered and jellied toast, and more coffee. These would rev him up. They would elevate his mood. Instead of being 10 feet deep in a hole of despair, he'd be elevated 3 feet, such that with effort, he'd be able to eventually pull himself out of the hole. Knowing that he had to do something positive, he picked up the picture of the pudgy teen, folded it into fourths, and placed it in his pocket. Reaching for pencil and paper he started writing his thoughts regarding what he knew and didn't know. He decided:

| What I Know | What I Need To Know / Do |
|---|---|
| 1) Vanda Mae was pregnant when she was | — |
| murdered. It doesn't matter who's the father. | |
| 2) "Pudgy" was seen putting on a belt | — |
| while leaving the scene of the crime. | |
| 3) "Pudgy" is most likely a student at CCNY. | — |
| 4) There are a lot of students at CCNY | Someone who knows how to |
| and identifying "Pudgy" from the rest | sort out the CCNY students. |
| of the students would be a problem. | |

| | |
|---|---|
| 5) The police would not seriously investigate the murder of a Colored woman; particularly one suspected of prostitution. | I will have to conduct this investigation. |
| 6) He would eventually find the killer. | Unsure - either kill him or get him to rat out his friends and kill all of them or report them to the police. |

Robin understood that he was going to have to think his possible actions through several times before setting them into motion.

———————

Rodham was watching Brown pull onto the parking lot. He decided to meet him at his car.

"Brown, I'm signing you up for a few hours of overtime this evening. I want you to take me out to Black Bottom Island. I want you to take me to the home of Cecelia Byrd."

"O.K., Captain. Let's go."

The officers left the city and drove the few miles down the dirt road to the one lane bridge which connected the mainland to the barrier island. Parking in front of Cecelia's house, Rodham told Brown to hold off on getting out of the car. Rodham then started unloading bullets from his gun. He put all but one of them into his pocket. Brown was watching this behavior and keeping his mouth shut. He was still hoping to get a promotion. The Captain stepped from the police car and started knocking on Cecelia's door. Cecelia's mother parted the curtain and looked at the Captain and asked, "What chu want Captain?"

"This is police business. Open the door Grandma."

"Cecelia ain't here. It's just me and the babies."

"Grandma," said the Captain, "this is the second time I'm telling you to open the door. Don't let it get to a third." As the curtain was closing, Rodham noticed that Brown was neither at his side nor behind him. His department's embarrassment was still sitting behind the steering wheel. Rodham was too disappointed to yell at him and so as the grandmother was opening the door, he waved him over.

"Good, Grandma. I don't hear any babies crying. You said you got babies in here."

"They're in their bassinettes. They're asleep."

The Captain walked over to one of the bassinettes and picked up a sleeping baby. Holding the infant with one arm, he took his gun out of his holster. Grandma ran toward the Captain to retrieve the child but Rodham was able to push her back to Brown with the hand holding the gun.

"Hold her Brown," he ordered.

When Brown had her in a firm grip, the gun was discharged into the ceiling. Now, Grandma was screaming as were both babies.

"Grandma, I'm gonna put this baby down and I'm gonna ask you a question. Now calm down." Rodham placed the crying baby back in the bassinette. He put his gun away and said, "Grandma, I hope you're ready for my question. Nod your head if you're ready."

Grandma nodded and the Captain then took his gun from his holster and pointed it at the bassinette. "Who killed Big Jim, Grandma?"

"Rocky."

"Grandma, you know that I can arrest you for lying to a policeman who's conducting an investigation? You know that right?"

"Yeah."

"You want me to handcuff you and take you to jail, Grandma?"

"No."

"So, tell me again, who killed Big Jim?"

"Rocky."

"And how did cripple ass Rocky kill big ass Jim?"

"I didn't watch the fight so I don't know how he did it. I know that he tricked him, though."

"Brown, take me to Rocky's house."

Grandma said, "He ain't there. He's gone. He left for New York. He was going there by goat cart. He hasn't returned since the day he left."

"Brown, let Grandma go."

Cecelia's mother ran to the bassinettes and placed herself beside them. That was the most which she could do while the police were still in the house.

In the police car, they watched the men coming back from the fishing boats. One of them had a red bandana on his head. The Captain watched him enter his home and then told Brown to slowly drive over to it. Before getting out of the car, Rodham took three bullets from his pocket and placed them into his gun.

Bobby was disrobing in the bathroom while water was running into the washtub. The first pot of scented water had been added and the second would be added soon.

Bobby was on the chamber pot relieving himself as Melissa was pouring more scented water into the tub.

Bobby started his cleansing routine the same way all of the time. He wet his hair. He massaged Madame Walker's Shampoo into the scalp and then he would rinse his hair with the clean tub water. He was on step 2 when Melissa entered the bathroom followed by the policemen.

"What's going on? What are you doing here, we ain't done nothing."

The Captain told Bobby that he needed to calm himself down. He then fired a bullet into the ceiling of the bathroom.

Returning the gun to his holster, he said, "I'm going to ask you a question Bobby, but before I do, I want you to rinse that soap out of your hair. I don't want it burning your eyes while we're conversing."

Bobby was suspicious, but thought it best that he comply with the policeman's suggestion. He had started rinsing the soap from his hair when suddenly his bushy hair was grabbed and his head was pushed beneath the water and held there. Brown was holding Melissa as she was screaming.

Rodham pulled Bobby's head up and waited for him to stop gasping for air. "Now that the soap is out of your hair, you can put the necessary thought into answering my question. . . Who killed Big Jim? You better tell me the truth."

Rodham took his gun from his holster and pointed it at Bobby's crotch. "You know Bobby, guns sometimes accidentally discharge. It's a lucky guy who's lightly grazed by the bullet. You thinking about your answer Bobby? I can't hear your answer Bobby; who killed Big Jim?"

"Rocky," whispered Bobby.

His head was immediately pushed below the water again. Rodham shouted, "You expect me to believe that . . . that cripple killed Big Jim?"

Melissa shouted, "It's true Rocky killed Big Jim. Rocky's smart and he somehow tricked him. Rocky killed him."

Rodham pulled Bobby's head out of the water. He told him to draw his knees up to his chest. When Bobby complied, Rodham shot two bullets into the washtub. It was like a Roman fountain; Bobby sitting in the tub motionless and blankly staring, while water was shooting out of it at different angles.

As Rodham was being driven back to the precinct, he said to Brown, "I hope that you learned something this evening, Brown."

"What was I supposed to learn Captain?"

"That you don't have to leave bruises when you interrogate a subject."

"Yes Sir, I learned that. Captain, can you sign my promotion?"

"No, Brown. You got a lot more to learn."

"Yes Sir, Captain."

———◆———

Jonathan had packed away his altar in one suitcase and his clothes in his other suitcase. He made sure that his recommendation from Carl was placed in the suitcase with his clothes. When Tunji arrived, he would be ready to leave.

Only Langston knew that he was headed for D. C. and he said that he would keep it a secret. The others would be told that he was going to Philly.

Langston let it be known that he had been offered a screen-writing job in Hollywood. It was to begin in January, so he would be leaving during the second week of December, nine weeks from now. Jonathan decided right then that he did not like the instability of an artist's life. Langston could live with it, Bruce could live with it, and Aaron seemed to live with it; but from Jonathan's perspective the only one who was really doing well materially and had financial peace of mind, was Wallace, the one with the steady job. In D.C., Jonathan understood that he would have to find a job and then get schooling at night. Art would have to be his last way of making money.

While packing the bags, feelings of incompleteness were flowing through him. He had paid for the extension cords, the hot plate, the light bulbs, the art supplies and now they were to be left behind. What would he need in D.C.? Water started filling his eyes at the realization that the things which could not be taken with him; the most important things which would be left in New York City, would be his friendships and even if he had known how to write, his special history prevented him from letting his New York friends know his full truth. Those friends of his which knew his special history, his Black Bottom Island friends, could not be told of his present truth. Rocky Johnson had to disappear. His whereabouts had to be unknown. His last known location had to be that dock in Charleston, South Carolina. There could be no connection between Jonathan Dunbar Hughes and Rocky Johnson. Jonathan began to realize that New York City was his cocoon and that he was a caterpillar. He had spun a cocoon around himself and he didn't even know it. He was destined to change and he hadn't fully accepted the inevitable. He told himself that it was time to accept his rebirth as Jonathan Dunbar Hughes. It was time to accept that he would have a tremendously different future life.

A vision of a butterfly filled his mind. It wasn't the best flyer, but it still got where it wanted to go and it still got to where it needed to go. It still retrieved nectar, it still pollinated flowers, and it still got God's work done. The butterfly was one of God's tools and he was one of God's tools. He realized that he was that small creature. He suddenly saw himself walking without a limp, in a garden, with butterflies flying around him. He resolved to place his trust in the Lord. He would let Rocky fall away like an old scab and in the place of the clotted blood would grow Jonathan Dunbar Hughes. Jonathan Dunbar Hughes, a man who was moving forward with his life and on towards Washington, D. C. He would not worry about the future, he would not lament for his lost friendships. He would consider his friendships to be like great meals, something to be savored at those times and remembered fondly. He would do God's work and he wouldn't worry, for the Lord was his Shepherd and as such, he would not want.

Jonathan's vision was interrupted by knocking on his front basement door. "Who's there?" he called out.

"Jonathan, open up. It's Tunji." Upon entering, Tunji said that since he thought that they should leave at 4:00 a.m., he ought to sleep over this evening. He then said with a laugh, I hope you haven't had beans for dinner.

"Choose a number between 2 and 4 and that'll be the number of cans of beans I've had this evening. I'd say make yourself at home but I know that your home is better furnished than this place."

"Things take time. Your life will change. All the things that you want, to make your life comfortable, will come in time. You got to keep marching towards your ideals, Jonathan. One step at a time and all that you want will come to you. Keep your angels primary in your life for they will show you the way and don't be impatient. Like I said, things take time. "

"O. K., Tunji, I hear you and I know that you are right, but I just wish that I had more things like the guys here have, then I could make you more comfortable. I like you, I respect you, you're being a tremendous help to me, I just want you to be more comfortable."

"Jonathan, I'm fine. I know how you're living. I'm here for you and not because you own certain things which society deems as status symbols. Jonathan, think back, when you were in South Carolina, hanging upside down and about to get your face kicked in, were you thinking about tables and chairs? . . . Were you, Jonathan? . . . Of course not, you were concerned about your safety. You got to put the basics in place before you can place antique tureens on top of antique tables and sit on antique chairs."

"Thank you, Tunji. Thank you for being my friend. Thank you for reminding me, first things first. . . .Tunji, can you write a letter for me?"

"Sure, but first things first. I went to a used book store today and got this old Bible. The family tree in it has not been filled in. I've used different types of pens and inks to create a family for you. Jonathan Dunbar Hughes, is the last of his line. He has no sisters, no brothers, no uncles, no aunts. It's up to him to create the next generation; if not, the line stops with him. So, pack this Bible away because you'll have to use it later to get official identification."

"Thank you, Tunji."

Tunji sat at Rocky's table and said, "Dictate the letter, I'm ready to write."

Rocky began:

Dear Langston, Bruce, Wallace, and Aaron,
   You all have been very kind to me. You have helped me in many ways and you didn't have to do anything. I am much appreciative of what you have done for me. It is time for me to move on. I'll be going to Philadelphia and staying with some friends of Tunji's while I'm looking for work. Tell Mr. Saperstein that I said thank you for renting the basement to me. I could only take so much in two suitcases. Please feel free to use those things which I left. The keys to the front and back basement doors and the main front door, are on the card table. I'll miss all of you.

Sincerely,
Your Friend,
**Rocky Johnson**

"Thank you, Tunji. Let's go to bed."

———◆———

Melissa was tightly holding Bobby. He wasn't speaking and his arms were hanging at his sides. The cops had been gone for five minutes. Confusion reigned supreme in his head. What to do first? Towel off he thought. Towel himself from his ankles up. No sense in toweling his feet. The washtub water had reached every part of the bathroom floor. He had made the floor especially well so that no critters could come up through the floor boards. The foundation of the bathroom was concrete. On top of the concrete, a layer of tar had been laid and on top of the sticky tar, the floor boards had been laid. Three coats of linseed oil had been used on the floor to make it water repellent. The water would stay right where it was, unless he mopped it up.

He had placed his heart, his soul, and his intelligence into making this bathroom a place of peace for himself and his wife. He had done the best he could with what he had. His washtub sat on cinder blocks and as such was elevated six inches above the floor. He had placed a draining faucet onto his washtub. After bathing, he would usually hook up a water hose to the faucet and let the tub water hydrate the lavender growing outside. Now his sanctuary had been defiled.

As his heart was no longer racing, he was beginning to think more clearly and he realized that life for him and Melissa could flourish only, outside of Dixie. He told Melissa to kill two chickens and to cook them this evening; that would provide their nourishment on the morning train. After dressing, he started packing his tools into two suitcases. There would be two suitcases of clothes and two suitcases of tools. They'd walk to the train station, leaving just before dawn. The suitcases would be in a wheel barrow which would be left at the station when they boarded the train. He had saved $1,800 which would help them get settled when they reached D.C.

———◆———

Half of the stools at The Blind Tiger's bar were empty this night. Kodak was sipping Southern Comfort when Brown entered, in his civilian clothes. Nodding to one another,

Brown asked if he minded company and Kodak replied with, "Join me. Want a Comfort? The first one's on me."

Brown took him up on his offer and then began talking about the hypocrisy of the Captain. He said that the Captain viewed him as a dumb tortuous barbarian. He said that he had never done anything that he didn't already see O'Brien do. He went onto tell how the Captain extracted confessions earlier this evening and how all he ever did was take things just a little bit further. He said that the thing which pissed him off the most was that the Captain released Big Jim's killer from jail.

"What? Why would the Captain do that?"

"Kodak, the man bent to Yankee pressure. A Yankee newspaper made a few phone calls and the next thing I know Rocky Johnson is being released from jail. But today, this afternoon, three different darkies told me and the Captain that Rocky killed Big Jim. Ya see what I'm saying? I'm the dumb one, but I'm the one who had him in jail." Brown continued, "Kodak, I got enough money for two beers. Shit, I'm essentially broke and that's because the Captain ain't gonna sign my promotion papers. He's the one that made the mistake and let the killer go, but I have to suffer the consequences."

"Brown, I'm gonna buy you two more Comforts. I want you to be good and mellowed out when you get home."

"Thanks, Kodak. . . You know that he wants your Grandpa's job. Captain's said it several times. He said that he doesn't want any negative publicity associated with his name nor with the police department. He thinks that next year will be your Grandpa's last year as Mayor. He's positioning himself to run right now. That's why he goes to the church picnics. It's more than good public relations for the police department. That's why you use his camera and his film. If it were really public relations, you'd be using your camera and your film and not the drugstore film. If it were public relations, you'd be developing the film and not the drugstore. . . Ya see, Kodak, I ain't as dumb as the Captain thinks."

"Brown, if three people told you that Rocky Johnson committed murder, then why don't you arrest him?"

"He's left town."

"Do you know where he went?"

"The first witness said New York City."

"The second and third?"

"Kodak, the Captain didn't ask them. He just wants to tidy up his paperwork. Multiple witnesses have named Rocky Johnson as the killer. The New York City police will be notified and if they catch him and if he's extradited, we'll see him again. If he's not caught, then we will most likely never see him. . . Kodak, Rocky did the state a favor; his killing of Big Jim, saved the taxpayers the cost of incarcerating him and the cost of executing him."

"Brown," inquired Kodak, "do you care more about capturing Rocky or getting a promotion?"

"The promotion, my wife is pregnant, she ain't working, and I got bills to pay. Soon, I'm gonna have another mouth to feed. "

Kodak signaled to the bartender. Upon his arrival, he ordered a fourth Comfort for Brown as well as a plate of fries. He also ordered the bill. After paying the bill Kodak said, "Things will improve for you before you know it. Just hang in there, you'll see. I'm gonna be goin'. You eat up and drink up and then go on home and go to sleep. Don't be beating on your wife and don't be giving me no strange looks; the whole department knows about her bruises. Your wife is pregnant Brown, you might trigger a miscarriage if you beat her."

CHAPTER 17

# THE NURTURING WOMB OF EDUCATION

———•———

## Tuesday, October 3, 1933

THE DISTANCE WAS NOT GREAT between the basement apartment and the subway station; still, it had been a good idea to leave at 4:00 a.m. because Jonathan moved slowly and his bags were somewhat cumbersome. He didn't know where he was going and his bags had to be taken down subway station stairs, onto the subway, through the halls of the subway station and Penn Station, and these same bags would eventually end up being lifted onto the overhead luggage rack. He was thankful that Tunji was his guide and that his island friend had carried both of the bags. Definitely, leaving at 4:00 was the right idea.

The main concourse of Penn Station was a beehive of activity. Jonathan had never seen so many people trying to get somewhere. Then he saw that Coloreds and whites were standing in the same ticket line and they were intermixed. Seeing this generated an odd feeling within him. The oddness increased when he realized that the Coloreds weren't deferring to the whites! Whites had to wait their turn to buy train tickets. Jonathan wouldn't have been surprised if a race riot had broken out, but it didn't. He didn't see any arguments going on this morning in the ticket line in Penn

Station. He knew that what he was watching was the normal way that Coloreds and whites behaved in this city. He also knew that it would take time for him to get used to how the races operated outside of Dixie.

Tunji had placed him in a corner near the ticket window and told him to wait for him to return with the ticket. While waiting, he saw other folks standing around looking up at a board upon which numbers would change and words would move. He liked the noise that the board made as everything changed. He figured that the board told of the comings and goings of the trains and he wondered, how many trains actually entered this station in one day.

Upon Tunji's return, the two men proceeded to the down escalator for Track 13. Jonathan was placed into a seat near the restroom, in a car which would be serviced by Tunji. His friend let him know that the train would be taking off in about fifteen minutes, just as soon as the other travelers boarded.

Before they had gone to bed, Monday night, Tunji had given his friend an address of a couple which would help him get settled in D. C.

"Are they with Daddy Grace?" asked Jonathan.

"No, Jonathan, they're Catholic. Don't worry though, this family will also help you get settled in D. C. They're the Lamonts. I phoned Mr. Lamont last night and he mentioned that he had a room for rent. They'll help you just like Daddy Grace's people would have helped you."

Mr. Alfred and Mrs. Lillian Lamont were a school principal and classroom teacher who had come north to provide their children with a better life than they could have in Georgia. Racism kept them from being hired by the D. C. School Board and so they made money initially by working as a porter at the train station and as a maid. Eventually, they both had gotten hired as clerks for the federal government and with time, they both had been promoted as far as Coloreds were generally allowed to go, GS 5. It didn't matter that both of them had more education than their supervisors' supervisors.

The Lamonts lived in a five bedroom wooden house in the far northeast D. C. community of Deanwood. They used one bedroom as a rental unit for single men needing a place to stay. They gave Byron a $25 commission when they took in someone he recommended.

Once the train arrived in Washington, D. C., Tunji had arranged for a porter to help Jonathan with his bags and into a taxi. Tunji had told Jonathan how much to tip the porter. He also told him what to say to the taxi driver to avoid a circuitous route to the home of the Lamonts. Lastly, he told him how much the fare should be.

The taxi brought Jonathan to a wooden home sitting on a large lot. A young man was sitting on the porch and got up from his rocking chair when the taxi stopped. Within seconds he was at the taxi.

"Hello, Sir. Are you Mr. Hughes?"

"Yes, I am. I'm here to see Mr. Lamont. Are you his son?"

"Yes Sir, I'm Martin. My parents are at work. They told me to get you settled in, after I collect $40. That $40 includes your meals. You can't go into the refrigerator for anything. You can give me the money once I get your bags onto the porch."

After the money was exchanged, Martin entered the house and took Jonathan's bags up to his room. "You'll have the room next to mine."

"It looks nice," replied Jonathan. Looking around, Jonathan saw a made-up bed, a chest of drawers, a full length mirror behind the door, a chair, and a lamp and a nightstand. It was the best living space he had ever had; it was also the most expensive living space he had ever had; but since food was included, he couldn't complain.

"Mr. Hughes, let me show you the bathroom." They walked a short distance and there was the standard sink and toilet but the bathtub had claw feet and there was a shower head on the wall. "Mr. Tolliver mentioned that you would be more comfortable sitting while showering so, dad got an old ironing board and cut it and reinforced it, so that it could comfortably rest across the top of the tub. He and I sat on it simultaneously and it didn't bend. It should easily support your weight. When you're finished showering, you can place it behind the bathroom door."

Martin continued, "Mom and Dad get into the bathroom early because they take the trolley to work. My sisters use the bathroom next, because they have to get to school. I'll use the bathroom next. I might just wash up because I've bathed prior to coming to bed or I plan on showering at school. After I've finished, then you can take a shower. No one takes long showers. That uses up all of the hot water. If you take a bath, clean the tub. Got it?"

"I got it," replied Rocky.

"There's another room I want to show you Mr. Hughes." Martin walked him to a room with a long table in its center. The table was covered by a plastic coated table cloth. There were several chairs in the room and several floor lamps and a light in the center of the ceiling. There were five book cases in the room, three of them were full, one had a few books, and one had no books. "This is our library Mr. Hughes. You can read anything you desire here, just put the book back. My sisters will be doing their homework here or I'll be doing mine."

"Martin, I'm ashamed to say this, but I never learned how to read. Colored folks in the rural South didn't get much education and Colored folks with club feet didn't get any. I got none. I want to learn how to read and write and do math. For math, right now, all I can do is make change. I know that I need night school classes and I know that I need a job."

"You're going to have to talk all of that over with mom and dad, they're the educators."

"How come you're not in school today?" inquired Jonathan.

"I attend Howard, Mr. Hughes. This semester, I lucked out and have no Tuesday nor Thursday classes. There are plenty of times when I'm on campus every day of the week. That means Saturday and Sunday as well as Monday through Friday."

"Ya seem awful young for a college boy. How old are you?"

"I'm 17 and I entered college at the age of 16. I seem young because I skipped two grades. I skipped the 2nd grade and I skipped the 5th grade."

"What ya want to do when ya finish college?"

"I'd like to be a college professor. I haven't decided what I want to teach, but that's what I'd like to do."

"Martin, I wish you well."

"Thank you, Mr. Hughes."

"Call me Jonathan."

"Sure, Jonathan. I've got French homework to do so I'm going to begin it. You are free to rest in your room, or on the front porch, or you can go into the back yard. There are some trees and some chairs back there. Do you have any questions of me?"

"No, no questions. Well there is one question, can I get a drink of water?"

"Yeah, you can get your own water. Just don't put the glass on a wooden surface. If you're at a wooden table, use a coaster. The kitchen table has a plastic coating, so it's o.k. to put the glass on it."

Jonathan reflected back a few nights to A'Lelia Walker's party and then said he'd drink the water while seated in the kitchen and at the kitchen table.

Descending the stairs, Jonathan was thinking that he still had to unpack. He really wanted to postpone that task so that he could fully savor this moment in his life, this beginning of new experiences, this place where he could finally relax. Jonathan was relishing the thought of being around financially stable educated Colored folks with "9 to 5" jobs. He was living with a family which had a room dedicated to reading books and they were ordinary people! They weren't rich like A'Lelia. It would take him time to process all the resources which were surrounding him. He felt though, that he was in a nurturing womb of education. In his mind, he saw an undifferentiated smiling mass, encased in a cocoon of silk.

The back yard of the Lamont home was a place of peace for Jonathan. The family had two apple trees, two peach trees, and two cherry trees. In between the fruit trees, there were benches. The family also had a large garden. A row of nasturtium was followed by a row of kale which was followed by a row of onions then a row of bush beans. He noticed that another row of nasturtium was followed by a row of watercress, then a row of onions, then a row of bush beans. Rocky noticed that these 8 rows were repeated once, for a total of 16 rows. The rest of the yard was grass. Sitting on a bench between an apple tree and a cherry tree, he wondered how two people with jobs outside of the home could have such a large and pretty garden. His answers came that evening when he met Mr. Lamont.

By 5:30 p.m. both Alfred and Lillian Lamont had arrived home. They welcomed Mr. Hughes to their home and gave him the same talk which their son had. They mentioned that they would help him get a job and that they would, over time, help him learn how to read, write, and do basic math. Mr. Lamont informed Jonathan that the family was very industrious; that they were always working to better themselves and that what he saw of their possessions was due to many years of constant working and saving and frugally spending their money. He told Jonathan that once a month, the family was called together to make decisions on purchases for the house or clothing. Howard tuition costs were discussed at these meetings as well as money for college for each of the daughters. The monthly calendar for the chores was drawn up at these meetings. Jonathan learned that it was at these meetings where everyone had to sign up for one hour a week of working in the garden. This involved weeding the garden or picking the vegetables or the fruit. Also, everyone in the family took turns canning the excess produce. There was little free time to be wasted listening to the radio. On Sundays, they went to church early. They caught the 7:00 a.m. streetcar so that they could arrive at St. Monica's by 7:45 a.m. The streetcar to bring them back home stopped across the street from the church, no later than 9:10 and they were on it. By 10:00 a.m. on Sundays, they were changing into more comfortable clothes and had the rest of the day to themselves. Mrs. Lamont mentioned that Martin did not always accompany them to church. She stated that frequently he would leave an hour after them. He usually attended Andrew Rankin Chapel on Howard's campus. He would then stay on campus and study.

That evening, out on the back porch, Alfred asked Jonathan if he had employment prospects.

"The only thing that I can hope for right now is that I can get some modeling jobs. I have a letter of recommendation from Carl Van Vechten, so, I hope that, that will help me. I was told that my bad foot and my brace would be something different for the students to draw."

"Have you written to the art schools or called them?" inquired Alfred.

"No, Mr. Lamont, I haven't. I never learned how to write."

"O. K., tonight, before you go to bed, I'll type out two letters for you. Those will be letters which will introduce you to the art departments. Tomorrow, while I have some free time at work, I'll call the Corcoran School of Art and the Art Department at Howard and talk you up at both schools. Maybe, you can begin making money this week." Alfred Lamont then asked, "Mr. Hughes, can you walk without your crutch? Can you use a cane or can you get around without any support?"

"I can get around. I'm not the best or swiftest on my feet, but I can get around, but I don't like climbing a lot of stairs without the crutch."

"Maybe you can get a job where you wouldn't have to climb stairs. Mr. Hughes, I've got the current layout of the Hecht Company Department Store, here in the house. I have diagrams which show the items and where they are located on all seven floors of the store. I want you to learn it. I'll help you memorize it and the rest of the family can quiz you on it. When you know where all of the products on the list are, I'm going to see about getting you a job there."

"Mr. Lamont, is there a specific job that you have in mind?"

"Elevator operator, they can sit on small stools during their shifts."

For the rest of the week, Jonathan listened to various members of the Lamont family read the list of what item was on a particular floor. By Sunday evening, he had practiced saying the words, writing the words, matching the oral word with the written word, giving the location of the item in the department store, and filling out practice job application blanks. Martin had told him that he would help him find his way on the streetcar to the Hecht Company on Tuesday. On Friday, October 6th, Jonathan got some good news. He was told to come to the Corcoran School of Art for a modeling assignment. That assignment would be on a Tuesday morning. Martin told him that he'd accompany him and that he'd bring two books to pass the time while he was waiting. He hoped that the weather would be pleasant because he knew that he would not be allowed to wait inside the school.

———◆———

Bartholomew Brown was lying in bed dreaming of his girl-friend. She was calling out his name. As he slowly woke up, he realized it wasn't "Sadie the Bad Lady" calling him, it was his wife. Ellen was telling him that he had overslept and that he had to quickly dress and get to work. He resented her telling him what to do. If he oversleeps, it's her job to wake him. He's the bread winner. What'd she done other than get pregnant? There'd be another mouth to feed in one or two weeks.

He had 15 minutes to get to work. No time for a bath. No time for a shave. There'd be the same underclothes and uniform as yesterday. Coffee was waiting for him on the kitchen table as was buttered toast with jelly, but he didn't have time for them. Brown left the house without saying a word to his wife. He jumped in the car and turned on the siren and drove as fast as he could to the police station. Pulling quickly onto the lot caused stares from his fellow officers, but it didn't matter because, he wasn't late.

Instead of attending the morning briefing, Brown went straight to the restroom. In the stall he dropped his pants and relieved himself. He told himself that he had to cut back on his drinking. Last night's Comfort was enjoyable, but he had too much. Going over to Sadie's apartment, after The Blind Tiger, was also enjoyable but he hated it when she asked him for money and he couldn't help.

"Don't you like my new perfume, Bart? Why don't you try to count how many places I sprayed it?!" Brown had had fun last night before coming home to his wife. Smiling, it occurred to him that the women in his life were similar and yet dissimilar in their traits. Sadie was pleasingly plump and Ellen had a grotesquely big belly. Sadie smelled good with her new perfume, but Ellen smelled like a hiney hole after a lot of broccoli and onions, because she was frequently passing gas. Sadie had a cute face with a petite nose, but Ellen's face seemed to be dominated by her nose. It looked to him that as her belly got bigger, so did her nose. They both had big tits but he didn't have to worry about Sadie's springing a leak. Sadie always had a nightcap waiting for him when he came over. Ellen, on the other hand, had started baking different types of bread during the last few months. He never knew what type of toast he was going to get in the morning.

"Brown! You O.K.?"

Why was the Captain yelling? Of course he was O.K.

"You missed the entire briefing this morning. If you're sick you need to be at home."

Wiping himself stimulated him to let his bowels loose, again. "I'm O.K. Captain; just a little bit of diarrhea this morning."

"Diarrhea means you're sick. I'm putting you down for sick leave and ordering you to go home. Oh, Brown, get rid of all your shit before getting in the squad car. Oh, another thing, my ordering you to go home doesn't mean that you stop at a speakeasy in your uniform and get a ½ pint. I'm calling your wife and telling her that you have diarrhea and that you're coming home."

"You can't do that Captain."

"And why not?"

"Cause the phone's been turned off." Flushing the toilet, he exited the stall.

"Brown, you look horrible. You look like you're half dead. I don't want you driving the police car. Give me the keys, I'm taking you home."

Brown complied with the Captain's request and handed him his keys.

Walking out to the parking lot the Captain told Brown, "I'll be back in a moment, I'm going to pull someone to drive your car to your home; then I'm personally taking you home."

As the Captain was walking back into the station, Kodak ambled by.

"You're not sick, not really sick, you're hung over Brown and we both know it. You know what else we both know?"

"What's that, Kodak?"

"The best way to get over a hangover is. . ."

In unison, they smiled and said, "to take a drink."

"Here's a ½ pint of Comfort. Put it in your front pocket. You'll feel better this evening. When you get home, tell your wife you want something with cheese. That'll bind you up. Take some coffee also. The coffee will make you a more alert drunk. You might like the feeling of a coffee buzz with a velvet touch."

Brown slipped the ½ pint in his front pants pocket and pushed it down so that the bottle's top would not show. Kodak walked away saying, "I hope you're feeling better soon."

That's when the Captain drove up. "Hop in, I'm taking you straight home." Getting in beside the Captain, Brown watched Mays, the oldest and fattest man with a badge and a gun, get in his squad car. He watched the cushion collapse as Mays's butt hit it. How Mays had avoided being forced to retire years ago was an unanswered mystery to all who worked at the station. Brown thought that he had to be blackmailing someone. As Brown was contemplating the absurdity of Mays's being on the force, he felt more intestinal movement and asked the Captain to wait a few more minutes before driving him home.

"I told you to get rid of all your shit before getting in this car. Make it snappy, cause I'm not taking a sick day today."

Brown had arrived at the station with a siren blaring and he left the station the same way. Once the Captain stepped on the gas, Brown passed out. Eight minutes later, Ellen was opening the door for her husband. Rodham was walking him from the car to the front door of the house. "He's sick, Ellen. I put him in for sick leave through Thursday. If he's out Friday he has to bring in a Doctor's note. I'm going to help him into bed."

"Ellen," shouted Brown, "fix me something with cheese and fix me some coffee."

Rodham got Brown in the bedroom and started undressing him. That's when Brown passed out again. The Captain placed the patrolman's head on the pillow and lifted his legs onto the bed. He grabbed Brown's holster buckle, unhooked it, and that's when he noticed the bottle of Southern Comfort. He removed it from Brown's pocket just to make sure that he saw what he thought he saw and then replaced the bottle. He then placed the gun and holster on top of the chest of drawers and left the room. As he was walking away, he thought that Brown smelled like a combination of alcohol, perfume, and a public toilet. He would note that Brown smelled of alcohol today and that he had a bottle of alcohol in his pocket when he'd been brought home. He'd also note the oral warning delivered to Brown in September and the complaints of the public the day that he shot Rocky's dog and goat. As he was about to leave he saw Ellen place two grilled cheese sandwiches on a plate with a mug of coffee on a tray. Looking at her he said, "Is he still beating you?" When she hesitated to answer he said, "You have the right to defend yourself."

"Thank you, Captain" was her downcast reply.

When Bartholomew Brown woke at noon that day, he realized that he was still in his police garb, so he reached into his front pants pocket and took out the ½ pint, sat himself up, broke the seal on the bottle and then poured two capfuls of the liquor into his coffee, tightened the cap on the bottle, and then placed it in his nightstand drawer. Standing now, he downed the doctored coffee, hung up his pants, removed his shirt, and put on his bathrobe. Grabbing the grilled cheese sandwich with his left hand and the coffee mug in his right, he descended the stairs, walked past his wife and onto his back porch. From his rocker, he told Ellen that he liked the bread which she had made and that the sandwich was really good with the onions and tomatoes and crumbled up bits of bacon between the slices of cheese. He ordered her to make him a few more and to also make some more coffee. He didn't intend to drink any more liquor that day, but the coffee with sufficient sugar along with the sandwiches, would meet his internal need for something filling and mood lifting. He rested the remainder of that day and all day Wednesday and Thursday. Officer Bartholomew Brown decided that he would enjoy this time off and not worry about anything. He would return to work on Friday morning. He would be on time and he would be sober.

———◆———

Bobby bought the tickets for himself and Melissa. Washington, D. C. would be many stops away, but it would eventually come. They would head to the Colored Waiting Room and wait the 90 minutes until the train north was announced. Upon entering the room, they noticed a familiar face, Cecelia Byrd. Stories concerning Rodham were exchanged. Cecelia stated that she planned to work as a maid and bring her mother and her children north with money she'd send to them. After buying her train ticket, she stated she had a total of $50. The rest of her savings had been given to her mother to take care of herself and the children. She hoped to have them with her by October 31st.

On the train, Cecelia sat towards the rear of the Colored Car and Melissa and Bobby sat in the middle. The couple discussed Cecelia's predicament of needing to immediately find work and shelter. Bobby suggested that they could give her $100, to which Melissa quickly interjected, "No. We can give her $50. D. C. is a big city and we may not see her again. Those babies and her mother are in a bad situation, but our generosity can extend only so far without it affecting our wellbeing. We got to do the same as her, find jobs and a place to live. Fifty dollars is very generous."

In the restroom of the train, Bobby unbuttoned his shirt and pulled two 20's and two 5's from his homemade money belt. He placed the folded cash in his palm, checked his appearance in the mirror, and then exited the room. Walking past Melissa to where Cecelia was sitting, he sat beside her and quietly said, "This is a gift from Melissa and me." He placed his hand on top of hers and transferred the funds. Upon slightly opening her hand and seeing the gift, she said, "Thank you, Bobby and tell Melissa I said thank you. I'd give you a hug, but that would draw attention to us and it might upset Melissa so, again, thank you." With a nod, Bobby walked back to his seat beside his wife. The three of them rode the 531 miles north with hope in their hearts, not knowing what the future would bring.

# CHAPTER 18

# THE LONE RANGER

---

## *Friday, October 6 - Saturday, October 7, 1933*

WORK WAS GOOD. IT HELPED dissipate the anger and the frustration. The tears didn't come when he was busy. The church ladies slowly began showing up for their special "movie star" shots. He had scheduled dates for photographing the Concert Choir, the Men's Choir, and the Youth Choir. Money was slowly coming in and more was on the way. It looked as though he would make the rent payment; but just in case, he had saved his dust money.

He knew that this transition period would test his skills as a businessman. He had already decided that he could cut back on consuming meat. He'd switched to eggs. Three of them a day, hard boiled or scrambled or utilized as part of an omelet, they would be his meat substitute. He'd consume no more than one baked chicken per month with the baking always taking place after church. Mondays, Wednesdays, and Fridays would have Robin rinsing black eyed peas and navy beans. Beans which were rinsed on Mondays would be sprouted, green, and edible in ten days, on the following Thursdays. Similarly, Wednesday's beans would be edible on Saturdays and Friday's beans would be edible in ten days, on Mondays. He wanted Vanda Mae and himself to have dedicated sprouting jars which were propped up facing the windows and drained into empty ice trays. Rice would always be cooked and consumed with the fresh bean sprouts. Watercress or kale, collards, cabbage, or spinach would also be steamed for the evening's meal. He liked the routine. The routine was simple and efficient. The routine presented a reasonable template for the future; at least as it pertained to meals. Its structure made him feel safe. If Vanda Mae had stuck to their routine, she'd have been dining with him this evening.

At the studio, the printing had ended five days ago. "Pudgy's" face had been placed on 26 - 8 X 10 posters announcing a look-alike contest with a prize of $100. The individual who looked most like the drawing would be paid the money after he participated in a one day photography session. Twenty-six posters went up around CCNY and each poster had a different letter of the alphabet on its back. Robin's notebook had the location of the placement of each poster. Directions listing the bench near the 136th Street entrance to St. Nicholas Park, were printed at the bottom of the poster. The directions also stated that the contestant had to bring the poster with him, with his name and address legibly printed on its back. Judging would take place on Saturday, October 7th at noon (rain or shine). The posters had been up for 5 days and as of the 7th of October, 16 young similar looking men appeared at the park bench to be judged.

Robin wondered about the accuracy of the drawing. How much different from the drawing was the contestant? He thought that the contestant which acted the most "unusual" would be Vanda Mae's killer. Several guys had brought their friends with them, so this complicated the selection by adding a diversion for Robin's attention. One of the "Pudgy's," though, was acting a bit more juvenile than the others. This "Pudgy's" friends were also more animated than the rest of the friends of the contestants.

Robin had all of the contestants line up and face him. One by one Robin closely looked at the picture and at individual contestants. He had brought his camera to the park. He then inspected each contestant through the camera's lens and compared what he saw through the lens with the poster in his hand. Robin kept returning to the "unusual" acting "Pudgy" and his juvenile friends. They had to be the killers and so he announced this "Pudgy" as the winner of the advertising contest.

He told "Pudgy" that his image would be placed into a scene of the Lone Ranger out in the dessert or on the plains, or in dilapidated buildings. He was told that he'd get the $100 at the end of the day and if his friends participated, they could get $50.00 each. They jumped at this offer.

The students were told to go behind the boulder and put on the jeans, chaps, cowboy shirts, bandanas, and cowboy hats which had been brought to the shoot, after which, he'd pose them. After 15 minutes of photographs, the students were offered rum and coke, to get them loosened up for the rest of the shoot. Robin didn't want them to be stiff in front of the camera. He told them that they had to look relaxed. Robin poured a bottle of Coke into a half of a fifth of Myers's Rum. He encouraged them to drink as much as they wanted and he took pictures of them in the cowboy garb, passing the bottle back and forth as they leaned against the boulder. The students were told that since Prohibition was going to end in December, this would be an ad for Myers's Rum. He told them that the label had to be facing the camera. The pimply faced friend asked if the Lone Ranger would be placed into this picture and he was told, "No, the Lone Ranger doesn't drink. A liquor ad would be placed in a magazine such as Field and Stream."

Robin mentioned to the students that they would soon have to move onto the next location, before the prostitutes came. He stated that prostitutes frequently used the very bench on which he had been seated. He asked the students if they were virgins and if not had they used the prostitutes in the park or did they have girlfriends who put out?

The students told of how they each had sex a few days ago with a hooker in the park. They told of how all she wanted to provide was blow jobs but how they encouraged her to perform other acts.

"Like take it up the ass," interjected Pudgy.

"Sounds like you guys had a lot of fun here in the park. When did your orgy take place?"

"Sunday," said Pudgy's good looking friend. "We wore the bitch out. She literally passed out draped over that bench."

"How much did she charge," inquired Robin.

"Twenty dollars a round," noted Pudgy's pimply friend, "but we each went twice with her so she walked away with $120 that Sunday afternoon."

"Y'all were certainly setting the grass on fire on that Sunday afternoon." Robin told the students that they would have to move to the next location, so they needed to change back into their own clothes. The next scene would be shot in the South Bronx and they'd be getting off at the Hunts Point Avenue Station. Upon disembarking the subway, Robin led his troop of fun seekers into a back room in an abandoned building.

Robin announced, "Just keep following me. There's more light coming through a window in the back." Once they reached the room, Robin continued, "O. K., in this scene, you're going to be in the jeans, the shirts, and the bandanas. Also, you're going to put the long johns on and the jeans over them. You're going to put these galoshes over your shoes and tie these small ropes tightly around the tops of the galoshes."

The students were drinking as they were changing clothes. When the students were dressed and the camera was set up, Robin stated:

> "O.K., the Lone Ranger is going to rescue you in this scene. You're going to place one foot in each bucket of tar. You'll be facing out towards the room. The long johns will keep any tar which works its way through the jeans, off of your skin. The turpentine over there will be used in case you get tar on your skin. Once you're in the correct positions, I'll tie this rope around you. Don't worry, it won't be tight. It just cannot look slack when viewed through the camera. This scene will be for a tar advertisement."

Robin had brought 100 feet of rope. He told the students that there would be a few more shots and that they would soon be cleaning themselves up and collecting their money. He told "Pudgy" that he might be called back for more work since he had won the contest. Robin then tied the rope around their shoulders, elbows, and hands.

"I need to check the sunlight from the windows," he said to the group. Satisfied that he saw no one walking near the building, Robin walked up to the guys, reached into his pants pocket, pulled out a .38 magnum, and shot each student in the heart. They really didn't have time to scream and even if they somehow lived and had enough energy to scream, no one would hear them because, today the New York Giants were playing the Washington Senators in the World Series; and as such, all ears would be focused on radios and not on unusual sounds coming from abandoned buildings.

Now it was time to clean up. That was part of his plan, the removal of all student identification. Their pants containing their wallets, were placed in a shopping bag. None of them was wearing a CCNY t-shirt nor shorts. He'd checked on that while they were changing. He now had to use the turpentine to wipe down the buckets of tar which had been brought to the Bronx via subway, from Jersey City, two buckets a day. A cloth and latex gloves were used to wipe fingerprints off of the bottle of turpentine. When the bodies would eventually be found by the police, the only finger prints would be the ones from the hands of the students, the same as the prints on the discarded rubber packets left in St. Nicholas Park.

Before Robin left his executed killers, he retrieved three packets of dust from his pocket. With gloves still on his hands, he rubbed both sides of each packet against his sleeve and then held the packet by its edge. Placing each student's right forefinger and thumb on the packets he then placed one packet each in the right pants pocket of each student.

He checked once more to make sure that all three students were dead and that he had no tar on himself. He placed the latex gloves in his bag along with Carl's chaps and the students' pants. After disassembling the camera and placing it in its case, he left for his home in Harlem.

Once in his home, he did not rest. After depositing the clothing of the students and Carl's chaps, he got his notebook and went to the 10 locations still having the look-alike contest posters and removed them.

Robin told himself when one catches rats, you've got to clean the area after disposing of the animals. There were rats in his neighborhood and he couldn't trust the police nor the District Attorney to carry out the laws of the land.

He was sad and anxious and disappointed in himself for becoming a vigilante, but it was a job which had to be done. If flies came into his apartment, he'd swat them. If mice came into his apartment, he set traps for them. These things would be done without thinking and without guilt. He told himself that he'd get over killing the students, before he got over losing Vanda Mae and the baby.

# SHADY LADY

———◆———

*Friday, October 6 - Monday, October 9, 1933*

THE DAYS OFF HAD BEEN good for Brown. He had been consuming a lot of coffee, vegetables from his garden, and Ellen's homemade bread. Not thinking about work had been good for his disposition. He wasn't angry with Ellen nor had he been angry with himself. He reasoned that whether he got a raise or didn't, he and Ellen and the soon to be addition to the family, would get by.

Bartholomew was wearing a smile as he walked into the station. He was 15 minutes early when he was told that the Captain wanted to see him. In the Captain's office he started to sit down when he was told, "Don't sit. This won't take long. Read this note which is being placed in your personnel file. You can sign it if you like or you can insert your version of events. It doesn't matter because I'm sending you home and docking you one day of pay." The note mentioned the citizen complaints of a drunken cop shooting pets on the dock. The note also mentioned that he had been given a verbal warning after the complaints were lodged. Finally, the note mentioned that he had smelled of alcohol on

Tuesday morning when he had diarrhea and that after he had been taken home by the Captain, an unopened 1/2 pint of Southern Comfort had been found in his front pants pocket after he had passed out.

Bart was silent. After dropping the paper on the Captain's desk, he quietly walked out of the office. It took about one minute before the calmness of the station was broken and there came a hard knocking at the Captain's door. When Rodham opened it, a bruised Kodak was pushed in. As his fellow officers looked on, Brown shouted, "He slipped the bottle in my pants. Tell him. Tell him, you cock sucking son of a bitch."

"Captain, I didn't put anything in Brown's pocket. You know I got a clean record and I'm not trying to mess it up. Brown's picking on me cause I'm small. Monday night, I admit, I bought him some drinks but Tuesday morning, I was here on time and sober. . . Captain, I don't know nothing about no bottle in his pants pocket."

That was when Brown charged Kodak. It took several police officers to pull Brown off of the photographer. After being subdued and cuffed, Brown's holster and gun were removed and he was to be placed in the back of a paddy wagon. He was told that the one day suspension had turned into a one week suspension, without pay and that he should report back to work on Friday the 13th.

It was utter humiliation. All of his peers were watching as he was being lead to the wagon, hands cuffed behind him. Riding home surrounded by the faint smell of urine only added to his anger. When the wagon stopped, he knew that it had arrived at his home. As soon as the front door closed behind him, he backhanded Ellen, then he slapped her again and pushed her backwards into a chair.

Heading upstairs, he was going to get out of his cop clothes and into civilian clothes and that was when the tears started. He was crying and then the tears turned to rage.

The first thing to hit the walls was Ellen's talcum powder. Then, the bottles of perfume, the clock, the lamps on the nightstands, hit the walls. The mattress was overturned and while all of this was going on, Ellen was downstairs screaming.

"How dare the bitch scream," he thought. He was the one in pain. He had something for her. He'd fix her. That's when he ran to the closet and grabbed Ellen's clothes and threw them down the stairs. His rage was not depleted. It was at that point when Brown got his hands on the chest of drawers and pulled it forward until it fell and landed on the bed. That was when the tears returned. Looking to his left, he remembered that the 1/2 pint was still in the night-stand drawer. He got the bottle out and sat on the floor and with two hands put the bottle to his lips and drank the alcohol. Leaning against the wall he continued to drink. This was his pacifier. The Comfort made the screams of his wife softer, until he couldn't even hear them. Sleep beckoned and he thought, "*O. K., a catnap's needed*" and he slept there while sitting and leaning against the wall. The open bottle of Comfort was held to his chest by both hands. Not a drop fell to the floor. When he woke up, ten minutes later, he finished off the Comfort and changed into his civilian clothes. The house was now quiet and peaceful, just the way he liked it.

As he was descending the steps, he kicked her dresses and handbags out of his way. Upon entering the dining room, he saw Ellen on the floor and his still born son at her ankles, the umbilical cord wrapped around his neck.

"Damn, bitch, you can't do anything right. Make sure you clean up that blood. I don't need to be slippin' when I come into the dining room" and then he was out of the door, walking down the street to the Piggly Wiggly.

At the supermarket, he found his favorite employee on the cash register. He let her know that he had to see her after she got off of work this evening but he was immediately rebuffed.

"Bart honey, this is short notice. I got other plans for this evening. Why don't you come around on Sunday evening?"

Bart got loud in the store and started accusing her of having another boyfriend. Multiple sets of eyes focused on the arguing couple when out of the crowd, stepped a policeman who recognized Bart and reminded him that the last thing which he needed was for someone to make a negative report concerning him. He was advised to leave the premises before things escalated and ended up out of control.

Brown got up in the patrolman's face and said, "Fuck you" and then walked out of the store.

Brown continued to walk and ended up at The Blind Tiger. Seeing the owner of the establishment, he asked him for a bottle on credit and swore that he'd pay him back on his next payday. Because it was still early in the day and there were no other patrons around, the owner capitulated for the sake of expediency. Brown received a fifth of Old Kentucky Bourbon. The owner told him that if he did not repay the whole sale price of the bottle by next Friday, that he'd ban him permanently from the bar; he then passed the bottle to him in a brown paper bag. Bart unscrewed the cap and immediately began his drinking right there in the Tiger.

Walking back to his home, he was nursing his bottle. When cops slowly drove by, he deliberately hoisted the bottle to his lips. He was daring them to arrest him.

Upon entering his home, Bartholomew looked to where his son was and saw only a smeared blood stain on the floor. "Where's my son?" he asked. Ellen told him that the baby was sleeping in the bassinette. "Crazy bitch," was his reply. "We're gonna make another one and you better not fuck that one up!" He ordered her to make him some grilled cheese sandwiches and to bring him some coffee. "I'll be getting myself in the mood to make another baby."

When Bart got in the bedroom, he saw a bloody sheet wrapped around a small object which was neatly placed in a bassinet. He went to the top of the stairs and called down, "Ellen, you're crazy. You've lost your goddamn mind!" While Brown was upstairs waiting for his sandwiches and coffee, Ellen walked to her small garden and got two tomatoes. Walking back she saw the belladonna berries. She knew that she had to get rid of the weed before the baby came but she hadn't. She thought that the plant could stay a little longer. She picked twenty berries and carried them in with the tomatoes. She would use them to add sweetness to the coffee for her husband. She squeezed all twenty berries into a cup and then placed five teaspoons of sugar in the cup. She then added the coffee. That's how he liked it, black with sugar. When the grilled cheese sandwiches were prepared, she took them up to him. When she entered the room, he was sitting naked on the back of the chest of drawers, stroking himself. She placed the tray on the nightstand

and told him it was too soon for sex. He told her, "Oh no it's not." He then grabbed the front of her house dress and yanked her forward. Her face slammed into the wooden chest and even though she screamed, there was no one to help her. He entered her from the rear. Her labia and birth canal burned with pain. He had a belt and he beat her as he rode her. Welts were forming on her legs and on her back. He pulled himself out of her, turned her on her back, and then said, "Bitch, we're gonna to do this until you get good and pregnant." He slapped her again saying, "We're gonna do this 'till your cunt gets good and tight." The rape went on and on and finally after ejaculating, he picked up her head by her hair and backhanded it, just to show her who's in charge. He wiped her blood off of his penis with the hem of her house dress. He then started eating a sandwich and drinking the coffee. He liked chasing the coffee with the Old Kentucky. He also really liked the sandwich. Ellen had done really well with this baking hobby. Tomatoes and onions and crumbled bacon were between two slices of cheese and this fancy Betty Crocker recipe bread. He was going to have to have her make this sandwich again. He saw from the corner of his eye that she was watching him eat the sandwich. He then told her that she did a good job on the baking and that the bread by itself, was delicious. He then said that the sandwich she had created was so satisfying that he wanted her to make more of them. Also, she should seriously consider entering the bread and the sandwich in contests when the fair came by in the spring.

Brown washed the sandwich down with several gulps of coffee followed by a mouthful of Old Kentucky. That was when the gagging started. Bart fell to the floor and started rolling around. He got up and started running and ran into a wall. While falling down the stairs, he was screaming Kodak's and Sadie's names. Most of his speech was incomprehensible. Naked, he ran out of the front door and collided with the fence. Turning around he ran to the back of the house and through the garden. Tripping, he collapsed at the base of the belladonna plant.

When Ellen felt strong enough, she rolled onto her stomach and backed herself off of the chest. Standing up and steadying herself against the wall, she took the coffee cup to the bathroom and poured its contents down the toilet. Flushing it, she turned toward the mirror above the sink. The bruises on her face would not be going away anytime soon. The full length mirror coupled with a hand mirror showed the extent of her body's beating. After washing the cup with hand soap it was slipped into the pocket of her housedress. Buttoning up her dress was followed by putting on her house shoes. The turned over chest of drawers precluded putting on fresh underwear. Taking her bundled child from the bassinette and the remainder of the sandwich, she slowly descended the stairs and headed for the kitchen. After placing the cup in the sink, she exited the front door and stood on the side of the road. Throwing the sandwich into the ditch, she waited until a car came along and took her to the hospital.

The triage nurse started yelling when Ellen entered through the Emergency Room. When things had settled down, Captain Rodham was called and told that she had delivered a stillborn son after being beaten by her husband.

She told him that when he came back home this morning, he beat her, then raped her, then beat her again, and then ran off. She did not know where he was. She wanted to file a complaint against her husband. She stated that she would file for divorce when she got out of the hospital. She stated that if the court would not grant her a divorce, then she would leave him.

Three days later, Ellen was picked up at the hospital by the Captain. He told her that her husband was found naked and dead at the base of a nightshade plant in their backyard. He apparently had eaten some of the sweet berries. "I guess he thought that it was a blackberry plant. An autopsy revealed that he was quite drunk when he died." He told her that she could go to the morgue and claim the body. She stated that there was no money for a burial and that he would have to go to the potter's field. She said that she might as well start the paperwork for the widow's pension. Rodham asked her what she would be doing while waiting for the pension to kick in and she said that she would go back to her job as a practical nurse.

# CHAPTER 20

# FROM DEANWOOD TO DOWNTOWN AND BACK

*Tuesday, October 10, 1933*

MARTIN AND JONATHAN WERE WATCHING the streetcar approach the stop. They had been waiting ten minutes and were nervous concerning what the day would bring. Martin was concerned with getting in enough study time to do well on two upcoming Friday exams. Jonathan was concerned with appearing nude in front of white women; nude in front of white men; whether he would get an erection or stay flaccid; whether he would be allowed to pose once the school discovered he was Colored; and if they would pay him that day. He also worried that when he got to the Hecht Company, that he would not pass the store test for elevator operator. He worried that Martin would leave him in an unknown part of town because he was tired of carrying him around and not being able to pursue his studies at college. Lastly, he worried that all of his worrying would cause him to perspire and that he would eventually become funky. He then worried that he had put on too much of Alfred Lamont's cologne before leaving the house.

At the Corcoran School, eyebrows were raised when the two Colored gentlemen entered. Two secretaries told them that there was a rear entrance for custodians. They were flustered when Martin spoke up and said that they were there as models and not as custodians and that if they checked their records, they would see the name, Jonathan Dunbar Hughes. He said that the students were being deprived of their chance to draw Mr. Hughes and that the school had offered Mr. Hughes the modeling assignment based on the recommendation of Mr. Carl Van Vechten of New York City. He suggested that they check with the department head to see if he were telling the truth. During all of this time, Jonathan was concerned that Martin was being too assertive with these white women. Washington might be the most liberal part of the South, but it was still a Jim Crow city as far as he was concerned. There were places for whites and places for Coloreds and everyone knew his place and rarely stepped away from it. Carl Van Vechten was the exception and he was in New York.

The secretaries told Martin and Jonathan to wait near the entrance and that they would go and verify their story with the head of the school. As the women were walking off, they were talking about how quickly race relations were changing and that the pace was much too fast. It was then that a white male came from a different direction and asked if one of them was Jonathan Dunbar Hughes. That was when Jonathan spoke up.

"I am," he said.

"Good, you're going to be in my studio for the next 90 minutes." Looking towards Martin he said, "You're welcome to wait in the studio or you can come back in 90 minutes."

Looking at the art instructor, he announced, "I'll return in 90 minutes." Looking at Jonathan he said, "When you're finished, come outside and wait for me. If you don't see me right away, go across the street and sit on the bench and I'll get back to you." With that said, Martin was off and Jonathan was being guided towards the drawing and painting studio.

As soon as Jonathan entered the studio, all talking stopped. This would be a first for all of the students, a Colored man with a limp. The instructor lead Jonathan to a tri-fold screen which had a chair and a robe behind it.

"Mr. Hughes, I want you to strip nude and then put on this robe. Stay behind the screen until I come back. O. K.?"

"O. K."

A few minutes later the instructor arrived back behind the screen with a pair of George Washington University gym shorts and a jockey strap. "The strap and the shorts are clean, put them on and when you're ready, let me know and come out and sit on the hassock and then take the robe off once you get to the hassock. You can drop it behind the hassock. Assume a comfortable pose. Your pose should have the brace in full view."

"O. K."

Everyone was very quiet during his time on the hassock. Everyone was busy using colored pencils to replicate his likeness. The 90 minutes went quickly and he was back behind the screen changing into his clothes. He had been told to show up at the same time tomorrow for another 90 minute session. "You'll be wearing the strap and shorts then, also. Can you make it tomorrow?"

"Yes, Sir."

"Call me Burke."

"Yes, Sir, Mr. Burke; but the secretaries didn't want to let me in the school today. You may have to meet me at the door."

"No, that won't be necessary. While you were posing, I told them that you were supposed to be here and that they were not to hamper you doing your job. They'll be paying you when you leave. Write your name on this bag and drop the strap and shorts in. You can give it to me as you exit the studio."

As Jonathan approached the secretaries, he saw one of them go into a desk. By the time that he got to that secretary's desk, she spoke first, "Sign the book here." She was pointing to a space in a ledger. "There's your money." The money was resting on the edge of her desk. Jonathan understood that she did not want her hand touching his. He wanted to curse this insulting behavior, but he knew that if he acted up, he would lose out on the chance to work here again. He took the twenty dollar bill and walked outside and waited for Martin to show.

Jonathan wasn't sure how long he waited. He knew that he had to get a watch and he had to learn how to tell time. He decided that when he had enough money, he would buy himself a fancy pocket watch. If he had had a plain wristwatch and if he had known how to tell time, he would have known that he had waited ten minutes for Martin to return.

"Hi, Martin. Where ya been and what 'cha carryin?"

"I took the streetcar over to the Hecht Company. I used your name and took the elevator test for you. You passed. You'll start on Thursday. You need to get there by 9:45 a.m.

You'll be making $18.00 a week for 30 hours of work. This is your uniform. You'll be working the morning shift. You'll be taking a pregnant woman's place. If they like you, they may use you more than 30 hours a week."

"But you don't look like me. They'll fire me when I show up."

"Relax Jonathan, I put a rock in my left shoe so that I was limping into the testing room. I took the test without my glasses. When I signed your name, I did it the way you do it. You already knew all of the answers on the test. Everything's going to be o.k. Besides, you know 'all of us look alike.' You'll be working elevator number two. You'll be working Thursday, Friday, Saturday, Monday, and Tuesday. Don't lose this name tag."

Martin showed Jonathan the stop for the Hecht Company. He showed him where elevator number two was. He showed him the employees' entrance and emphasized the importance of using that entrance. Lastly, he showed him how to get back home. Where to transfer streetcars and what the landmarks were at those stops.

Jonathan had a lot to absorb. He had to get back to the Corcoran tomorrow morning, without the help of Martin. Then, he had to get back to Deanwood. He would do it. He would have another $20 bill by this time tomorrow.

CHAPTER 21

# FUNERALS ARE FOR THE LIVING

———◆———

*December 22 - December 31, 1964*

THE THERMOMETER ON THE BACK porch read 33 degrees. The high today was predicted to be 40. The t. v. weatherman was not predicting rain, so a heavy jacket would be enough to keep her warm as she walked toward the bus stop. On the bus, she observed a young lady in high heels, holding the grab bar. She hoped that her heels would not break and that if a heel did, that the young lady wouldn't take a bad fall. She, on the other hand, was a Hush Puppy lady. It was a comfortable shoe, the black version of which paired well with her black and white uniform. She could be on her feet inspecting the work of the maids, the janitors, the child care providers, and the rest of the hospitality staff. She had done all of their jobs except janitor. She had come a long way since she first arrived in October 1933. She was no longer homeless and unemployed. The Phyllis Wheatley YWCA had extended her a lifeline back then and she had grabbed hold and never let go.

Back then Cecelia hoped that her children and her mother could join her by Halloween. She never thought that they'd come just prior to Halloween 1934. It took that long to find a place which would accept two adult women and two babies. Cecelia had slept on the sofa for ten years, preferring that her mother and children have the bedrooms. It wasn't until the twins were in the fourth grade that Cecelia and her mother agreed that the children were responsible enough to let themselves in after school and stay indoors. Their goal now would be to acquire a house; so both ladies had to work. They did, Cecelia as a desk clerk with the YWCA and mama as a maid for a family on Kalorama Road. It took five more years, but with the help of Melissa, who had become a real estate agent, she was able to acquire the house near the corner of Georgia Ave. and Irving Street. The location was perfect; mama could easily take the crosstown bus and she could easily take the downtown bus and the children's school was within easy walking distance. They moved in, in 1948. During the fifties, the twins graduated from Miner Teachers College. Mama lived long enough to see both of the grands get their Masters Degrees from Howard. Cecelia had been in the home by herself since '58 and that was O. K.

Rather than transferring buses at Rhode Island Ave., Cecelia liked walking the remaining few blocks to work. She'd buy a newspaper on the way and when at her desk, use a red ink pen to mark articles that looked interesting which she'd read either at lunch or when she got back home. This morning, she scanned the headlines. There were two stories concerning Vietnam and a story about President Johnson being against a federal employee pay raise. She always looked for articles about Mrs. Kennedy, Caroline, and John-John. Their goings on had always brought a smile to her face. Now, she could identify with Mrs. Kennedy's widowhood; a young woman with two babies to raise, whose husband had been murdered. . . . Lastly, she checked the obituary and saw the picture of the white guy. Who was this Carl Van Vechten? Why was he famous and why had she never heard of him? She'd save this article for this evening's reading.

———◆———

*20 E. 127th St - 3rd Floor*
*New York, N. Y. 10035*
*December 22, 1964*

*Dear Jonathan,*

*I hope that you are doing well. I am doing o.k., for a 62 year old man. I certainly am not ripping and running the way I did when I was younger. Now, I'm much more likely to engage in gently tugging and walking when I want something.*

*My friend, I have some sad news to convey to you. You may already have heard from the television broadcasters, but if you haven't, I wanted you to know that Carl Van Vechten died yesterday. I know that you remember modeling for him. It was the only money which you made while you were in New York.*

*Many friends, which he and I shared, turned against him once "the book" was published; but I didn't turn against him. I defended him; we really were quite close.*

*Fania Marinoff, his widow, said to me this morning, that the funeral was going to be for family only. I tried to convince her that many Negroes would come to pay their respects if the funeral were open to the public but she would not budge on her desire to keep it within the family. As a consequence, I thought that you, Bruce, Robin, Tunji, and I could get together on December 31st for dinner, reminiscence, forward thinking, and general merriment. At that time, we'll be able to raise a cup of kindness for Auld Lang Syne. If you can make it, let me know which train or bus you'll be taking north and I will meet you at the station. You are certainly welcome to spend the night on my sofa just like you did 31 years ago. The sofa is different, though; this one pulls out to a bed. You'll be comfortable if you stay with me.*

*I'm hoping that you can make it. I've already called Sylvia's Restaurant and reserved a table for that evening. I hope to hear from you soon.*

*Your Friend,*
*Langston*

Letters from friends were like flowers to Jonathan. They were to be savored, appreciated, cared for, kept, and systematically catalogued. Since learning how to read and write, he had saved all of the letters he had received from Tunji and Langston. Now, he was being invited back to New York City to discuss old times and current events, to see Tunji, Robin, and Bruce again, and to sleep on a different sofa.

Langston had traveled so much since Jonathan had last been in New York. He had met all of the famous race men and women. He knew important people outside of the country. He knew heads of state in the Caribbean and in Africa. It was Tunji who sent Langston's new address to him in '47. He had gone to one of Langston's plays, seen him, and asked for his address so that a friend could write to him. Tunji said that Langston immediately recognized him although he had forgotten his name. Tunji thought that Jonathan would want Langston's new address but he also cautioned him to be very careful about writing to him because he was probably under surveillance by the F.B.I. and Jonathan did not need to be accused of being a Communist mole.

Jonathan really didn't need Tunji's advice. The Red Scare had reached every person holding a job in Washington, D. C. Reflecting back to that 1947 letter triggered later memories of newspaper photos of Langston in '53. Back then, Jonathan could have reached out to Langston, but he chose to watch him from the safe distance provided by a television screen and one day later newspaper reports. Langston was on the hot seat then. Sitting before the House Un-American Activities Committee. At that time, Jonathan had not extended a comforting hand to the man who had saved his life. Doing so would have cost him that hand. He knew that he would have immediately been fired and so he waited, year after year after year for the Red Scare to die down. He had felt like he was Peter denying Jesus, except in his case, no one was accusing him, other than his conscience.

Sixteen years after Tunji's 1947 letter, Howard University awarded Langston an honorary doctorate. Because of its courage, Jonathan sent a letter to Langston inviting him, Bruce and Robin to stay with him and his cats during the week of the March on Washington. He let it be known that Tunji had already agreed to come. Langston had replied that they would come but that Robin had already planned to stay with photojournalists which he knew. He would be working as a freelance photographer for the Negro press.

Jonathan's guilt-ridden memories, as well as his good memories, had been triggered by Langston's current letter, a letter which had arrived almost one year and four months after their righteous indignation peaceful protest march for jobs and freedom. Placing the letter on his desk, Jonathan got his phone book and found the number for Union Station. It was his plan to leave work on the morning of the 31st and take a bus to the train station, that way he'd be in New York City no later than 2:00 p.m. The phone clerk at the station would give him all of the information he needed.

Getting writing paper, a stamp, and an envelope from a drawer, Jonathan wrote:

> 692 Harvard Street, N. W.
> Washington, D. C. 20001
> December 24, 1964

Dear Langston,

It was a pleasure to receive your letter although, it is regretful that it was generated by the death of Mr. Van Vechten. I am though, looking forward to sharing a cup of kindness for Auld Lang Syne. I'll be on train number 174, the Northeast Regional, which should pull into Penn Station at 1:44 p.m. I'll arrive on December 31st. I'm looking forward to seeing you, Bruce, Robin, and Tunji.

> Sincerely,
> Jonathan

Stepping off the train, Jonathan remembered immediately one of the things which he did not like about New York City; there were too many people. A bottleneck developed as those persons with whom he had just shared a train, tried to get onto the escalator. To him it was like 10,000 ants all of which were trying to move through a small passage way at the same time. It would take time, but all 10,000 would get through.

On the main concourse, right off to the side of the escalator was his friend, Langston and beside him, Robin. He walked over and hugged both of them. His tears started flowing but he couldn't explain to them why he was crying. He was caught in an emotional moment which had to run its course, and it did; as the multitude came off the moving stairs and as the crowds walked past, oblivious to the common history of these gentlemen.

The three guys were walking towards the subway when Langston informed Jonathan that, "We're taking the subway to my place. Bruce and Tunji will meet us there."

At their destination, Robin asked Jonathan how his ankle was holding out as they were ascending the second flight of stairs going towards Langston's apartment.

"I'm doing fine. Once I got on with the federal government, I was able to save enough money to pay for surgery. I don't use the brace any longer. "

"Thank you for opening up your home to us," said Jonathan as Langston walked to his china closet. From the middle shelf he removed an unopened bottle of Johnnie Walker Black and three glasses. From the freezer he brought an ice bucket with a pair of tongs and from the refrigerator he brought two bottles of ginger ale.

"O. K., it's catch up time. I got champagne for later on and a special sherry for the same." Langston continued, "You've got Planter's Walnuts and Cashews and bacon wrapped around hot dog slices and held together with a toothpick. Robin, why don't you fill Jonathan in on how you have been doing?"

"Well, Jonathan, Langston knows a little something about how I've been doing since he and I attend the same church, St. Philip's Episcopal. I also attend Abyssinian Baptist. I've got a thriving photography business. I take pictures of groups within churches such as the various choirs, but I also take glamour shots, baby pictures, wedding pictures, passport photos, and high school yearbook pictures. I've branched out into lithography and I've done the posters for the political campaigns of several Negro politicians. Business has been good enough so that I could buy the building housing the studio. I did that with Carl's help. Carl used the studio right up until he died, but he had long since sold the equipment and the business to me. He continued to take the portrait photographs of the famous and near famous, but he also had his private photo sessions. You know, those photo sessions, the special private ones, didn't bother me. They went on while I was developing film or doing the books, or when I was absent. Jonathan, you know my history; his private life was his business. Live and let live is my motto. It was a little awkward though when I turned over all of his photos to his wife. At this point, I've already given everything to Fania. I did remove though, a few sets of photos. Mine are in my apartment above the studio. Yours are in this envelope." Pushing the envelope toward Jonathan, he said, "They're for you. You've got the photos and the negatives."

"Thanks. I remember that night well. It was because of that night, that I got some modeling jobs in D. C. . . . . Robin, were Vanda Mae's killers ever found?"

"Yeah, they were murdered. It was in the newspaper. Their fingerprints matched the prints on the rubber packets found on the ground."

"I'm glad they were taken out."

"Yeah, me too. . . . So what's life been like for you?"

"Robin, Langston, I've been working my butt off. After getting hired as an elevator operator at the Hecht Company, I started taking night school classes. It took me six years to get my reading, writing, and math skills up high enough to pass all of the tests to get a high school diploma. I also had to pass history and science courses. I took the night classes at Cardozo High School. It was hard work but I stuck with it. When the war came along, I knew that I wouldn't be drafted because of my bad ankle but I thought that there would be vacancies in the government and that maybe I could get one of the vacated jobs, so, I applied to be a switchboard operator at the State Department. Well, I didn't get accepted for the training, even though I had taken switchboard courses at Cardozo. I was accepted into the State Department though, as an elevator operator. So I started working over there, taking people from one floor to another when I happened to notice that the person who rejected me for the training program was pulling a double shift and was pissed about it. He told me that one of the operators had left to give birth and he didn't have anyone to take her place. So,

I spoke up and said that if he trained me, I wouldn't get pregnant. He started laughing, then he told me to come to his office when my shift was over. When I got there, he told me that my application for training had been approved and that my class would start the next morning. He told me to first go to personnel and sign the paperwork and then come to the classroom. I was told that males used to do switchboard jobs but that they tended to be rude to the callers and eventually they were removed from the boards. I was also told that I had to speak clearly and that I couldn't sound Colored. Well after six years of courses at Cardozo, where they tried to get rid of any southern accents and after living with the Lamonts for that entire time period, where proper enunciation was expected and declamation was appreciated, I had lost my southern accent. To make a long story short, I passed the training and was assigned to the night shift and I've been on that shift since 1939. I was the only male and for a long time, was the only Colored person working the switchboard at the State Department. I'm now in charge of the night shift. I'm still the only male operator at the department. No one messes with me because I work a shift which no one wants. There are plenty of people that make more money than I, but I've got a good job with excellent benefits."

"But," said Langston, ". . . did you get pregnant?"

As the laughter was dying down, they heard the doorbell ringing. Langston recognized Bruce's voice on the intercom and buzzed him in. Moments later he and Tunji were hugging Langston, Robin, and Jonathan. After two more glasses were filled with spirits and bacon wrapped hotdogs were passed around, Jonathan continued his story.

"After one year of doing my job with a steel brace on my leg, I used my vacation time to have an operation on my foot. As soon as my vacation time was up, I came right back to work. I didn't tell anyone that I was going to have an operation and I especially did not tell the women with whom I worked. I used my crutch and a brace again until I could get around without them. After my surgery, I started saving money again, this time I wanted a house. After 5 years of saving, I bought a small house in D. C., on Harvard Street. It cost me $7,000 and I had saved $4,000. It's been paid off for a long time now. Melissa, Bobby's wife, they're friends from Black Bottom, found the house for me. Bobby fixed it up after I bought it. I ran into Melissa at Cardozo High School when I was there, but she was in the day program and I was in the night program. She works for a real estate broker. Her husband went to Armstrong Vocational and got training in plumbing, electricity, and in carpentry. This is the second house that he's fixed up for me. They both work for J. R. Pinkett Real Estate. I've been working for 25 years at the State Department. I'll have my 30 years in before I turn 65 so I'm not going to retire until sometime between 1975 and 1981. I have lady friends but I do not have anyone with whom I want to settle and make a home."

"Maybe you need a man," said Bruce.

The silence was followed by nervous laughter and then by Jonathan's reply, "You're not moving in, Bruce. I don't care how much you try to tempt me with your charms. You're a wild one, an untamable beast and my cats won't like you and they're good judges of character. So get that notion out of your head."

"I'll drink to that," said Langston.

As the glasses clinked all around and the men imbibed, Jonathan asked Langston if he could get out his special sherry and if they could toast Carl and Vanda Mae.

"Of course, I'll get fresh glasses also."

When the glasses were filled, Jonathan said, "To Carl and Vanda Mae, the two people that have had an impact on everyone in this room."

"To Carl and Vanda Mae" and the glasses clinked.

"There's one more toast that needs to be done before we go off to dinner," said Jonathan. This is my toast to each and every one of you. . . Robin, you got me out of Black Bottom. I didn't like the way it was done, but my life is better because I left. You're an inspiration Robin. You have a business and an apartment building. You've totally gone legit. You're proof that God works miracles. Langston, you were there for me when the bullets were flying and the blood of my two pets was staining your clothes. You were there to rescue me from that horrific scene. You were there to get me settled in New York and you got me my first paying job in New York. Bruce, you were there for me when I needed art supplies but you did more than provide me with art supplies, you provided me with a glimpse of your immense artistic talent. You were the gold standard against which I would measure my artistic aspirations. You are a true gem of the African Diaspora. Tunji, you helped me to begin my new life. You understood that I had a naive country backwater Black Bottom framework for operating and you knew that I needed a sophisticated urban framework to do more than subsist outside of Dixie.

Thank you for placing my feet on that urban path. You are a true conductor of the Underground Railroad. All of you gentlemen, are my African Angels and I raise this glass in your honor. Ache'."

Clinking their glasses, their responses were, "Ache'."

## The End